D1280201

Cockspur Island

A Novel of the Coast Guard

Bradley K. Adams

ISBN: 147746400X
ISBN-13: 978-1477464007

This book is dedicated to....

My amazing wife and daughters who give me unconditional love and support.

My family, here and gone, who always believed.

My shipmates who shared the ups and downs of twenty-five years.

Patricia Cornwell, who taught me the writing process.

And, foremost, to **God** and the blessings of faith.

Acknowledgements

I would like to extend my most gracious thanks to Mr. Charles Cornwell and Mrs. Allyson Conroy who accompanied me on this writing journey.

Savannah, Georgia

Summer

Savannah, GA: Tropical Storm Danelle has been upgraded to Hurricane Danelle and is barreling toward the Georgia/South Carolina coast and is predicted to make landfall as a strong, category three hurricane. Danelle is packing winds of up to 85 miles per hour and is expected to strengthen significantly as she passes over the warmer waters of the Gulf Stream. Danelle should develop into a category three storm by late Tuesday evening. Landfall is currently predicted to occur anywhere along a line between Oglethorpe Sound on the Georgia coast and Charleston, South Carolina. The entire Georgia coastline, north to Georgetown, South Carolina is under a hurricane warning with watches issued for the northeast coast of Florida and barrier islands of North Carolina. Mandatory evacuations are occurring within the warning area. Residents as far as twenty miles inland are being asked to voluntarily evacuate. The Coast Guard has issued warnings and advisories encouraging all mariners to immediately return to port. Larger vessels (including U.S. military vessels) are being directed to steer south, out of Danelle's path. At present, meteorologists at the National Hurricane Center are predicting sustained winds in excess of 100 miles per hour at landfall and a possible storm surge greater than 12 feet.

Savannah, GA: Hurricane Danelle made landfall at 2:30a.m. local time as a category two storm, in the vicinity of Myrtle Beach South Carolina. Sustained winds of 100 miles per hour have been reported with gusts greater than 115 miles per hour. Storm surge levels range from 10 feet on the leading edge of the storm to five feet along the Georgia coast. Low-lying areas have experienced significant flooding in the affected areas. Reports of widespread power outages and structural damage to beach and inland, waterside homes, have been received. Savannah was spared the brunt of Danelle's winds and storm surge but still experienced significant coastal flooding along with straight-line winds and tornados reported. Storm surge along the coast at Tybee Island was reported at six feet, occurring during slack tide, causing inland flooding across Wilmington Island and Thunderbolt. Power remains out across the majority of the low-country and emergency crews are fanning out across the region commencing recovery efforts. The Port of Savannah has been temporarily closed to commercial and civilian traffic.

Bradley K. Adams

1

The low country bathed in oppressive, sweltering heat. Eight hours ago the barometer had bottomed out as the fringes of Danelle passed over Savannah bringing cooler temperatures and nearly immeasurable volumes of rain. Now, it was just hot. The wind that had howled such a horrific tone the night before was gone. Not a breeze could be felt and every breath of humidity laden air burned the lungs. Such was the way of post-storm operations.

Boatswain's Mate First Class Henry "Hank" Morgan ripped the ball cap from his sweat-drenched head and ran his forearm across his brow. Hank couldn't recall a time when he had sweat this profusely without being engaged in physical fitness activities or playing softball (which he didn't consider exercise). Looking forward of the boat Hank could see the broken marsh filling his immediate environment and smell the acrid odor of exposed mud and marine life baking in the heat. Of course, it didn't help that Danelle had drowned a significant number of animals with her storm surge. Already, Hank and his crew had passed the half submerged carcasses of raccoons, deer, opossums and dogs. If it was a mammal and was unfortunate enough to live within the sprawling bog… it was probably dead.

What Hank and his crew were doing was standard operational procedure, SOP, in the wake of a violent storm. Twenty four hours ago they'd been holed up inside an aircraft hangar at Hunter Army Airfield near the center of Savannah. Hunter was constructed on one of the few pieces of land that would not be submerged in the event of catastrophic flooding. The rest of the city be damned but the base would survive. Hundreds of those who hadn't packed up and headed for Columbus, Macon or Atlanta had arrived at Hunter's gates in the hours before the storm, and the hangar that housed Hank, his crew and his boat had turned into a very full and very uncomfortable shelter. Hank found it extremely difficult to maintain military discipline amidst the crying and screaming evoked by the din of hurricane winds. Hank was glad the storm passed so quickly. Now, the task at hand was survey work.

After the storm passed Hank was contacted by his officer in charge, Master Chief Marc Braden who'd spent the event inside a warehouse at the Port of Savannah. Hank was directed to trailer his 25-foot response boat small (RBS) to the nearest accessible ramp and complete a thorough investigation of all navigable waterways within Station Tybee Island's area of responsibility. Of course, the mission was limited by the availability of fuel but, with tanks full, Hank was confident that he could sustain several hours of investigation.

Armed with machetes, a chain saw and a tow strap, Hank and his crew set out for a boat ramp on the Wilmington River in the early morning hours. By noon Hank and his crew had hacked their way through the debris ridden streets of Savannah. The ramp, surprisingly, was clear and serviceable with only a small hump of debris left resting on the sloping concrete. The smell, however, was less than palatable. The marsh, to Hank, always smelled of decay. Today's smell was different, overpowering. All that had decayed and all that decayed had been stirred together at once. Hank didn't expect the smell to get any better as the day unfolded.

Hank's friend and fellow crewman, Boatswain's Mate Second Class Mike Harwood, slowly backed the 25942's trailer into the water. With a slight surge, the boats luminous metal hull gained buoyancy, her orange all-around flotation resting smoothly on the water's surface. Seconds later, the crew was aboard. Hank eased the engines into gear piloting the 942 into the Wilmington River and through a maze of vegetation-lined waterways toward the city of Thunderbolt.

Thunderbolt, Georgia was little more than a small spit of land that had somehow managed to maintain its autonomy from the larger city of Savannah. Essentially, Thunderbolt was a buffer-zone between Savannah and Wilmington Island, which had grown significantly over the past decade. Thunderbolt was a quaint area with a small population but supported several marinas and the bulk of the areas fishing and shrimping fleet. In Coast Guard terms, Thunderbolt was the Mecca of the local small-boat and commercial fishing communities. Hank had spent many hours here, on the water, during the past two years of his tour. Hank loved Thunderbolt, but it didn't look the same now.

The "Lady Marie", a large shrimp-boat that Hank had frequently boarded, had broken free of her moorings and was pushed hard aground in the marsh opposite her docs. Her sister ship, the "Gina Marie" drifted nearby, its starboard outrigger torn loose and lying in the water. Hank nosed up to both vessels as Rachel and Ryan called out. There were no replies. Before Hank put a boarding team aboard the "Gina Marie" a shout had come from the Thunderbolt side of the river where Paul Sulsky (the "Gina Marie's" owner) was launching a flatboat. Hank knew, with a wave of Paul's hand, there was no one aboard either vessel.

Fletchers Marina, further down the river, was a nightmare. The thirty-some boats that hadn't been hauled out prior to Danelle's arrival were in varying states of ruin. The mooring lines hadn't been rigged to allow for the sudden rise of the storm surge and the boats had been held fast in their places as floodwaters spilled over their gunwales. As best as possible, Hank maneuvered the 942 through the debacle, collecting vessel registration numbers and recording present and potential petroleum spills. There were several. Departing the marina, Hank heard several loud, angry, yet imperceptible exclamations coming from the "Gina Marie" as she bobbed outside the marina exit. Paul Sulsky stood on the boats forward deck, trying to attach a line to the downed outrigger. Apparently, his efforts weren't working.

"Paul's gonna have a tough day," Hank thought. "Hope the insurance is paid up."

The rest of the river transit was uneventful, until a flash of reflected sunlight indicated a boats presence deep in twisting waterway of Romerly Marsh Creek. Mike was the first to spot the distant flicker. After bringing the 942 to clutch speed, Hank caught the glinting reflection of sun on glass. Hank piloted the 942 into the tight spaces of the creek with a keen eye on his fathometer. When the tide was flood, the branches of the creek were difficult to navigate without running aground. Now, as the tide was starting to ebb, deep water would be progressively harder to find. One bend, two bends in the creek and the shape of the boat appeared along the muddy bank.

The boat was small, twenty five feet in length from the looks of it, white with blue trim, a cabin in the forepart and an inboard/outboard engine design. It lay tipped to the port, the keel sunk deep into the mud. The port quarter of the boat dipped below the surface of the water and the creek communicated freely with the vessels deck. The cabin windows, along the port side, were a spider's web of breaks, apparently struck by wind-blown debris. A radio whip antenna, snapped like a twig, lay in the long grass of the marsh.

"Maybe it drifted in here?" Petty Officer Rachel Stone said as she leaned out the port side door of the 942, trying to get a clearer view.

"Maybe?" Hank replied as he reached for the chart plotter, activating the man overboard feature to record the GPS position of the wreck for later use.

"Onboard the small boat...." Seaman Ryan Beck yelled from the bow of the 942, "This is the United States Coast Guard. Is anyone aboard?"

Hank brought the engines to neutral and increased the volume of the listen-forward feature on the loudhailer. There was no audible reply.

"Odd that they're here..." Hank commented as he nosed closer to the wreck. "I know the wind and tides are crazy during a hurricane. But here of all places... kind of interesting."

Mike leaned in the cabin door from the back deck, "Gonna have a look, Boat's?" Mike asked.

"Absolutely." Hank responded, "I'll nose us up and you and Ryan can jump over."

"Sounds good, boss," Mike responded then wiggled his way along the sponsons of the 942 to join Ryan on the bow.

"Distances?" Hank called out to Ryan and Mike as he watched the fathometer move from six to five feet of water depth.

"Ten feet off!" Ryan yelled.

"Plenty of water." Rachel added from the navigator's seat next to Hank.

The nose of the 942 cleared the cabin of the wreck giving Mike and Ryan a look into the flooding deck.

"Fuck me!" Ryan exclaimed and turned his head with a wince of disgust.

"Holy God." Mike said added in surprised astonishment.

With incredible force, the odor of decomposition washed through the open doors of the 942's cabin and into Hank's nose as he brought the 942 alongside the wreck. Ryan leaned over the bow and wretched as Mike

14

grabbed a mooring line from the forward compartment, quickly making the bow off to one of the wrecked boats cleats.

"I don't think this is good" Rachel said as she leapt from her chair and proceeded to the back deck.

"Someone dead Mike?" Hank asked as he pulled off the engine kill -switch lanyard and wiggled from his seat.

Mike looked into the aft deck of the wreck and nodded "Yeah, real dead."

As Rachel rigged a stern line, Hank exited the cabin through the forward hatch. Coming onto the bow, Hank looked into the wreck as Ryan commenced another, stronger, fit of vomiting. Hank understood why. The body had been a man, young, mid-twenties maybe. His...its back was blown open exposing muscle, bone and spine. Definitely a shotgun wound, Hank thought, as he found himself choking back his Adams apple. Ryan may have to scoot over soon.

The body was incredibly bloated. Flies swarmed the open spaces of torn flesh. There were no maggots yet. Maggots would have tipped Hank over the edge. Hank had seen dead bodies before, floaters, to include the ones that strained through the mesh of recovery litters or whose skin fell off at the slightest touch. These things Hank had developed a tolerance for, but maggots… not ever. Hank cautiously took a step from the 942 onto the leaning and water-slick deck of the wreck.

"What is it guys?" Rachel called from the cabin.

Mike turned to Rachel grimacing "It's pretty bad. Dead guy…."

Mike could feel, physically, Rachel's heart sink as her level of fear and apprehension rose. Mike had never asked, but he didn't believe Rachel had ever seen a body.

"Stay put Rachel," Mike motioned with his hand.

"Tell her to try to raise Incident Command. If not them then try Sector," Hank spoke over his shoulder as he knelt down over the body.

"I heard," Rachel shouted, apparently the listen-forward was still on. She picked up the microphone on the 942's primary radio.

Mike stepped onto the wreck behind Hank, careful not to lose his footing, "Only one aboard?"

"Ever hear of a guy committing suicide by shooting himself in the back?" Hank stood, gathering as fresh a breath of air as he could. The smell of decay remained overpowering.

He turned to his left and noticed the door to the wreck's cabin. Behind the door was darkness save for a sliver of light piercing draped windows.

"If there were others then they were in the cabin...damnit!" Hank reached into a small pouch on his weapons belt and produced a pair of latex gloves. This scene was nasty, bloody and Hank had no intention of picking up HIV or HEP or God knows what other disease may be lying around. Mike and Ryan followed suit.

"Any luck with the radio?" Hank looked into the cabin of the 942 where Rachel stood speaking into the microphone. Rachel raised a finger, letting Hank know that she was conversing with someone. Hank knew she could raise Incident Command and Sector Charleston both. Communications had been good when they left the launch ramp. He was stalling. He didn't want to go into that cabin. He didn't want to see what may be inside. His mind was conjuring up the grizzliest scenes imaginable. Every childhood terror from every corner of Hank's psyche was darting across his synapses playing out vivid horrors.

"Act your damn age!" Hank thought as Rachel's voice returned him to the moment.

"I reached them, Boat's," Rachel stated as she leaned out the side door of the cabin. "They want us to confirm whether or not anyone else is aboard. Get the registration numbers and take pictures if we can. But, don't touch anything we don't have to."

"No problem," Ryan responded as he rose from his leaning position, wiping a line of phlegm from his chin.

"Looks like we get to go inside," Mike tugged up on his gun belt and slapped Hank on the shoulder.

"Ok then," Hank exhaled the words. "Ryan, grab the camera from the Boarding Kit. Mike and I are going to have a look in the cabin."

"Roger," Ryan responded and crawled through the forward hatch into the 942's cabin.

"Ready?" Hank rolled his eyes then placed his focus on the cabin door. Reaching out, he grabbed the door handle and cautiously pulled.

The smell of the body on deck could not compare with the rush of putrid stench that exited the cabin. The sound of buzzing that accompanied the odor was intense, reminding Hank of a bee hive he'd disturbed when he was seven. But, these weren't bees. The flies were syrup- thick and swarming around the cabin's dimly lit interior. At the far end of the cabin, near the bow, Hank could make out the form of another body, another male. He reached for his flashlight as he placed his forearm over his mouth and nose to block the odor.

Mike bent down, peeking into the cabin through the space between Hanks legs. "Starboard side... heads up, Boss."

Hank flicked on his flashlight and moved the beam to the starboard side of the cabin, illuminating a pair of what appeared to be rotting female legs.

"Yuck," Mike commented dryly.

Hank moved the beam forward, settling on the man's body. The body was recumbent with a Mossberg twelve-gauge pump lying across its lap. In the neck was a knife, not horribly big but apparently big enough. Dried blood lead from the stab wound down the man's chest, lap and legs and into a coagulating pool on the deck. At the side of the body, against the bulkhead, was a small stockpile of tightly wrapped brown packages.

To get a look at the woman Hank had to enter the confines of the cabin one cautious step at a time. The cabin deck was thick with drying blood. The flies swarmed in and out of Hank's vision, landing on his face and arms haphazardly. He swatted at the air to no avail. Once inside, he brought the light to the woman's feet, tracing the body past the waist and chest to the head. He recoiled violently.

"Shit!" Hank exclaimed with a start.

"Boss?" Mike poked his head into the cabin, seeing what Hank saw. "Shit!" Mike backed out of the cabin. It was his turn to choke.

The right side of the woman's head had been completely removed by a gunshot. Shredded brain matter hung from her opened skull by thin lines of sinew. Behind her, unidentifiable bits of tissue and bone covered the bulkhead in a spray pattern. The woman's remaining eye was open, the gaze fixed eternally in a form of fear and disbelief.

"My God, what happened here?" Mike said as he peeked back into the cabin, using his own flashlight to illuminate the dead man.

Hank's eyes scanned the cabin, coming to rest on a duffel bag at the woman's feet. The bag's zipper was open. He carefully reached down, opening the bag further to reveal the color of green.

"Damn," Hank said as he illuminated roll upon roll of bills. He guessed the bag contained nearly a quarter of a million dollars in tightly rolled, large denomination currency.

"Crank?" Mike said, making Hank turn to where Mike illuminated one of the brown packages at the bow. The package was torn open on one corner, spilling a rusty brown material onto the cabin's vinyl seats.

"All right. Let's back out of here for a minute," Hank said as he scooted backward and out of the cabin.

Hank gulped the semi-fresh outside air into his lungs as he shook his head toward Mike. Mike nodded his agreement. Neither man had ever seen something so violent.

"Here…"

Hank and Mike turned to find Rachel and Ryan standing on the bow of the 942. Rachel handed over bottled waters. Hank accepted the water eagerly, took a long drink, swished the water around his mouth and then spit into the marsh. Mike poured half his bottle over his head, face and arms.

"It's worse in the cabin?" Rachel asked, her eyes fixed on the body lying on the deck.

"Much worse," Mike commented, taking a drink.

"It's obviously the leftovers of a drug deal," Hank started. "Looks like the woman and this guy were the buyers and the guy at the bow was the seller."

Hank took a drink. "I think this guy…" Hank motioned to the body, "… or the woman, stabbed the poor bastard and then he shot them both. This guy here was trying to get off the boat when he ate it."

"Which means there was someone else here… another boat?" Rachel added.

"More than likely," Mike commented.

"Damn," Ryan said softly, staring into the distance.

There was a tense, silent moment before Mike broke in. "One hell of a deal. There's a shit-load of money in that cabin and a shit-load of meth."

"Meth?" Rachel said. "Methamphetamines?"

"It's a favorite around here," Hank responded. "There are labs cooking the crap all over the place in the swamps and marshes."

"What do you mean by shit-load?" Ryan asked.

"Well…" Hank looked back into the cabin, then to Ryan. "I'd say there's a couple of hundred thousand dollars in that lady's bag… that kind of shit-load."

"Damn."

Hank took another drink, spit again, then gathered the way forward. "We need to call Sector and tell them exactly what we've found and we need to take lots of pictures."

Rachel pulled her personal cell phone and Hanks Coast Guard issued cell phone from her pockets. "We didn't have a camera. We can use these. They both have cameras."

Rachel had been in the cell phone box. Any other time Hank would have dressed her down for having a personal phone out while on mission. The Coast Guard had taken a hard-line stance against personal cell phone use as of late. Station Tybee policy was that cell phones had to remain in the cell phone box if taken underway.

"If you take pictures with that it'll probably be seized as evidence," Mike told Rachel.

"I don't care. I've been looking for an excuse to get a new one," Rachel smiled. She was handling this situation very well.

"Let's just use my issued phone," Hank reached out and took his phone from Rachel.

"That phone sucks. The images will be way too pixilated," Rachel responded.

"Ok then we'll use yours," Hank rolled his eyes, foregoing an argument.

"I'll call Sector while you guys handle this," Ryan interrupted.

"You okay, Ryan?" Mike asked as he flashed a look of concern to Hank. Ryan was the youngest of the crew but was also very seasoned and had seen his fair share. Mike was surprised to see Ryan distancing himself from the scene. But, everyone had their limits.

"Yeah, I'm doing good. Just need a little fresh air is all," Ryan responded without looking at Mike.

"Good then, Ryan, go ahead and make the call. We'll handle things out here," Hank reached across the bow and patted Ryan on the shoulder.

Rachel stepped onto the deck of the wreck and started snapping photograph after photograph. Hank and Mike watched in wonder as she crouched down over the bodies in the cabin, the flash on her cell phone camera illuminated the space with incredible frequency.

"This is pretty nasty," Rachel said as she leaned close to the woman's body and lined up a shot of her pulverized skull.

"You doing alright down there?" Hank asked.

"I aint scared," she responded... a Rachel-ism that she frequently used.

"Don't touch anything, Rachel, just take pictures. This is a crime scene," Mike shouted toward the cabin.

"Oh, you can bet I don't plan on touching anything." Rachel responded.

Hank and Mike exchanged raised eyebrows. "She's tough," Mike commented.

"You think?" Hank added as he and Mike stared into the cabin, watching Rachel move nimbly about.

After a three-minute eternity Rachel emerged from the cabin with thirty or so photos saved to her camera's memory.

"Get pictures of the whole boat and her registration number too, Rachel."

"Already done, Boat's," Rachel smiled at Hank. "I knew we'd end up using my phone so I took those pictures before you guys even asked."

Hank frowned. "Please don't do that again. Not without being told."

Rachel's smile sank, slightly, "Just being proactive."

"Boat's!" Ryan called urgently from the 942's cabin, "You better have a listen. It's urgent!" Ryan waved the radio microphone in the air as Hank climbed back onto the 942 and into the cabin.

Hank took the microphone from Ryan "Who?"

"Sector." Ryan moved to the back deck of the 942 and stood by the stern line.

"Here we go," Hank said as he cued the mic. "Sector Charleston this is 942."

"942 this is Sector..." came the almost robotic sounding voice of the watch stander at the Sector Charleston Command Center. "...divert immediately to a report of explosions and fire at Turners Creek Marina," the voice was well trained, not urgent, but insistent.

Hank rolled his eyes, exasperated at the thought of being diverted from a scene of this type to any other case. "Sector, 942, you are aware of our situation here? Over..."

There was a brief pause then a different voice, a female voice, came over the radio, "942 this is Sector. We are fully aware of your situation and have notified the Chatham County Sheriffs and Savannah Police. They are dispatching assets to the location you provided. For now, you are to proceed at best speed to a potential loss of life situation."

Hank didn't answer. The people they'd discovered couldn't be any more dead were dead and the Coast Guard's job was saving lives, first and foremost. "After a hurricane, response assets are limited. Other resources will come," Hank thought.

"Let's go folks!" Hank shouted to Mike and Rachel who hurriedly climbed aboard the 942. "We've got SAR."

"We're leaving?" Mike asked, taking the bow-line down to a single turn.

"Saving lives trumps babysitting dead folks," Hank responded as he climbed into the boat coxswain's seat, easing the 942's engines into reverse. "Take off all lines."

"Stern's off!" Ryan shouted.

"Bow's off!" Mike called.

Rachel moved to the navigator's seat where she had left the cell phone box. Rachel opened the lid, staring at two full and two empty cut outs in the foam liner that held the phones in place.

"That's weird," Rachel said as she placed her and Hank's phones in the empty slots.

"What's weird?" Hank asked as he turned the bow of the 942 and started cautiously out of Romerly Creek.

"Nothing... I'm just being paranoid." Rachel placed the box in stowage under her seat then plopped down in her chair.

"That's a lot of money to leave sitting out here." Mike wiggled into his seat behind Hank, finishing the last of his water. "It'd be like winning the lottery is anyone finds it before the cops get here."

"And it's getting toward low tide," Hank added. "Chatham County had better bring a flat-boat or they'll never get up in there."

"Who would know it's back there?" Ryan asked as he stood at the aft door of the cabin.

Rachel turned her head, looking at each member of the crew. "The phone box isn't right." Rachel thought. "They aren't where they were when I opened the box."

As Hank found the deeper water at the exit of Romerly Creek he pushed the throttles forward, bringing the 942 on plane.

Romerly Creek, the wreck and Rachel's concerns fell into the distance.

Ten days later....

Monday

2

6:30AM

Hank kissed Lori and Allison, and hopped into the cab of his ancient Ford F-150 to head for work. Hank and Lori had been married for three years and the partnership seemed to get better with every passing anniversary. Lori had been a city girl, immovable from her family and roots in the small town of Muncie, Indiana where she and Hank were raised and had dated in high school. When Hank went off to college at Indiana University their relationship remained intact, though strained by the relentless string of sex starved males pursuing Lori at Ball State. But the strain was more a creation of Hanks jealousy than any physical reality. Lori remained unswervingly true throughout their separation.

At the end of Hank's freshman year at IU the money had run out. Hank's family fell on hard times and was forced to close their furniture store. The economy was drying up, so were sales. Without some financial support from his parents, Hank couldn't afford to stay in school. So, Hank joined the Coast Guard. Hank figured the G.I.

Bill would give him enough money to return to college after a four-year enlistment and with the added bonus of the post-9/11 G.I. Bill he may even be able to swing some graduate work. All these thoughts were six years ago. Hank was on his second enlistment now.

Hank's first assignment out of boot camp had been to the Coast Guard Cutter Cheyenne in St. Louis. This was Hank's top pick, mostly because it placed him a weekend's drive away from Lori. Lori visited Hank often and vice versa over the first three years of his assignment to the Cheyenne. Often times they would meet half-way in Decatur or Peoria Illinois… get a hotel room, see a movie. It was on one particular half-way trip that their lives had been completely changed.

Lori conceived Allison during a half-way weekend. The news was joyous to Hank and Lori but less than welcome to Lori's very traditional parents. A hurried wedding was assembled by Lori's mom in order to conceal the coming "baby bump" that would undoubtedly show under Lori's wedding dress if she didn't act quickly. Two months after the positive pregnancy test, Hank and Lori were married and sharing a very cramped apartment.

Though the pregnancy had pushed Lori to college disenrollment, she had managed to complete her Associate's Degree and had been able to find part time employment as a receptionist in a Dentist's office. Lori was good with people and with accounting. Someday Hank intended to put Lori back in school, full time, to finish her degree. She was taking online classes sporadically now but, for Hank, that wasn't good enough. Lori had sacrificed a lot to chase Hank around on his Coast Guard adventure. Though she said the decision to make the Coast Guard a career was mutual, Hank still felt guilty...like he had robbed Lori of her life in some ways.

Allison arrived on a brutally hot and stormy August day. The power in the hospital had briefly gone out while Lori was in labor thanks to a lightning strike on a nearby transformer. But, emergency lights and all, Allison arrived a healthy eight pounds and twenty inches long. She was their pride and Joy. While Allison had been forming in her mother's tummy, Hank had managed to make E5, second class Boatswain Mate, which meant a little more money for the family and fewer days of hotdog and macaroni and cheese dinners at the end of pay periods.

Not three months after Lori and Hank had brought Allison, "Ally", home Hank received orders to Coast Guard Station Tybee Island. From a cutter to a small boat station... probably the most typical career path a Boatswain's Mate could follow. Lori didn't take the news well and neither did her parents. While they lived in St. Louis, Hank and Lori were constantly visited by Lori's parents. Now, Lori was coming to grips with moving well beyond the half-way weekend and being on her own. Through tears and anger Lori had watched their household goods packed and loaded onto the Mayflower truck. Lori's parents were there when Hank, Lori and Ally pulled out of town. The farewell hugs took forever (none were for Hank). Lori didn't speak for the first three hundred miles of the trip to Georgia.

The first year in Savannah was tough. Lori writhed in a combination of post-partum depression and the anguish of being separated from her family. Hank made sure she had internet access at the house and unlimited talk and text on her cell but nothing really helped. Her family was still distant, she was alone. Hank had to stand duty, port and starboard duty, which meant two days on then two days off with sliding weekends. Even though Hank only "worked" fifteen days a month, he had to get qualified to operate the unit's boats, stand the watch and conduct law enforcement. During that first year Hank guessed that, even though he was on a "cake" duty rotation, he was home less than three days a week. It made things hard on Lori.

The breakthrough had come when Mike was assigned to the station. Mike, Mike Harwood, was a Coast Guard fixture. Mike had been in the service for ten years already and had bounced back and forth from assignment to assignment, never anywhere for more than two years. Mike took all the real "hell no" billets that no one else wanted. He was on the Polar Sea, an icebreaker, when he came out of boot camp... then, onto the Cutter Sherman. Next, he was a part of Pacific TACLET (Tactical Law Enforcement Team). The majority of Mike's tours were spent away from home and away from his wife Debbie and son Andrew. Mike arrived at Station Tybee because Debbie had put her foot down.

Hank recalled Mike's explanation, "She said she was tired of using a vibrator and unless she started getting the real thing from me she would have to whore around."

Debbie, rough edged as she was, was a blessing for Lori. Debbie was a no nonsense military wife. Her father had been a Gunnery Sergeant in the Marine Corps so Debbie had lived the perpetual relocation life since she was born. Debbie was fiercely independent, headstrong and not the least bit intimidated by new surroundings. Lori cleaved to Debbie immediately, drawing strength from Debbie's type "A" personality and assimilating coping mechanisms that turned Lori into the quintessential "military wife." Lori became strong, self sufficient. Hank hated to think of the future when Debbie and Lori would be parted. For now, Lori had become a new person and a force to be reckoned with in their relationship. Hank loved it.

Hank drove over the Thunderbolt Bridge, looking out on the sunrise over the marsh, thankful for the privilege to experience the excitement of the skies twisting pastels. If there was one thing Hank could never fathom it was the power of nature to generate such a beautiful spectacle and yet, such a horrific tempest as had been last week's Danelle. Nature was fickle, no doubt, but Hank took the good with the bad in equal sums of appreciation.

The drive to Cockspur Island took about ten minutes. Just enough time for Hank to listen to the morning news on 103.9 FM and enjoy a couple of oldies, which had become his favorite music. The new stuff was too new for Hank. The younger folks at the station were incessantly tuned into Eminem, Lil Wayne or some other music that Hank had little in common with. He supposed his musical taste was the product of growing up with a brother who was ten years his elder. Hank's outdated musical taste was a common point of focus for his duty section and lent to his labeling as an old man at age thirty because he preferred Van Halen. Such were things. The mantel of being an "old man" was one that all Coast Guard leaders took on regardless of age.

U.S. Highway 80, the only road linking Savannah to Cockspur and Tybee Island was free of traffic. It was Monday and that was to be expected. Yesterday at noon the road would have been packed, bumper to bumper, in both directions. Hurricane or not, the tourists and locals flocked to the beaches on Tybee Island every weekend. Luckily, beach erosion hadn't been that significant so the local beach haunts were open for business and not losing a summer dime. Hank reached his turn onto the bridge that spanned the South Channel of the Savannah River to Cockspur Island. The Station rested on the islands western tip.

Across the bridge Hank could see Terry Macomb sitting in his National Park Service squad car just off the road in a spot Terry thought inconspicuous. It was an ongoing game between Terry and the crew of Station Tybee. Cockspur Island was home to Fort Pulaski National Monument. As such, a strict speed limit of fifteen miles per hour was enforced. With the weekend tourists gone, Terry (as usual) turned his ticketing attention to the members of the station crew. Terry had passed out seven speeding tickets to Station personnel in the past six months for as little as one mile per hour over the speed limit. Terry was, as the crew called him, a dick.

Hank came to a stop in front of Terry's squad and rolled down his window, "Morning, Terry," Hank yelled out the window as Terry rolled his eyes. "How's hunting this morning?"

"You're gonna be late for work," Terry responded, leaning his head out the driver's side window.

Hank snickered and rolled away from Terry at a crawl. As soon as Hank was out of sight he accelerated to thirty. Hank knew it was brainless to act this way but, Terry really pissed Hank off.

"Follow me if you've got the balls," Hank thought to himself but Terry was nowhere to be seen. Hank slowed as he headed down the road to Fort Pulaski. Hanks morning visits to the Fort had become a tradition. He left home fifteen minutes early just to be in the Fort's presence.

Fort Pulaski was history, which Hank loved. He pulled into the parking lot as he sipped the cup of coffee Lori unfailingly provided every duty morning. Hank soaked in the sunrise over the Fort's thick masonry walls. The American flag flapped lazily in the breeze from a pole inside the Fort as the sun crested the walls sending brilliant spears of yellow and orange across the horizon.

The Fort played a part in the Civil War, not a monumental part but a part just the same. In April of 1862 the forces of the Union had arrived on Tybee Island across the South Channel of the Savannah River bent on seizing the Fort from the Confederacy. The determined Confederates refused to surrender the Fort until the Union unleashed its latest development, the rifled cannon. Cannon fire poured onto the unsuspecting Confederates who stood in awe at the range of the Union guns. The Fort was surrendered in short order.

"How startled those poor bastards had to have been," Hank thought for perhaps the hundredth time. For him, the story of Fort Pulaski's fall was a reminder to expect the unexpected and to always be wary of what you don't know. Over confidence and failure walked hand in hand. He put the truck in drive and headed off to work.

Cockspur Island lived up to its name to a fault. Several times Hank and Loir had brought Ally to the island for a picnic and, on each occasion, Hank had spent the remainder of the evening picking cockspurs out of clothing, blankets and anything else that had touched the ground. The Island was replete with the damn things. When the crew played a game of football in the field adjacent to the station (no matter how short the mower cut it) every pair of tennis shoes and socks were covered. The football games were fantastic morale but the spurs deadened the mood almost immediately.

Driving between thick stands of pines, Hank could feel and taste the hint of salt air that hung over the island. In days of old, when there was no bridge, Hank imagined that this had been a very isolated place... regardless of its importance. This island guarded the entrance to the Savannah River. Hundreds, if not thousands, of men had stood the watch in the dripping heat of the Georgia summer. God only knew how many were buried here and there. It was a perfect place for defense or a perfect corner to be backed into with no ready escape at hand. It still felt that way at times, when a storm came through knocking out power as it went. The emergency generator at the Station did its job but only the most essential of circuits (communications, refrigeration) received power. In the midst of a storm the near dark of the Station was ghostly.

The blast of an over-loud car horn interrupted Hank's musings. It was Seaman Shawn Jones, racing past Hank as the station buildings came into view. Shawn's meticulously polished and outlandishly accessorized Mustang roared past Hank, who gave a cursory wave.

Shawn was a darn good worker and a member of Hank's duty section, with which he would be spending the next two days. In his rear-view Hank saw Terry's squad approaching at high speed.

"Shawn… you're gonna get it," Hank thought aloud. But, just as Terry reached Hanks rear-end, Shawn turned into the station parking lot. Terry slowed to a stop.

"Better luck next time buddy," Hank said as he reached the Station entrance.

Station Tybee was more of a complex than a single unit structure. Collocated with the Station were an Aids to Navigation Team and the eighty-seven foot Coast Guard Cutter Tarpon. The Aids to Navigation Team (ANT Team) occupied a small building and garage on the Station's east side. The Tarpon moored at the end of the pier. The station was a large two-story building with administrative offices, a training room, recreation room and galley on the lower level and twelve hotel-like berthing rooms for unaccompanied (single) members and duty standers on the second deck. Between the Aids to Navigation Team's buildings and the main Station building was a small but sufficient structure divided into shop areas and garage spaces used by the Station's Deck and Engineering departments. The Station pier structure consisted of one long L-shaped pier and a single-leg pier along which the Stations two assigned small boats were moored.

On the grounds of the station, near the water, stood a screened-in pavilion, a recently installed BBQ pit and a basketball court which in an extreme emergency, could double as a landing pad for Coast Guard helicopters. Though Hank had never seen this particular use personally, he was aware that it had been a common occurrence in the past.

Hank parked, grabbed his duffel bag and headed toward the Station. Shawn stood at the Station's side door smiling like the Cheshire Cat.

"That was close," Shawn said, referring to Terry.

"Very close," Hank shot Shawn a judgmental and scolding look. "Getting another speeding ticket and having to tell Master Chief about it would not be the best way to start a Monday."

"I suppose you're right," Shawn looked scolded.

Hank slapped Shawn on the shoulder, "No blood… no foul. Get your uniform on."

"Aye, aye..." Shawn said then turned and headed up the metal steps to the second floor. Stopping, Shawn turned back to Hank, "You know who that is?"

Shawn's pointing finger directed Hank to where two unfamiliar cars were parked in the visitor's parking spots. "No clue. But, with all the post - Danelle things going on, we should expect lots of visitors."

Shawn shrugged his shoulders and bounded up the stairs as Hank entered the main building.

The main hallway of the Station was abnormally busy this morning. Hank watched as members of the off-going duty section scampered about hurriedly, nervously, the way they did when Master Chief was in a bad mood or was put in a bad mood by something stupid the crew had done. As he passed the open door of the Master Chief's office, Hank peeked inside. A man in a suit and tie and another in a Chatham County Sheriff's uniform sat conversing with the Master Chief. Master Chief was in early, very early.

Hank stopped at the bay window that looked into the Station's communications room. Inside, BM2 Joe Jarvis stood filling out the morning relief paperwork while Fireman Stacy Olesheski tended the unit's radios...

nothing out of the ordinary here. Hank walked into the training room and headed for the back office that he shared with Mike Harwood.

"What's going on, Boat's?"

Hank startled as Rachel shot him the question. She was standing, out of sight, at the front of the training room. She looked concerned.

"Going on…?" Hank replied.

"Hey, Bubba…" it was Mike, calling to Hank from the doorway of their office, "You got a minute?"

"You got a minute," was universal code for "We need to talk, off-line," at any Coast Guard Station. Mike rarely talked "off-line" Hank's concern rose to match Rachel's.

Hank entered the office, Rachel trailing after, to see Ryan and the Station's Executive Petty Officer waiting. Hank tossed his bag onto the floor next to his desk as Mike closed the office door. No one said a word, which was odd. Hank looked around at the silent faces then grabbed his coffee cup, finding it warm and heavy.

"I got it for you already," Mike said as he plopped down, cockeyed, on his desk.

"I'm grateful," Hank said, "Morning, XO. What's up?"

The Executive Petty Officer, the second in command, Jennifer Brooks, fidgeted in her chair then smiled unconvincingly at Hank. Jennifer had been the XPO of the Station for two years and had been in the Coast Guard for twelve. Jennifer was a model First-Class Boatswains Mate who, as Master Chief put it, had her "Shit in one sock!" She was single, thirty-five years old, never married. Jennifer was whole heartedly dedicated to her career and a very effective leader. She was strong-willed and independent, more of a man than half the men on the crew but betrayed her femininity by keeping fresh cut flowers and a scented oil warmer in her office. Above all Jennifer was a pro, could be trusted and wasted no time on bullshit. She spoke to Hank.

"An agent from CGIS (Coast Guard Investigative Services) and Savannah-Chatham Narcotics are in the Master Chief's Office. They came here to talk to the four of you about that boat full of dead people, drugs and money you found."

"Okay," Hank thought. "Time for some Coast Guard math."

"CGIS, plus the locals, plus a nervous Station and the crew of the 942 all sequestered to a back office," Hank sighed at the thought. This was not going to be a good Monday.

Jennifer continued, "The four of you are going to be interviewed singly, soon. Master Chief will be in the room with you." Jennifer stood from her chair. "Until then, you four stay in here and stay quiet until the interviews are over." Jennifer gave them each a steely, authoritative gaze. "Got it?"

Each of the four, Hank, Mike, Rachel and Ryan nodded their acknowledgement. There was a knock at the door as it opened. It was Master Chief.

Master Chief Boatswain's Mate Marcus "Marc" Braden, forty-four years of age medium build and height and a twenty-six year veteran of the Coast Guard entered the office with his usual dead pan face on full display. Hank had rarely seen Braden exhibit any other facial expression. Even when you knew Braden was upset, pissed even, his facial expression never changed. Once, only once, at last year's Coast Guard Day party, Hank had sat across the table from Braden mulling over sea-stories from Braden's career when Braden had laughed, subtly and not for long. Braden always preached consistency. Hank supposed the lack of emotion was a part of the consistency Braden strove to provide. Braden never got excited when things got rough or dangerous. He never lost his cool no matter how much shit hit the fan. Hank respected Braden greatly.

Marc Braden was the poster boy for minority success in the Coast Guard. Braden, an African-American, stood out as one of the few black Master Chief Boatswains Mates in the service. Moreover, Braden was one of the few, regardless of race, enlisted men who had successfully served through five tours as Officer In Charge of Coast Guard units. Braden was constantly being asked to events that focused on the future of minorities in the Coast Guard and on each occasion Braden answered with a stout "No!"

Hank clearly remembered last year's Civil Rights training. Braden had stood in front of the crew and said, "I am Master Chief Braden. I am not Master Chief Braden… the black guy. I put my pants on one leg at a time and any success I have earned is because I have worked… hard. Race, religion, gender… are non-factors at this command." Hank remembered Master Chief bristling, "Don't think that they ever will be. God help the person who makes them one." No one ever had. Braden was, simply put, the best Officer in Charge Hank had ever served with. Knowing that, Hank knew that this particular situation must be serious.

"Folks… good morning," Braden said, shutting the door behind him.

A chorus of subdued good mornings came from Hank, Rachel, Mike and Ryan as Braden took a sip of his coffee.

"Ok," Braden began. "To begin with, none of you has done anything wrong. You're not going to jail and you're not losing your birthdays."

Braden's statement immediately lightened the atmosphere of the room. Hank knew the Master Chief was about to drop the big "But."

"But…" Braden continued "The boat you found in Romerly Creek has become a significant concern for local law enforcement. Apparently, the bodies were those of some known drug pushers locally and in the Charleston area and…"

"That's why CGIS is here?" Mike asked.

Braden held up a finger, "Let me finish, Mike. Chatham County wasn't able to reach the boat until the next high tide after your discovery. When they arrived, the bodies and the product were still there but the money was gone."

Rachel, Mike, Ryan and Hank exchanged glances.

"They think one of us took it?" Hank chimed in, saying what everyone else was thinking.

"Did I say that, Hank?" Braden's tone was forceful.

"No, Master Chief, you didn't."

"None of you are being accused of anything. Is that clear?" Braden looked around the room. Everyone nodded.

"But, you are going to be given the Rights Advice prior to the CGIS and Chatham County agent's interviews with you. Its procedural and I expect each of you to cooperate fully."

"So..." Hank thought, "We aren't being accused but we are being suspected. Great."

"When do we start?" Mike huffed as he took a drink of coffee.

"Right now, they want to talk to Ryan first, for no particular reason." Braden opened the door, motioning with his head for Ryan to follow.

"Everyone else just sit tight. We'll get this over as quick as we can and you can start your duty period."

Braden winked at the group, a rare display meant to calm the nerves, then accompanied Ryan out of the room.

"This sucks," Rachel said then sank into a chair.

3

7:45AM

Briny water, mud and plant decay shot through the wheel wells and over the hood splattering violently across the windshield as the Jeep Cherokee rocketed along the swamp road. Deer darted across the path as the vehicle gained firmer traction on an island of hardened clay then turned toward a blue-white gleam of metal amidst the thickening pines. The Ogeechee was the perfect place to hunt, to fish and to hide. Mile upon unknown mile of ATV trails crisscrossed the Ogeechee and, with a strained budget, the Georgia Department of Natural Resources couldn't hope to deter anything illegal. The Ogeechee was Dennis Taylor's production floor.

Dennis Taylor, Denny, D.T., thirty two years old, twice married, father of two girls from one wife and one mistress, was the epitome of entrepreneurial prowess where methamphetamine was concerned. Growing up in an impoverished home with an abusive father and alcoholic mother, Dennis had perceived early that his options for success in life were few. At age twelve he and his departed older brother had embarked on a life of crime starting with petty theft. By age sixteen Dennis had graduated to couriering marijuana for the local dealer and automobile theft. After his brother (at age twenty) had been shot dead by a convenience store clerk, Dennis moved away from anything as risky as robbery and settled on drug dealing as his forte. Dealing drugs was reasonably safe, if you were smart. The customers were legion and the money was abundant.

At first Dennis thrived on the sale of prescription medications like Percocet, Valium and Demerol to addicts in Macon, Savannah, Valdosta and Jacksonville. Supplied by a well organized chain of pharmacy and hospital employees, Dennis had engaged a substantial clientele and had propelled his income to the six-figure range by the age of twenty-six. But, the risk became too great. Dennis had had to personally kill one of his long time suppliers in Jacksonville when the poor dolt had been arrested and released on bail after swearing to name the "head" of the organization. Dennis didn't mind the killing. It was a part of business. He had shot men and women before, but preferred that things didn't come to that point. The cleanup was time consuming and marked an organizational failure.

The move to meth was logical, timely. Dennis needed to get separation from his previous product and was grateful he could step away easily, having not exposed his identity to more than a few persons in his previous dealings. Besides, meth was a better fit for profit. No matter what form methamphetamine took it was fairly cheap and quick to produce with the added plus that it could be "cooked" in almost any location. Most importantly, meth was extremely addictive which meant a captive customer base. Though the product could put a user in their grave in a matter of years, it's addictive properties meant a steady stream of new addicts to replace any loss. Dennis actually monitored the number of new customers very closely to ensure one, continued patronage, two, consistent income and three, his relative invisibility to law enforcement. Too many users meant too much demand and too great a chance of "loose lips."

In the past, Dennis had a soft spot for his users. He had seen some of the long-term addicts turn from twenty-five year old starlets to thirty year old zombies and had felt initial pangs of guilt when the undertakers came calling. That was the past. The users made a decision to use and Dennis was happy to oblige. Their decision to destroy themselves was as much their own as his mother's was to drink herself to death. The folks at Canadian Club had no remorse about his mother's addiction. Dennis shared the same philosophy where his customers were concerned.

On days like today, as the jeep entered the miniscule clearing where one of his "cook houses" was located, the subject was loss. Dennis hated losing product and he hated losing money. He had recently, no more than a week ago, done both. Just before Danelle made landfall his associate, Bernard Cummings, insisted on making a waterborne transaction with a dealer from Charleston. The transaction would take place near Wassaw Sound in Romerly Creek. Bernie assured Dennis that this was a "sure deal" considering the preoccupation of the cops and the Coast Guard with Hurricane preparations and evacuations. The deal was twenty pounds of powder in exchange for a quarter million dollars. The deal would go down the evening before expected landfall, giving the folks from Charleston an opportunity to run up the coast to Beaufort before the weather got to dicey. It didn't work.

The Jeep slammed to a halt in front of the twenty foot Airstream trailer, the "cook house." The rapid stop was for show, to convey Dennis's anger. Inside the trailer Dennis saw several shadows scurry past windows. The door to the trailer opened and Bernard, followed by two cookers, exited. Dennis didn't know the names of the cookers but he'd seen them several times in other locations. Personal association with employees wasn't something Dennis wanted. Cookers came and went. Dennis could train a no-name addict to cook meth in a matter of a few days. Keep them supplied with product and give them a little oversight (like Benny) and product flowed like a river.

"I bet the fat bastard's nervous."

Dennis looked at his driver, Evan Gregory, the one and only employee he had allowed to bond with him on any level. "He should be."

Dennis and Evan climbed out of the Jeep as Benny moved forward; smiling as if all was well.

"Boss, whatcha doing out this far?" Benny asked as he offered a hand.

"How's product Benny?" Dennis said, refusing Benny's hand as the two cookers, nasty gaunt junkies, lit cigarettes and leaned against the trailer.

"Product is damn good boss," Benny smiled. "Aint no damn Hurricane gonna keep us off line for long."

"That's good to hear Benny. That's good to hear." Dennis leaned in the front door of the trailer, examining the beakers, pots, tubes and burners used to cook. "That's real good to hear Benny, cause you fucked up and you owe me."

Benny heaved a slight laugh as sweat began to bead on his forehead, "Yeah, yeah... I heard about Wassaw." Benny pulled a cigarette from his pocket. He shook as it was lit.

Evan opened the rear door of the Jeep as Dennis looked over the cookers.

"I didn't know shit would get that ugly Denny, Boss. Those fuckers have never done that kind of shit before." Benny sucked nervously on his cigarette.

Dennis eyed the cookers. "Damn you two are piles of shit. Like your boss." Dennis looked toward Benny. The cookers didn't speak.

"You said you knew those folks...said they were a good deal," Evan said as he pulled two fifteen-pound propane tanks from the Jeep.

Benny tossed his smoke to the ground, having "hot boxed" to the filter, "Well, I thought I did. It's what I was told...you know?"

"No. I don't know Benny!" Dennis voice rose, "You know Benny! You know we don't fuck with wild cards. We sell to sure things and sure things only. That's standard. That's the way we run."

Benny nodded his head, agreeing with Dennis. "They weren't a wild card, Boss. I knew that broad, Tracy from high school and she was legit. She was in with a dealer in Charleston that had credentials."

"Yeah, credentials like you getting a piece of ass for selling her shit for cheap." Evan snickered as he set the propane near the front of the trailer.

"But you didn't check anything else did you Benny?" Dennis stood in front of Benny, staring him in the face, "You didn't do a buy to screen their product or their dealers. You didn't work our people for background." Dennis shook his head. "You just wanted a piece of ass, didn't you, Benny, from some whacked out high school skank?"

"It's not that way, Denny." Benny said as he lit another cigarette.

"BULL SHIT!" Dennis punched Benny in the stomach sending Benny sprawling onto the ground.

The cookers both sprang up but Evan produced a .38 special that caused them to recoil in fear.

"Your shriveled up cock just cost me a quarter million Benny, and your girlfriend killed one of my best couriers!" Dennis kicked Benny in the side as Benny choked.

"I'm sorry. I'm sorry." Bennie said as he struggled to his knees.

"He didn't mean anything to go wrong," one of the cookers added.

"Shut your mouth!" Evan shouted and struck the cooker in the face with the revolver.

Dennis laughed. "That isn't the worst part Benny. The worst part is that now the cops are looking around. I don't like that shit, Benny."

Benny stood, holding bruised ribs. "I tell you, Boss, that broad showed me numbers, good numbers on her organization. And, and the cops won't find shit. Chatham will make sure of that, right?"

Dennis had connections all over Southeast Georgia and Northeast Florida. Cops, judges, lawyers, shrimpers…hell, even garbage men were on the payroll. But this was one instance that might be hard for his "people" to bury. Dennis had heard that the Feds, the Coasties up in Savannah, had found the boat, the product and the money. When the Feds got involved things got very complicated. Meth was not a top priority in the Governments "War on Drugs" and was largely left for the locals to handle since most meth operations were piecemeal…small. But, let the Feds find a large bag of cash and some bodies and they would swarm all over the place. His people couldn't stop that. He'd have to bury this mess himself.

When Chatham, Dennis' contact within the County Sheriff's Office, had phoned to relay the news about the busted deal Dennis immediately hatched a plan. Dennis and Evan drove to the dead currier, Pete Meyers, home, planted cooking apparatus, ingredients, completed product. Next, they drove to the marina where Pete rented a berth. Pete never took his boat registration out of the glove box of his unlocked truck. Lastly, today, Dennis and Evan made a stop at Benny's mobile home outside of Savannah where they planted Pete's registration, five thousand in cash and several ounces of product. All this lead to now. Now came the end of the cleanup.

Evan left the cookers and went to the front of the trailer where he replaced half empty propane bottles with the full ones he and Dennis had brought.

Dennis heaved a sigh then reached out, patting Benny on the back "You have a lot of faith in the way I run things don't you, Benny?"

Benny smiled. "I always have. I always will. I wouldn't have shit if it wasn't for you, Boss. I owe you."

Dennis smiled. "Probably true, Benny, but up till now you've done a real fine job. I'm sure you can make it up to me."

Benny brightened, he was off the hook. "Sure can, Boss. The boys and I have been cooking all morning."

The cookers both nodded their heads.

"I bet we can roll out enough product to make up for what got lost by the end of the week." Benny's tone was confident.

"Well…" Dennis said as Evan went inside the trailer. "Don't rush things fellas. I don't want shitty product and I sure as hell don't want any accidents." Dennis produced a silver flask from his pocket and passed it to Benny.

Benny accepted the flask eagerly, taking a long draw then handed it to the cookers who drank in turn. Sharing his flask was one of Dennis' trademark "that-a-boy" moves designed to relax and inspire the troops.

Evan exited the trailer giving Dennis the slightest of glances. The glance spoke.

"Follow me up to the car boys," Dennis said as he turned toward the Jeep. Benny and the cookers followed.

At the Jeep, Dennis reached inside and produced a carton of Marlboro Reds. Benny and the cookers all smoked Basics and their eyes lit up as Dennis handed over the carton of premium smokes. Dennis snatched a pack from the carton, tapped it on his palm to pack the tobacco then offered a smoke to Benny.

Evan started the Jeep as Dennis climbed in. "Get back to work boys," Dennis said as he leaned out the window, offering Benny a light.

Benny pulled deeply on the cigarette until the tip glowed cherry red, "We're on it, Boss," Benny said as the jeep backed away. "Ya'll get inside," Benny urged the cookers who retreated to the trailer.

Benny waved as Dennis and Evan disappeared around a stand of pines. Benny and his boys made lots of product, more than anyone else. The fact that they weren't dead made Benny think Dennis needed, perhaps even liked him. As Benny reached the trailer the door swung open.

"It stinks in here, Benny...bad," the cooker said. Benny didn't smell anything.

"What the hell you talking about boy? A cook house always stinks." Benny took a draw on his smoke and leaned in the front door."

The explosion was monstrous as Benny's cigarette ignited the propane gas that filled the trailer. The fire ball leapt into the sky producing a mushroom cloud of boiling flame that spewed bits of aluminum and human tissue across the swamp. It was common for a cook house to have an "accident", blowing itself sky-high. From their position, several hundred yards away, Dennis and Evan leaned on the hood of the Jeep, watching. In a few minutes Dennis and Evan would drive back to the spot to make sure everyone was dead or dying. This far back in the swamp a dying man was as good as dead. Ambulances couldn't reach them fast enough and chances were that no one had heard or seen the explosion.

Later, Evan would drive the Jeep to Jacksonville where the vehicle would be given a complete overhaul. There would be new tires, paint, and plates…at a chop-shop that Dennis frequently used. After, the Jeep would be sold to some two-bit auto auctioning house and would disappear across the border of Texas into Mexico. Cleanup work would be finished.

"So much for that…" Evan said.

"For that part anyway," Dennis said as he watched the smoke rise from where the trailer had been.

"What part? You mean there is another part?"

"I want my money, Evan," Dennis coolly responded. "Some little assholes took my money. They left the bodies and the junk but they took my money. I want it back."

"Just who do you suppose has it? It could be anyone?"

"No, Evan, right after a Hurricane it couldn't be just anyone." Dennis climbed into the Jeep. "I have my ideas."

Dennis pulled out his cell phone, scrolling through the contacts until he found one labeled "WSAV."

"All I need are names," Dennis said as Evan started the Jeep and headed for the trailers smoldering hulk.

4

8:30AM

"Some of these pictures are graphic. Are you ok with that?" Special Agent Jeff Nguyen asked as he opened the folder.

"What kind of a dumb ass is this guy?" Rachel thought. "I took the damn pictures."

In actuality, Rachel Stone understood the question and why it was asked. When the crew of the 942 returned to Hunter Army Airfield after discovering the bodies, they had a mandatory meeting with an on-site Critical Incident Stress Management team. It was standard procedure in the Coast Guard and in all armed services for that matter. The CISM team would sit you down, ask you to explore and express your feeling about seeing or doing traumatic things, and offer their help through situations that could be difficult for the human psyche to process.

Of course, in keeping with her "tough guy" persona, Rachel had listened to the team then politely dismissed any further intervention. At twenty-three years old and the most junior (in age) boatswains mate at Station Tybee, Rachel decided that she had to maintain a rugged exterior or risk losing any form of respect from her peers and subordinates. Two days later when the post-hurricane frenzy subsided she had found the bottom of a fifth of Bacardi, cried for two hours then passed out. The next morning she felt ok.

"No, no problem," Rachel said as Jeff laid two pictures in front of her.

"This is Tracy Wilmot," Chatham County Deputy John Martin began, sitting up straighter in his chair. "She's the woman you found."

Rachel looked at the picture of Tracy, before her brain was blown out, seeing a haggard looking blonde that was probably pushing fifty. If first impressions were anything, Rachel would have categorized Tracy as a dirt-bag, living or dead. Next to the "living" picture was the picture of Tracy with her brain evacuated. The picture was less traumatizing than the real thing had been.

Nguyen laid out the next set of photos.

"This is Peter Meyers," Nguyen said. "He's a known drug courier, a good one supposedly."

Rachel looked over the mug shot of a middle-aged black man. To Rachel there was nothing especially significant to see. The other picture, the one of Meyers dead, had as much impact as the picture of Tracy.

"And this guy... we can't identify." Deputy Martin pointed to a picture of the third body on the wrecked boat. Apparently the police had turned the body over, revealing the face of a young black man, perhaps twenty, contorted by bloating and decay. Rachel hadn't taken this picture.

"The question, Petty Officer Stone, is whether or not you recognize any of these people," Nguyen began. "We aren't asking if you know them. Rather, we're asking if you recognize them... from a bar or restaurant, from a boarding or...well, anything?"

Rachel answered immediately, "No. I don't believe I've ever seen any of them."

"Fair enough," Nguyen said, and then placed the pictures back in the folder.

"Now, when you found the boat, you and your friends spent some time investigating the scene, right?" Deputy Martin asked.

"Deputy, my coworkers and I spent *some* time investigating the scene. A grand total of ten minutes, maybe, before we were called for SAR," Rachel answered, agitated.

"Were you or any of your coworkers ever alone on the boat, the wrecked boat?" Martin added.

"None of us were ever alone on that boat, Deputy. The closest to *alone* that anyone got was BM1 Morgan and only because he was the first one to go aboard."

Rachel's temper was gaining steam. If there was one thing she knew about military folks, especially the real good ones, they couldn't hack any inference that impugned their integrity. She was one of those people.

"From the time you left the boat until the time you got back to base, did you make any stops?" Nguyen asked.

Rachel fought to maintain her composure, looking behind her to where Master Chief sat. Braden stared back at Rachel, chin up and confident, projecting the image he wished her to convey.

"We left Romerly creek and went straight to Turners Creek. When the case was over we went to the ramp and trailored back to Hunter."

"Ok then," Nguyen smiled at Rachel. "We appreciate your time and cooperation, Petty Officer Stone."

"I'm done?" Rachel asked, rising from her chair.

"For now..." Nguyen smiled again. "Oh..." Nguyen added as Rachel straightened her uniform. "If you think of anything that seems peculiar or different about this case...please let Master Chief know and he'll get in touch with us."

"Peculiar, maybe..." Rachel thought. The phones weren't right... or were they? Rachel choked back the urge to mention it. There wasn't any sense in making these squirrelly pricks any more curious than they already were.

"You bet," Rachel said. "Can I go?" Rachel looked at Braden.

"Thanks, Boat's, you can head out," Braden responded as he rose from his chair, ready to summon Hank to the inquisition. "I'm bringing in Petty Officer Morgan."

Braden had sat through the questioning of Seaman Ryan Post, Petty Officer's Harwood and Stone and was growing tired of having his crew under a spotlight of accusation. Braden wanted the inquisition to end, fast, and to get on with the daily routine. Still, there was precedent for distrust of folks in a Coast Guard uniform.

Braden was privy to a history of criminal behavior within the Coast Guard. There had been several incidents of espionage; the selling of intelligence to drug cartels. It certainly wasn't uncommon for members to use government purchase cards to redecorate their house. And, there were plenty of incidents in which government property had been sold or pawned. But, these actions represented only a meager fraction of the workforce.

"I trust my crew," Braden thought as Hank entered the room.

****

Hank had been down this road before, not for the same reasons, but the tension felt the same. Hank hated to admit it but participating in "official investigations" wasn't as foreign to him as he would like. In boot camp there had been the kid who threw himself out the third story window of Healey Hall, shattering his legs and lower spine. Hank, and the rest of his company, had to give statements about that incident for the better part of a week. In the end... the kid was just nuts. On the Cheyenne, the engineering petty officer had been caught having sex with the wife of a Coast Guard Auxiliary member at an annual Christmas party. Hank had to give statements and testify at a Summary Courts Martial over that business. Really, those cases were fairly trivial compared to this, but the consequences seemed substantially more dire this time around. They were.

Hank took a seat in front of Nguyen and Martin after being given the Rights Advice. There was nothing about being told you had the right to remain silent or to an attorney that evoked comfort. The fact that he was involved in any situation that questioned his personal ethics and morality made Hank furious. Hank strove, every day, to be his very best and to give his very best in service to the country. Hank was an idealist, wrapped in the flag. Honor, Respect and Devotion to Duty, the Coast Guard's core values, were something Hank tried to live, despite how cliché they seemed to his shipmates.

"Boatswains Mate First Class Henry Morgan?" Nguyen asked, knowing the answer.

Henry Morgan. Hank had never managed to forgive his parents for deciding on that name. Of course, he understood that his grandfather was named Henry and that his mother wanted that name to carry on through the family lineage. But, being named after a pirate and popular rum was a chore. Hank spent the majority of his life having people yell "Arrrgh, Captain," in the halls at school and there was scarcely a time he could prop a foot up on the handrail of a boat without someone asking, 'Got a little Captain in you?" all this enveloped in laughter and additional taunts. There were moments when Hank wished it were the days of old when he could have exercised his authority as a pirate and flogged his chastisers at the mast. In the end, Hank had to join their laughter and…take it.

"Aye, aye," Hank responded, robotically.

"Petty Officer Morgan…" Nguyen continued, "I want you to understand that this is a part of an investigation that the Chatham County Sheriff's Department has asked to be performed. That is the reason why Deputy Martin is here."

"I understand."

"In the wake of Hurricane Danelle we all understand that your duties had you and your crew running all over this area without very solid command and control. And, we understand that you did the best you could in a difficult situation."

"Get on with it," Hank thought.

"The reason we are taking such an interest in this particular case is the fact that your crew was the first response at the scene of a homicide and that a large sum of money disappeared from that scene between the time of your arrival and the time Savannah-Chatham Officers were able to reach the scene," Nguyen finished.

"I understand that completely, Special Agent, but I want to remind you that my crew reported the existence of the boat, bodies and the money immediately after discovery. It seems to me that if we had the desire to take the cash we could have simply said nothing," Hank responded. "It's not our fault that we were called away prior to the arrival of local authorities. We wanted to stay."

"I understand…" Nguyen replied, penciling Hanks remarks onto a lined pad.

Nguyen was a "Coastie" the same as any of the 942 crew. CGIS agents were pulled from within the ranks of the Coast Guard and were a de-facto form of Internal Affairs. Nguyen had been with CGIS for the past six years. Before that he had been a Chief Food Service Specialist, a cook, and had served on several Coast Guard cutters and shore units. Nguyen could weed the good Coasties from the bad Coasties easily. To Nguyen, Hank was as honest as they came.

"We realize that, and we have listened to the tapes of your radio conversations with Sector Charleston," Nguyen said.

"Why am I here then?" Hank asked.

"Hank...." Deputy Martin leaned forward. "Each of the people you found dead were part of separate organizations... bad ones. This guy..." Martin pulled out the picture of Pete Meyers, "... he is a part of a methamphetamine operation, a big one that we've been trying to take down for the better part of five years. This girl...." Martin pulled out Tracy's photo, "...she is a part of a particularly violent gang in the Charleston area."

Hank could feel apprehension building somewhere in his stomach.

Martin continued, "We have a body count from these folks but we haven't been able to pin it on them yet. God knows we're trying."

Apprehension and even fear, definitely. Hank could feel each welling up as his thoughts turned immediately to Lori and Allison.

"Look..." Martin's leathery façade dropped to reveal true concern, "If you or one of your crew took that money there are going to be consequences."

"We didn't!" Hank shot back, infuriated by the inference.

"Wait a second..." Martin held up a hand to calm Hank. "Even if you didn't, Hank, there may still be consequences. You need to listen and listen good."

Hank fought for composure as Master Chief rose from his chair and moved closer.

Nguyen spoke next. "Petty Officer Morgan, anyone could have taken that money. There was a period of eight hours between the time you left that boat and the time local authorities were able to reach the scene. Some *local* could have come up through the marsh in a flat-boat. Hell, even one of the *bad guys* could have shown up. But, the fact is that a quarter of a million dollars was taken while the product remained. That means the bad guys probably don't have the money. No drug organization in the world would have taken only one of the two."

Hank could see the logic but was unsure where Nguyen was headed.

"Listen, Hank," Braden chimed in calmly "You and your crew had full access to that money. I'm not - we're not saying any of you took it. What is being said is that someone took it and that that person or any other person these drug organizations perceive may have taken it... might be at risk."

"For what..." Hank asked, fully aware of the coming answer.

"These people are going to want their money back," Nguyen said, "There are some drug cartels in the Caribbean or the Baja of Mexico that could write off a quarter million as business expenditure but we're in Georgia. That much money is a significant payday for these people and they aren't likely to dismiss the loss."

"And they will try their best to find out who has it," Martin chimed in. "They will go through everyone who could have taken it until they reach the one who did. That means you and your crew."

"Hank…" Master Chief Braden placed a hand on Hank's shoulder, squeezing softly "I know you are a damn good Coastguardsmen and I know you run a tight ship. If you tell me that you didn't touch that money then I believe you and so should everyone else." Braden shot a glance at Nguyen and Martin.

Braden continued, "I also know that we don't make near as much money as we should for what we do and that much money could be a serious temptation."

"We did not take it, Master Chief," Hank sighed the answer.

"I believe you, Hank, but I want you to stay alert. I want you to keep thinking about all the things that happened from the time you found that boat to the time you got back to Hunter…every detail, even the smallest." Braden looked into Hanks eyes, "If someone from your crew took that money, and I am saying *if*, then I have to know so I can protect the rest of you."

Hank looked at Nguyen and Martin as he considered each member of the 942 crew. Hank found it hard to believe that any of them would have been capable of stealing the cash from the boat without him noticing. A twenty five foot RBS was far too small a platform for anyone to hide anything. The bloody sack full of money would have been completely conspicuous. Besides, each crewman had a job at the time they left the wreck. Ryan was on the stern, Mike was on the bow and Rachel was in the cabin. Ryan and Rachel were the only people who had been alone, when they were on the radio in the 942's cabin. There was simply no way one of his people could have taken the money.

"Master Chief, if I had any idea that one of my crew was responsible for taking that money I would tell you right now. But, for the life of me, I don't see how they could have snuck it past the rest of us. The boat's too tight and there is no place to hide the cash if they'd tried."

"That's what we all believe, Hank, but we have to keep all possibilities open." Nguyen smiled at Hank. "But, that doesn't lessen our concern for personnel safety."

"You think we're in danger?" Hank questioned.

"Maybe..." Martin placed the pictures back in the folder as he talked. "The one thing you have going for you is that the bad guys only know, thanks to the media, that the Coast Guard found the boat. They don't know who."

To some extent Hank felt relieved. Coast Guard units were typically small which meant they were part of the community in which they existed. Crewmen were often on a first name basis with the same people they saved or censured which made for some uncomfortable moments around town for Coasties and their families. Knowing that there was the potential for very violent people to be after you, especially in this case, was disturbing. But, if names were kept close to the vest then Hank, and his family, could feel relatively secure. Questions remained.

"You honestly think these people would risk exposing themselves and collapsing their business? " Hank asked.

"No. I don't think they, the leaders, would risk it but I wouldn't put it past them to send a few of their lackeys out to hunt," Martin responded.

"You have to understand, Hank, there are some very desperate people in the low-country. There's a big gap between the rich and the poor. A lot of folks live paycheck to paycheck. Some have gotten wrapped up in the drug trade. They'll do what it takes to feed their kids, pay the bills or get their next hit," Nguyen asserted.

"Once, I scraped up the guts of a meth-head that jumped in front of a Semi on a twenty dollar dare. That's about how much a hit costs. And once, I saw a father of three try to rob a gun store with a pocket knife because his kids needed shoes. He died." Martin's face sagged, the memories surfacing as he spoke. "With desperate folks like that in this world you can bet someone would be willing, for a very small price, to come after you."

Hank sat, silently, feeling the anxiety well up inside his mind. There were times when Coasties truly got to touch the dangerous side of their job. Contrary to popular belief, the Coast Guard was on the front lines, every day. You never knew when you would board a boat and find yourself staring at the barrel of a gun. You never knew which SAR call would suddenly propel you to the brink of disaster. Coasties just took those things as they came because there was never any real time to think about them. But, this time, Hank would have hours and days to look over his shoulder and worry about his family. How long would he have to? Would he ever *not* have to?

"So, what now?" Hank asked, somberly.

"For now you stay quiet. We all stay quiet." Master Chief perched on the edge of a desk. "You keep your mind, ears and eyes open for anything that suggests trouble, including where that money could have gone."

"But..." Nguyen said, tossing the folder of pictures in his briefcase, "... you do not play CSI on this. Investigating this kind of thing is my job. Deputy Martin and I will be working together closely for as long as it takes to become comfortable with a conclusion." Nguyen closed his briefcase then straightened his tie. "You just need to keep doing your job, Petty Officer Morgan, but with a bit more vigilance."

"Are our families in danger?"

"If they don't know who you are then they don't know who your families are. It's that simple." Martin replied as he rose from his chair.

5

5:10PM

I'm live outside the entrance to Coast Guard Station Tybee Island where I had the opportunity to meet some of the brave men and women of the Coast Guard who were so instrumental in the aftermath of Hurricane Danelle." Trisha Jordan, WSAV field reporter, flipped her sandy blonde hair as she smiled her way to a segment recorded earlier.

Hank sat in the galley muscling his way through the plate of lemon chicken that was on the menu for tonight's crew. Coast Guard galleys served pretty good chow for the most part with breakfast and lunch being the cook's forte. But, by the evening meal the culinary creativity was reduced to minimum levels. Tonight was lemon chicken, rice and almond green beans. Hank hadn't seen an almond yet, and the lemon in the chicken must have been chicken flavored. Still, it was chow that he didn't have to make, was cheap as meals go and was, unfortunately, a mandatory purchase that kept the station's galley functioning. Hank would have seconds at breakfast to make up for this.

On the television, the image of Station Tybee shone brilliantly in the late-day sun as Trisha Jordan rattled off some uninteresting banter. Everyone in the duty section, except for the person standing radio watch, was gathered in the galley to watch the report. No one really cared about anything the reporter was saying. The crew waited to hoot and whistle when the face of one of their shipmates appeared on the screen. It was common practice to rib the hell out of those unfortunate enough to have to conduct an interview, except for the Master Chief and the Executive Officer, if they were still around.

It was well after five in the afternoon and Master Chief and BM1 Brooks had departed for the day leaving Hank, the Officer of the Day, in charge. As the Officer of the Day or OOD, Hank was the direct representative of the Command in their absence. His job was to ensure that the unit remained secure, clean and ready to respond to the mission. Hank was a second-class Boatswains Mate when he reported to the unit and had recently advanced in rank. Despite the fact that he was a first-class Petty Officer, his billet still called for him to be a member of a duty section. He was the only first class in the duty rotation. Until he transferred, he did what he had to do.

The face of BM2 Laura Hill appeared on the screen to a round of joking cheers. On camera, Laura explained that she had been a part of a crew that headed into the unit's area of responsibility (AOR) after Danelle, searching for damage and distress. The combined images of Seaman Shawn Jones, Fireman Gabriel Ortiz and Petty Officer Steve Lyle were the next to appear. These were the members of Laura's crew, one of two crews that made up Hank's duty section. In turn, each of them took a healthy bit of razzing, were called "stars" or "Hollywood." and then the segment ended cutting back to Trisha Jordan's live feed from her spot in front of the Stations sign at the entrance to Cockspur Island.

"You guys looked good," Hank said as he pushed another fork full of rice into his mouth.

"I didn't know they stacked shit that high," Mike said as he chomped ice from his near-empty cup. Mike leaned closer to Hank, "I think Master Chief overreacted about us doing TV."

Hank had taken the phone call earlier in the day, when WSAV requested an interview. Master Chief was very uneasy. In keeping with the need to hide the identity of the 942 crew, Master Chief had initially turned down Trisha Jordan's request but, after a lengthy phone conversation with the Sector Charleston Public Affairs Officer, Master Chief reluctantly apporved the activity. The plan was simple. Laura and her crew would be the face of the Station's post-Danelle response but would repeatedly state that the entire crew engaged in recovery activities. Laura herself was directed to say that she and her crew had been active in the Hilton Head area though they never made it out of the Savannah River.

Master Chief had been present for the entire interview process. Jordan asked the typical questions; what boats did you use, how long were you out, what did you see? Jordan was hunting for a sound bite for tonight's broadcast. When Laura responded to a question by saying, "Things were a real mess. I've never seen devastation like that before." Master Chief knew Jordan was happy. That statement was the only one included in the finished report.

After the interview, Jordan engaged in friendly conversation with the crew, inquiring about their duty schedule, asking if their job was tough on their families. Jordan and her cameraman walked to the dock to record footage of the station's assigned boats. The forty-one foot Utility Boat, CG 41683, and the 942 were photographed in turn.

Hank remembered how nervous Master Chief was when he saw Rachel replacing the national ensign on the 942 but Rachel was only visible for a moment. When she spotted the camera she leapt into the cabin, out of sight. When Jordan finally left the station, Master Chief was still uncomfortable about what had transpired.

Half an hour after dinner, Trisha Jordan came back to the station with follow-up questions. Hank met her at the gate.

"Petty Officer Hill indicated that she was in the Hilton Head area. So you guys were spread out in different spots?" Trisha asked.

"Yes, around the Savannah area and north to Port Royal Sound," Hank answered reluctantly. He didn't have time to confer with Master Chief before engaging Jordan.

"I see. I see," Trisha said, busily writing on her notepad. "Now, your big boat…the UTB, she has a ton of range right? She's the real heavy lifter?" Trisha glanced a smile at Hank then went back to her notes.

"That's true," Hank responded as he saw Mike walk out the door of the station, headed to the smoke pit.

"So you guys did some short and long range recovery work with your boats?"

"True again," Hank said as Mike lit a smoke and walked toward the impromptu interview.

"I think I remember Master Chief Braden saying that your big boat was kept somewhere up the Savannah River during Danelle. Where did ya'll keep all your other boats? Trisha asked with another smile and innocent yet inquisitive tone.

"We kept the smaller platforms at Hunter," Hank responded.

Trisha jotted down the information as Mike approached. "Where were you during the storm…" Trisha looked at Hanks nametag "…. Petty Officer Morgan?"

"He was with me," Mike said, blowing smoke into the space between Hank and Trisha. "And right now…"

Mike continued, "…we need Petty Officer Morgan inside the unit."

"Oh…." Trisha offered her hand to Hank. "I'm so sorry. I need to let ya'll get back to work."

Hank shook Trisha's hand. Mike didn't bother.

"It's ok, Ma'am," Hank smiled. "Have a good evening."

"You too guys. I'll make you look good," Trisha waved, hopped in her car and sped away.

"Thanks, man," Hank said, turning to Mike.

"Don't mention it," Mike said, patting Hank on the back. "She's got a great ass but I wouldn't want to get stuck talking to her."

****

By seven in the evening Trisha had finished at work and was seated in a booth at the Bayou Cafe on River Street. Her first dirty martini of the night was half gone and another had already been ordered. This was a normal night for Trisha. After work she went out for drinks and to wallow in the plethora of men who made their advances. She would unbutton two buttons on her blouse, exposing her cleavage, and pull her skirt up to mid thigh. She was thirty five years old, unmarried and attractive. She loved to flirt. She loved the attention. She rarely went home with a man unless she knew the evening benefited her socially or monetarily. She wasn't a prostitute but she walked a fine line. She liked money and success and wasn't afraid to use her looks to gain either.

"Your report was another gripping look into the utterly inconsequential."

Trisha peered up from her drink, catching Dennis Taylor staring down her shirt. Trisha met Dennis two years ago at a fundraiser for a nameless, failed, city political candidate. Dennis was intelligent, charming, relatively good looking and very well off. She spent the majority of that evening in his company. The conversation had been stimulating and intelligent and she eagerly shared a bed with Dennis at evening's end. She also shared some drugs, cocaine, to which she was addicted. In the months and years that followed, Dennis always made sure she had an ample supply. In exchange she did him favors from time to time. A certain news story here and there or some small piece of research into someone or something was all Dennis ever asked. They hadn't slept together since that first night. Trisha liked the arrangement. It was cordial and mutually beneficial.

"Don't be an ass, Dennis," Trisha smiled and scootched over, allowing Dennis to sit. "You asked me to do a story about them and I did."

"I'm sorry love," Dennis smiled his reply as he motioned for the waitress to bring more drinks. "So, what we're our fine Guardians like?"

Trisha sipped her martini, "They are great. I've talked to some of them before and they are always very nice, very cooperative and very formal," she ate the olive. "It must be part of their training."

"I'm not surprised."

"Why the interest?" Trisha asked, adjusting her blouse.

"I have a nephew who's interested in joining the Coast Guard. I figured that seeing them as the heroes of Danelle might finally push him into a recruiter's office."

"Good plan. I can think of a lot worse career choices." Trisha accepted her next martini from the waitress as she delivered the round of drinks.

Dennis sipped his martini then set the drink down with a smack of his lips. "I just can't imagine what those poor kids had to go through during that hurricane, being separated from their families...."

"It wasn't too bad on them from what I was told. The storm only glanced us so most of their families were back at home within three days."

"Even then..." Dennis trailed off, sipping again. "Where the hell did those poor guys go during the storm? They couldn't have stayed at their base?"

"Some went to a warehouse up-river with their larger boat. Some went to Hunter with their smaller boat."

"Makes sense." Dennis said.

"After the storm they responded... picking up the pieces."

"We didn't hear much about that. What kind of pieces?"

"Well, we didn't talk about it today but I know they went to a big fire at Turners Creek Marina the day after the storm. They actually saved a transient who was hold-up in a burning boat."

"That's incredible. I hope Teddy, my nephew, joins." Dennis smiled, "You know...my friend keeps his boat at Turners Creek. I'd like to thank those folks at the station for what they did."

"They would probably like that. But, I don't know who went to that call," Trisha said as she flashed an inviting smile toward a husky, grey-haired man across the room.

"No idea?" Dennis asked as he surveyed Trisha's target, a member of the city council... if Dennis identified him correctly.

"There are twenty eight folks stationed out there, Dennis. Some of them were at Hunter and some were in other places. The only person I can guess was at Hunter and would have been close to Turners Creek was a guy named Morgan and maybe this other one named.... Harwood... I think. But, I don't know." Trisha leaned forward onto the table causing her blouse to gape open in full view of the councilman across the room.

"Those two work together?" Dennis asked.

"It seemed that way."

Dennis looked across the room at the councilman who was obviously staring at Trisha. He knew this guy, and knew he had a wife and three kids at home.

"Ok then, Trish," Dennis stood. "Did you bring a copy of your footage?"

Trish reached to her side, digging through her purse and producing a DVD. "Here it is. It's everything we took today."

Dennis bent over, kissed Trish on the cheek and dropped a small bag into her brazier. "Thanks Trish."

"You know, Dennis, that's a lot of trouble to go through for your nephew." Trish leaned back in the booth, fishing the cocaine out of her blouse and dropping it into her purse.

Dennis looked over his shoulder as he walked away. "Anything to better my family."

The councilman stalked up to Trish as Dennis walked out the restaurant door.

Tuesday

6

9:00AM

Jeff Nguyen was operating outside his mandate. It wasn't part of a CGIS agent's job description to pursue possible wrong doing on the part of Coast Guard members into and through the intricacies of civilian law enforcement yet, here he was. He was supposed to have returned to Charleston right after interviewing the crew of the 942 but Deputy Martin had convinced him to stay on. A couple of phone calls and a couple of lies about "tying up loose ends," and Jeff had been cleared to stick around for another few days. For some reason Jeff felt he needed to.

"It'll be just up here on the right," Martin pointed toward the next right hand turn, a dirt road in the middle of nowhere, as he slowed the squad car.

How old is the scene, John?" Jeff asked as he pulled his briefcase into his lap, fishing out a pair of latex gloves.

"A few days anyway. This is the house of one of the dead guys ," Martin replied as he turned onto the dirt road leading to Benny Cummings double-wide trailer.

This morning, Martin had received a call from the Park Rangers in the Ogeechee telling him they'd located a burnt out, blown up lab in a remote part of the swamp. Three bodies were found at the scene, all badly burned but not so burned that the Rangers hadn't been able to read Benny Cummings name on what was left of his driver's license. After the call, Martin ran a check on Benny, found an address and asked investigators to head for the residence. What they found inside was interesting, relevant. Martin threw the SUV into park as they stopped in front of the trailer. Two other vehicles shared the dusty patch of gravel, one from the State Police and another from the Savannah-Chatham Anti Narcotics Team.

As Jeff and Martin climbed out of the car a State Police Officer appeared in the door of the double-wide.

"Good afternoon," Martin addressed the officer.

As was customary, the State Police Officer merely waved a hand in Martin's direction. For some reason, the GSP felt as though they were just a little bit better than county or city PD. Their uniforms were more elaborate and their jurisdiction was certainly larger… almost as large as their heads. Benny's home, the site of the burned trailer and now, other evidence, made this affair extend across several counties. That, unfortunately, made it a State matter as well.

"Anything?" Martin asked as he and Jeff stepped onto the dilapidated wooden porch that had been added to the double-wide.

"More dumb ass redneck meth-pusher shit," the officer responded.

Martin hated these guys. "Well then…ya'll should be able to handle this pretty well." Martin patted the officer on the shoulder as he and Jeff stepped into the home.

The home appeared exactly as Jeff imagined it would. Growing up in Seattle, Jeff was far out of touch with anything "southern" or "redneck." Every time Jeff thought about "southern folk" all he could see was Larry the Cable Guy in a sleeveless flannel shirt. All Jeff could hear was Jeff Foxworthy saying, "You might be a redneck if…." A mobile home on a dirt road in the country was the crowning jewel in Jeff's hillbilly stereotype. The place smelled of cigarettes, spilled beer and sweat.

"You're here!" a voice called from the kitchen space.

"Hey, Mitch…" Martin responded as he looked around the unkempt living room.

Mitch Dailey came out of the kitchen, giving Jeff the once over. Mitch was a seven-year veteran of the Savannah-Chatham Anti Narcotics Team and had earned his weight, which was considerable, in gold as far as investigation and interdiction were concerned. Mitch was known to be the roughest of all the teams members, the most unorthodox and the most effective. When Mitch made a case against someone they were either convicted or, for some reason, never returned to drug trafficking. Martin had seen a few black eyes and a couple of casts on Mitch's suspects before. No questions asked.

"Mitch Dailey, meet Jeff Nguyen," Martin said, motioning toward Jeff.

"Howdy," Mitch said and delivered a pulverizing handshake.

"Nice to meet you, Sir," Jeff responded, ignoring the pain shooting through his knuckles.

"Special Agent Nguyen is down here from Charleston. He's from the Coast Guard."

Mitch raised an eyebrow. "That explains calling *me* sir." Mitch released Jeff's hand, "That boat business has got ya'll's attention too?"

"That it does, sir...Mitch." Jeff smiled.

"Sir- Mitch is ok. I like sounding like royalty." Mitch laughed.

Martin walked over to a small desk on the far wall of the room and started sorting through a pile of unopened mail. "What do you have so far Mitch?"

"Well..." Mitch pulled a can of Skoal from his back pocket. "...Mr. Personality outside found a few thousand dollars in the bedroom closet." Mitch placed a heaping pinch of tobacco in his bottom lip. "The money was all a damn mess. Fifties, twenties and a few tens were mixed in there... only a couple of hundreds in the bag."

"That's strange?" Jeff questioned.

"Damn sure is, given what all has happened," Mitch responded.

"Meth dealers, the small-time ones, would have cash in those denominations, Jeff." Martin continued to flip mail from his hand onto the desk. "Small bills indicate small sales... small quantities. This guy, Benjamin Cummings, we never heard of him. That means he is very, very small time."

"Mix that with this and a strange picture gets worked up." Mitch reached, grabbing a small square of paper from the top of the desk, then passing it to Martin.

Martin looked the paper over then rubbed his chin as he passed it along to Jeff.

"Interesting...." Jeff said as he looked over the boat registration. The registration belonged to Pete Meyers, the owner of the wreck. "It looks like we've found the perpetrators," Jeff said, handing the registration back to

"Case closed then?" Mitch said, disingenuously. "This small time pecker-wood and ole Pete were business partners, and things went to hell in a hand basket. I can go home now."

Martin laughed. Jeff tried desperately to sort the sarcasm from the sincerity. "It seems crazy to me," Jeff said.

"Go on..." Martin responded.

"Well, to me it seems that all this Cummings had going, as far as production, was some tiny lab in the swamp. I know people can cook meth in a hurry but, a quarter million dollars worth?"

"There you go," Mitch said as he spit tobacco juice into a soda bottle.

"And this guy Pete Meyers... he's a known currier for seemingly notable drug runners in this area. Why throw in with a nobody? And, would he be so stupid as to leave this..." Jeff held up the registration, "...here?"

Martin eased into a creaky wooden chair by the desk. "I doubt it, Jeff."

Jeff sighed, his brain whirling. This wasn't the kind of thing he was used to. Most of the time he didn't really have to think to do his job. Jeff investigated things according to policy. Hell, even the guys working intelligence for the Coast Guard followed an approved game plan. Last week he was investigating a kid who had used a government travel card to rack up a five thousand dollar Best-Buy bill. Today, the shit was getting thick... and challenging. Jeff liked it.

"So, here is what we have in front of us," Martin started his summary, "Cumming's manages to land a major order for meth from a dealer in Charleston. He spends the better part of a month cooking the shit, then hires Pete Meyers to make the deal happen. Pete does the deal the day before Danelle hits, on the water, since all of us law enforcement types were busy saving the world." Martin motioned to Mitch who handed over the can of Skoal. "The deal goes bad. People get dead, and a week later this piss-ant dealer, Cummings, a guy with very little capital, probably nervous as hell, is back in his lab making the next batch." Martin loaded his bottom lip with tobacco and handed the can back to Mitch.

"And the son-bitch's lab blows up and burns him to a crisp. Bullshit," Mitch scoffed.

"Definite bullshit," the GPD officer agreed as he entered the room.

Martin, Mitch and Jeff turned, surprised, toward the officer.

"I just got off the phone with the coroner's office in Savannah. They say Cummings was dead before he burned. There is evidence of trauma to the back of the head, from a fall or maybe from being blown into the ground. They found fragments of pine bark and dirt embedded in his skull."

"What does that mean?" Jeff asked, turning to Martin.

"It means that maybe Cummings was tossed into the fire. It probably wasn't what his killer wanted, but that's what they had to do." Martin accepted the bottle from Mitch and spit.

"I don't like this shit at all," Mitch said as he stuffed his hands in his pockets and gazed out the front window.

"It wasn't Cumming's deal. Was it?" Jeff asked.

"No. It wasn't." Martin replied.

"Mr. Coast Guard, this is gonna get real complicated," Mitch said, smiling.

"Look…" Martin began. "Cummings was just a player. He probably had something to do with arranging the deal but he wasn't the mastermind. When it all fell apart, whoever the *real* boss is decided to cover his tracks by killing Cummings and making it look like Meyers was Cumming's partner."

"That's my bet," Mitch said as he wallowed the snuff in his mouth.

"You don't know that for sure," the GPD officer said, leaning against the doorframe.

"No. We don't. But it's a pretty damn good theory," Martin replied.

"And it hasn't got a thing to do with why I'm here," Jeff interjected.

"Really..." Mitch said, sarcastically.

"Jeff." Martin climbed from his chair. "I think it has a lot to do with why you're here. Cause this guy, this boss, whoever he is... he isn't even trying."

"Trying what?" Jeff asked, mildly provoked.

"Trying to be invisible, Jeff. Oh, he is making an effort...." Martin pointed at the boat registration in Jeff's hand. "He planted that here. He went to the trouble of killing Cummings...but, he thinks we're all stupid. He's overconfident and careless. He thinks he's untouchable."

"Speculation," the GPD Officer chimed in.

"I trust my gut and my experience," Martin shot back. "We've seen this type before." Martin motioned toward Mitch, "They get so big, so rich, so powerful... they start believing they're bullet proof. Believe me, I know the type. They make mistakes. They get aggressive."

"It's a god complex, Mr. Coast Guard." Mitch spit into his bottle.

"Everything this guy thinks, to him, is right," Martin said, staring at Jeff.

"What's he thinking, Martin?" Jeff folded his arms.

"He thinks one of your people has his money."

7

4:00PM

Evan Gregory nearly tripped over a basket of mud-caked oysters, fresh from somewhere in the low country, as he walked into the Thunderbolt Fish House. Evan didn't mind being Dennis's hired gun. The pay was excellent. The benefits were vast. But some of the people and locations he had to pay calls on were not to his taste.

The smell of the Fish House inundated Evan's senses. The oysters, shrimp, crabs and slabs of fish laid out in ancient-looking cases were the likely source of the overpowering reek. Perhaps the catch was a little older than the fresh, the sign on the front door advertised, but "fresh" was a very objective term in these parts. Some of the shrimp boats brought their bounty to the dock every couple of days. The long-liners rarely came back to dock within a week of their first string. Paul Sulsky was the type who left the dock and didn't return until the hold was full or his onboard supply of beer was exhausted. When Sulsky made port you could expect very little ice remaining on his catch and one of the first things off-loaded were the empty bleach and ammonia bottles, both chemicals having been used to preserve the catch and/or control its smell.

Before entering, Evan had scouted around the dock where the Gina Marie was tied up. The boat looked relatively unscathed in the wake of Danelle though Evan remembered the pictures of the Gina Marie's outrigger torn off and lying in the river. The local news channels were quick to catch that imagery. There was no one on the Gina Marie, her decks were relatively clean and Evan noticed that the outrigger had been repaired making the boat ready to fish. The Lady Marie sat in the parking lot next to the boat dock. Evan could tell, from the looks of things, that she was undergoing repairs. The large hole that had been poked in her starboard side by a submerged piling was already patched with new planking. The fresh epoxy resin that coated the planks reflected the midday sun. With no sign of Sulsky around the boats, Evan decided to check inside the store.

"Afternoon, Sir." Paul Sulsky peeked his head out from the walk-in refrigerator at the back of the store, greeting a possible customer. "How can I help you today...." Paul stopped short of finishing his sentence as he recognized Evan.

Sulsky was what Evan, via Dennis, referred to as a "hider." It was no great secret that shrimp boats had a knack for becoming a refuge for criminals and ex-cons. Most of the men Sulsky hired for his crews were either hiding from the law or had just been released from jail. The men were desperate and that helped Sulsky. He could pay them under the table for their work, at a lower wage, and never hear a complaint. After all, a few days on a shrimp boat was usually more than enough time for a desperate man to evade detection. Often, when Sulsky returned to port, he would hand the crew a cash payday and they would never be seen again. Dennis Taylor was well aware of this fact and over the years Sulsky had helped hide more than one of Dennis' miscreant associates. For Sulsky, there was no tremendous benefit in the arrangement though he saved a little money but somehow Sulsky knew that Dennis was not someone you crossed.

"How's things Paul?" Evan asked, leaning against a refrigerated display case full of shrimp, oysters and fish fillets.

"Not bad, Evan. Not bad." Sulsky wiped his hands on his pants then offered a shake to Evan.

Evan reluctantly returned the gesture, knowing he'd be hard pressed to wash away Sulsky's stink.

"Shrimp today? Just came in this morning. They aren't more than a few hours from the sound." Sulsky tapped on the case, indicating a pile of shrimp that was, definitely, more than a few hours old.

"No shrimp," Evan said as he spied through the rest of the case. "But I might take a half-bushel of oysters off your hands later."

"Half-bushel? Hell, that's just a warm up," Sulsky said, smiling, chuckling. "I'll just throw in the other half... on me. That'll get you right."

Evan smiled back, sharing a cordial laugh, "That's ok, Paul, but I appreciate it."

Things got quiet as each man tried to size up the other. Evan broke the silence.

"Paul, Dennis needs a favor... just a little help."

Sulsky shrugged his shoulders, "I don't mind that at all. What's Denny need?"

Evan reached into his jacket pocket, pulling out a manila envelope and exposing his revolver.

"I'd appreciate it if you took a look at some pictures." Evan said as he opened the envelope and placed several photos on the top of the case.

"Women?" Paul said jokingly.

Evan smiled, "No, no. Not the kind you're thinking of anyway."

Paul picked up the first photo. It was obvious that the photo had been captured from some kind of television broadcast. In the picture was a fair haired young lady in a Coast Guard uniform. The second picture, showed a group of boys, along with the first girl. They all looked so young. The kids, the Coasties, were a pain in Paul's ass. They boarded his boats at least four times a year to check his nets for the TED's (Turtle Excluder Devices) that allowed Sea Turtles to pass through the shrimp nets unharmed. The Coast Guard and the TED's had cost Paul a lot of shrimp.

"Why am I looking at the Coast Guard, Evan?" Paul asked.

"You were out on the river the day after the storm. Right, Paul?" Evan asked, ignoring Sulsky's question.

"Sure was," Paul said as he looked at the third photo. another girl with brown hair hanging a flag on the Coast Guard's little boat.

"You see the Coast Guard out that day, Paul?" Evan's tone became subtly intimidating.

Paul didn't like where this was headed. Like most fishermen he didn't love the Coast Guard but he respected them. On more than one occasion those "kids" had saved someone Paul knew, or their boats... their livelihoods. What the hell did Dennis want with them?

"Yeah...I saw their little boat right up here in Thuderbolt," Paul answered.

"You see anyone in those pictures that you recognize, Paul?"

Paul scanned the pictures again. He definitely recognized the Mexican-looking kid from a time his boat had been boarded earlier in the year. He recognized the fair-haired girl from the same time. But, the girl on the boat changing the flag, Paul thought he saw her on the little boat the day after Danelle, maybe.

"Hell, Evan, I've seen a few of these kids at one point or another. The Coasties make my boats a pretty regular stop when they're out patrolling."

Evan chuckled, "Ok, ok… I mean, did you see any of them the day after the hurricane?"

"No," Paul answered quickly.

Evan raised an eyebrow at the quick response, sensing Sulsky's deception.

"Are you sure about that?" Evan crossed his arms over his chest. "You did see the Coast Guard that day…right?"

Sweat beaded on Paul's forehead as he pondered his answer. It was the last thing in the world that Paul wanted, dragging some poor kids into this mess with Dennis and Evan. "I was out. I saw them."

"Anyone in those pictures?" Evan leaned on the case, jacket gaping open, gun clearly visible.

"Maybe this one." Paul pointed a quaking finger at the photo of Rachel. "It's hard to say if it was her though. She was inside the boat."

"Good. Good, Paul, that's a great help," Evan said as he gathered the pictures and placed them back in the envelope.

Paul sighed with relief, perceiving that the inquest had ended. "So how about those oysters?"

Evan stuffed the envelope back in his jacket then peered into the case. "Let me have a look."

"They are real beauties. I got them from the beds over in Ossabaw and had some for lunch today. A little hot sauce and a squirt of lemon and they'll...."

"You suppose if you saw the kids on that boat you would know them by their face?" Evan cut Paul short.

Paul's heart sank. "Yeah, I'd know."

Evan smiled at Paul, "I think the oysters can wait then. Let's go for a little drive."

8

5:05PM

Evan came to a stop in the visitor's parking space in front of Station Tybee. The road onto Cockspur Island would be closing in an hour, plenty of time for Paul Sulsky to have a look around. The grounds of the station were quiet. Evan could see two young men in uniform fishing off the pier. Only the larger, white, Coast Guard boat was at the dock. The smaller orange boat was apparently gone and the big boat, the Coast Guard cutter, was gone as well.

"Get out. Make it fast," Evan said as he put the car in park.

Paul Sulsky was nervous, sweating. The ride to the island had accelerated the "on edge" feeling Paul had had since Evan first walked into his store. Evan stopped at a Little Caesars Pizza on the way, purchasing five large pizzas and an equal number of two-liter bottles of Coke.

"These are gifts. You're going to say thank you to them for their service," Evan insisted.

"They know me. They know I'm a fisherman and that they piss me off sometimes."

"All the more reason for you to offer them an olive branch," Evan smiled.

Now, as Sulsky crawled out of the car, pizza and soda in hand, his nervousness rose to a crescendo. Sulsky didn't know exactly what Evan wanted with these kids but it couldn't be anything good. Guys with guns and questionable liaisons didn't choose to go anywhere near the law without a good, really good, reason. The fact that Evan was perfectly comfortable carrying a concealed weapon onto a military post was proof positive that trouble was brewing, or had brewed and was looking for a place to land. Sulsky wished now that he hadn't admitted to seeing the Coast Guard at all.

"I'll be waiting here. Make it quick," Evan said as Sulsky moved away from the vehicle.

The doors to the station opened and Sulsky was greeted by a slender young man he recognized. It was Mike Harwood. Following Mike were two other Coasties…the girl from the television report, Laura Hill, and a young Latino, Gabriel Ortiz. Of the three, Sulsky could only identify Mike as having been on the Coast Guard boat the day after Danelle.

"Afternoon everyone," Sulsky said with a hard-to-conjure smile.

"Mr. Sulsky..." Mike addressed Sulsky by name "...what brings you by today?"

Sulsky was surprised that Mike knew his name without prompting. But, in all likelihood, the entire crew of this unit was familiar with Sulsky. Sulsky was a common customer and a perpetual griper.

"I'm doing fine young Mr. Harwood," Sulsky replied, reading Mike's nametape. "Here..." Sulsky handed the pizzas to Laura and the two bags of soda to Gabriel.

"What's all this for?" Laura asked, suspiciously.

Sulsky swallowed hard, "I just wanted to come and say thanks to ya'll...for everything."

Mike couldn't believe his ears. "Well. Thank you."

"I know. I know. I've been a pain in the ass to you folks. But, I know ya'll busted your asses after that damn storm...getting things put back together so guys like me can keep fishing." Sulsky extended a hand to Mike. "I appreciate it."

This was teetering precariously on the edge of a conflict of interest and Mike knew it. In the past two years, Sulsky had been issued violations for at least ten different federally regulated items. If Mike remembered correctly, Sulsky had been dished out close to five thousand dollars in fines as a result. Like most of the fishermen in the area, Sulsky's relationship with the Coast Guard was love-hate, with the majority on the hate side. Taking this present from Sulsky might give the impression that the Coast Guard would be more lenient the next time Sulsky broke the law.

"I know it's like the Greek bearing a gift here..." Sulsky said, reading Mike's facial expression, "...but I don't expect anything in return."

Mike shook Sulsky's hand, "Sir, I appreciate the gift but I don't really think we can accept it. We were just doing our job."

Sulsky looked at Gabriel's face as Mike commented. It was apparent that Gabriel was dying to tear into the pizza. "Look, Mr. Harwood, if ya'll don't take this stuff I'm just gonna march over to your dumpster and pitch it inside. I'm not a big fan of pizza or Coke," Sulsky smiled.

"Well..." Mike sighed, "...give me just a second?"

"Sure," Sulsky replied as Mike produced a cell phone and stepped away. Obviously, Mike was getting another opinion or authorization.

"Just ya'll three here?" Sulsky asked Laura.

"No sir. We have a radio watch stander, another crewman and our duty cook. We're just the greeting committee," Laura smiled.

"Bet that cook would be happy to take the night off," Sulsky laughed out the comment.

"Not as happy as we'd be to see him take the night off," Gabriel responded.

Sulsky laughed. "You know, I recognize that boy..." Sulsky pointed toward Mike, "... from the other day but I don't see the other folks that were out there. I know I've talked to one of them... kind of a good looking kid, probably thirty, had three of those," Sulsky pointed to the chevrons on Laura's collar.

"Probably Petty Officer Morgan," Gabriel blurted out, without thinking.

Laura shot Gabriel a scolding glance. Gabriel was going to get a royal ass chewing later. He knew he wasn't supposed to be discussing personnel with anyone right now. But, the cat was out of the bag.

"Maybe, Mr. Sulsky, but we have several First Class Petty Officer's on the crew. They all look alike," Laura said with a chuckle.

"That's a good one," Sulsky laughed as he sensed Laura's purposeful disclosure.

"Who's your friend?" Gabriel motioned toward Evan, sitting in the car.

"Oh…" Sulsky paused, conjuring an answer. "That's Charlie…" Sulsky lied, "…he helps out at the fish house from time to time."

There was a click as Mike closed his cell phone. "Mr. Sulsky." Mike approached, "I just talked to my Officer in Charge and he said we could accept the gift. He also asked me to thank you."

"That's fantastic," Sulsky said. "And please thank him for me. He's got a good crew that does a hell of a job."

"Thank you, Sir," Mike said, shaking Sulsky's hand again.

Sulsky turned and headed for the car. "Make sure you share with everyone."

"We will, Sir. If they find out we hoarded the pizza we'd never hear the end of it."

"If ya'll need more then I'll bring some by," Sulsky opened the car door. "When do ya'll work next?"

"That's classified," Mike smiled the response.

Sulsky laughed, "Ok then. Take care." Sulsky closed his door.

"Well…" Evan asked.

"They're on duty right now. I'm pretty sure all of them are."

"Names…" Evan demanded as he backed out of the parking space.

"Harwood, for one, and Morgan for another." Sulsky felt ill as he spoke.

"Names help, Paul. We'll have to get in contact with those nice folks and express our thanks too." The lies and sarcasm bleed from Evan's mouth.

"You're an asshole!" Sulsky thought as he looked out the car window, delivering a wave to the Coasties as the car sped off.

On the steps of the station, Mike watched Sulsky's departure, "That was pretty damn weird." Mike turned to Laura and Gabriel. "Throw that shit away. I don't trust that prick!"

Gabriel and Laura shot Mike a look of disappointment then headed for the dumpster.

Wednesday

9

11:45AM

Hank got home just in time for lunch which was typical of an off-going duty morning. The crew woke at 0600, had chow, cleaned the boats and the unit then attended all-hands quarters and training along with departmental meetings and completing the relief process. It was a solid six hours of work on top having worked for the past forty-eight. Of course you got to sleep, but it wasn't home, the beds weren't comfortable and Mike, Hank's roommate, snored like a freight train. In a little more than thirty-six hours Hank would be on his way back to the station for weekend duty, Friday through Sunday.

"Say hi to Daddy." Hank heard Lori's voice coming from the screened in balcony of their apartment.

Hank looked up to see Lori standing on the balcony holding Allison. Allison smiled excitedly at Hank's approach and waved her arm as hard as she could. Hank loved having a family to come home to. It didn't matter how ridiculous or stressful work had been. When he got home he had people he loved, and that loved him back, waiting. Hank and Lori had discussed Lori going to work on many occasions but had decided that it was in Allison's best interest (despite having to live on a tight budget) to have Lori at home being a mom. Hank knew having Lori there was in his best interest too.

The door to the apartment flung open as Hank reached the top of the stairs. Allison stood in the doorway, hands held high, urging Daddy to pick her up. Hank was happy to comply. Dropping his duffel bag, Hank scooped Allison up and gave her a big hug and kiss.

"Hey there baby girl," Hank said as Allison planted a forceful kiss on his cheek. "And how's my beautiful wife today?" Hank kissed Lori.

"We're doing great today." Lori's language had changed since Allison was born. Any reference to "I" had now become a inference of "we." It was as if Lori and Ally were the same person.

"We slept all night in our bed. And this morning we had a bath and ate a good breakfast." Lori smooched Ally on the cheek.

"That's awesome!" Hank smiled and bounced Ally in his arms.

"How was Daddy's work?" Lori asked, moving Hank inside and shutting the door.

"The usual," Hank shrugged. "Helo Op's. No SAR calls this time around, and two patrols...uneventful." Hank tried to bury his true emotions concerning the investigation, but Lori knew how to read him.

"Really?" Lori questioned.

"Yeah, really." Hank placed Ally on the ground. "Mike had another five-alarm snoring session last night so I didn't much sleep. I'm just a little tired."

Ally ran off to the corner of the living room, collapsing into a pile of toys she had drug out from the closet as Lori moved toward the kitchen.

"Ready for some lunch?"

"Starving, yes, please." Hank followed Lori into the kitchen, opened the fridge and grabbed a beer.

"Early for that." Lori said as she leaned in after Hank, grabbing the lunch meat.

Hank didn't respond, only faintly smiled then grabbed the stack of mail off the kitchen counter.

"Bill, bill, credit card offer, bill and twenty five percent off carwash..." Hank tossed the pile back onto the counter.

"There was a letter from your sister. I opened it," Lori said.

"What's she up to?" Hank said as he walked into the living room and sat down next to Ally.

"She was writing about your father...about finances."

"Oh boy." Hank took a drink then set the beer on the coffee table.

Shortly after Hank and Lori came to Savannah, Hank had learned that his father was ill. Hank's father was suffering from prostate cancer and the disease was progressing. Stubborn as he was, Hank's father had never heeded the warning signs, the trouble urinating, bone pain and leg swelling the nervous issues that had developed. Now, things were serious enough that Hank's father had had to quit his job, leaving Hank's mom as the sole provider. The money his parents had gotten from the sale of their furniture business was nearly gone and the cost of prostate treatments and medication had already forced Hank's parents into a cramped, two bedroom, third floor apartment in Muncie.

"She wants us to send money regularly," Lori said as she exited the kitchen with a sandwich for Hank.

"How much?" Hank asked, accepting the plate from Lori.

"She says, and I quote..." Lori sat on the couch, "... two hundred dollars a month is a more than fair contribution." Lori didn't like Hank's sister. She loved Hank's parents, but his siblings, a sister and a brother, were arrogant and dumb-ass respectively.

"Wow!" Hank said, stuffing a bite of sandwich into his mouth. "Shannon is married to a damn orthopedic surgeon that makes a six digit salary and she thinks everyone is made of money." Hank washed the bite down.

"Honey..." Lori leaned forward staring into Hank's eyes. "We can swing it if we need to."

Hank sighed. He knew his parents needed the money desperately but he also knew that his tight budget couldn't get much tighter. After his father was diagnosed, and knowing his parents financial situation, he had explored the process of his parents becoming recognized as his dependents by the Coast Guard, making his father eligible for military health insurance which was much better than MEDICAID and MEDICARE. But, being "dependents" meant that his parents would have to live with him and Lori. No matter how much better things would have been, his sister fought the idea vehemently. She wanted her parents nearby, more than likely to take advantage of having a free babysitter around. Hank's brother, the deadbeat, still lived with mom and dad and was irate at the thought of having to support himself. In the end Hank's folks decided to stay put. Hank wished he could have been face-to-face with his siblings to argue this out. Such was the cost of the miles that separated them. Hanks voice was seldom, if ever, given any countenance.

"What would we give up if we did that?" Hank asked.

"Well…" Lori looked around the living room. "We could go to basic cable. I could cut your hair myself and we could sell your truck." Lori was hesitantly serious. "We don't need two cars."

Hank appreciated what Lori was trying to do but, though honorable and plausible, Lori's suggestions were unacceptable. They were both paying off student loans. Though the F-150 was paid for, their Corolla required a monthly payment. Then there were groceries, electricity, phone, cable and a host of other expenses that ate away at Hank's paycheck. Most important to Hank, something he would not forego, was the money, however menial, he and Lori socked into an IRA every month. They had to plan for their future. Hank hated bottom-lining things, so did Lori. But, the bottom line was that they had offered a solid option to the family and that option was ignored. It was the best he and Lori could do, given their circumstances.

"No, Honey. No." Hank looked at Lori, solemnly. "We have to have a life here and we have to have some security. We already send my folks fifty dollars every paycheck and that has to be good enough for now."

"I could go to work," Lori suggested.

"We already talked about this and we agreed on what was in the best interest of our family, Lori," Hank sighed. "There has to be a line that we draw, regardless of how shitty it feels to do it. Mom and Dad don't expect us to go broke looking after them. They want us to have some security."

"Alright, sweetheart. But, if we have to then…" Lori kissed Hank gently on the forehead.

Lori admired Hank's ability to back away from an emotional situation and focus on the priorities of his immediate family. It made her feel comfortable… secure. There was no doubt that she an Allison were at the top of Hank's to-do list every second of every day. But, Lori also knew that it was her responsibility to keep some emotion in play. She didn't want her husband becoming hardened. Her father was that way. Her father was a stone wall, reclusive and miserly. In the time since Lori had married Hank and had Allison her parents had never offered so much as a dime to help out, despite any need. Lori wouldn't allow Hank to become that way.

"We can do a little more, Hank." Lori touched Hank's hand.

Hank's thoughts drifted away from Lori's voice and to the bag and the boat. There was no one else around after they left. What if they had all agreed to say nothing and just take the money… divide it up? That much could have made a big difference.

"We could have done a lot more." Hank mumbled the words as he stood, heading to the kitchen for another beer.

"What did you say, Honey?" Lori asked as she walked to the balcony door that Allison had opened.

"Nothing, sweetheart, just talking to myself."

Hank reached into the fridge for a beer, chastising himself for his thoughts. "You're out of your damn mind!"

He twisted off the bottle cap, "How would you ever hide that? How would anyone ever hide that?" Hank took a drink. "How *could* someone hide that?"

Lori bent over, snatching Allison into her arms before Allison ran onto the balcony. Allison loved to open and shut the sliding glass door, almost as much as she liked re-arranging the plastic bowls in the cabinet by the stove.

"Come on silly," Lori said as Ally shook her head from side to side.

"No?" Lori asked playfully, then noticed the car again. It was the car that had been through the apartment complex three times already. It was a champagne colored sedan, a Buick if she guessed right with a husky-built young man behind the wheel.

"Honey…" Lori called for Hank.

Hank came from the kitchen and stood at Lori's side, gazing out the door. "What's up?"

Lori pointed. "That car has been prowling around here all day long. It was parked out there this morning when we got up. It cruised through here right before you came home, and it's back again now."

"Might be someone looking for a home," Hank said, moving his head around, trying to get a look at the driver. "Maybe it's a lawyer. The neighbors downstairs are always in some kind of mess."

Lori shrugged. "Maybe. It just feels uncomfortable. The guy is always looking this way."

"Well…" Hank rubbed Lori's back, "The next time he drives through I will try to get his license plate number."

The presence of the car could mean something or nothing at all. Hank felt paranoia welling up in his mind. This would be the cost if a person took the money. This was the price for even the slightest involvement. Hank turned away.

Lori slid the door shut as the sedan headed off.

10

4:30PM

Mike turned down Butler Avenue smiling, rocking out to AC/DC's "Thunderstruck" on his Chevy Tahoe's stereo. The sound of the music boomed from the vehicle drawing mixed reviews from the faces of tourists Mike passed. Mike was extremely pleased with himself. Behind the Tahoe, Mike towed a trailer containing two, brand new, Sea-Doo GTS 130's. These were on Mike and Debbie's summer wish list. They'd wanted to get a pair of "Jet Ski's" since the day they found out they were headed to Savannah. Mike decided to pull the trigger on the purchase. If Mike got home soon enough, he and Debbie would have time to take their new toys out for a spin. The thought of hopping across the waves off the beach at Tybee Island thrilled Mike to the core.

Of course, Andrew was way too young to go out for that kind of fun. Mike would have to give Lori a call to see if she and Hank would watch Andrew for a few hours while he and Debbie whooped it up. Lori babysat a lot for Mike and Debbie, mostly because Lori came off as a serious homebody. She never went anywhere, neither did Hank. Debbie and Lori would go shopping together once in awhile. They took the kids to the pool together, went to the park...but "serious fun" was never on the plate for the Morgans. Every time Mike asked Hank what he did on a weekend, Hank would say, "We just hung out." Mike thought that was dreadful.

Mike and Debbie made a fair amount of money. Debbie's job as a loan officer at Sun Trust Bank paid her well, more than Mike brought home. Mike and Debbie weren't savers. They spent what they had and were often times chastised (by both sets of parents) for being impulsive sensualists. They liked their toys and they liked having a good time. Mike and Debbie were loving parents but not the least bit conservative in their lifestyle or Andrew's upbringing. Mike predicted that, based on the example he was being given, Andrew would aspire to sell T-shirts on a beach as a chosen career. Everyone laughed the notion off. Andrew's grandparents would never allow it.

Another left, then a short right and Mike stopped in front of "Harwood Casa" as stated on the sign in front of the piling-raised beach house they rented on Tybee Island. The house was wonderful for Mike, Debbie and Andrew. Large bay-windows let sun stream into the kitchen and living room of the house. Sliding glass doors opened onto a wooden deck that encircled the residence and, at its height, provided a partial view of the beach. On the back deck was a Jacuzzi, bar, stainless steel grill, and, cleverly concealed in a wooden box, a 47 inch flat screen with surround sound. Mike and Debbie hosted a lot of social gatherings.

Debbie's car, a newer Lexus, was in the carport under the house letting Mike know that she was home from work. As usual, she was off early on Wednesdays when she was scheduled to work a Saturday. She would be surprised. Mike honked the horn then eagerly jumped out of the Tahoe, racing to pose himself atop one of the Sea-Doo's before Debbie could reach the front door.

"Oh my God!" Debbie yelled in excitement as she flung open the door, "You got them!" Debbie raced down the steps and ran to the trailer, "They're gorgeous!"

Mike beamed, smiling from ear to ear as Debbie climbed onto the Sea-Doo next to him, giggling.

"Thought you might like them?" Mike smiled.

"Like them?" Debbie grabbed the crafts handle bars, "I love them!" Debbie leaned over, kissing Mike passionately. "I thought we were going to wait until the end of the season... when prices were cheaper?"

Mike patted Debbie on the thigh, "I gave it a thought then said, what the hell. We're not getting any younger."

Debbie kissed Mike again, "How much were they? Can we afford this?"

Mike hopped off his craft and climbed onto Debbie's, sliding in close behind her, "They were a bargain. I've been haggling with the dealership for weeks." Mike reached his hands around Debbie, squeezing her sides.

Debbie's eyebrows shot up. "Did you open up a separate bank account? That's not very fair Mr. Harwood." Debbie always called Mike "Mr. Harwood" when she was unhappy with him. In this case, the presence of the new toys overwhelmed any discontentment.

"We are supposed to agree on things like this," Debbie shot Mike a half-hearted look of disapproval.

Mike sighed with a smile, "If I'd told you then it wouldn't have been a surprise. You just need to trust me on this, babe. This isn't going to make a dent in our portfolio." Mike took Debbie's face in his hands. "What it is going to make a dent in is the summertime blues!" Mike laughed, kissed Debbie, then hopped off the trailer. "Where's Andy?"

Debbie climbed off the trailer. "He's having a snack, watching Disney."

"Well..." Mike headed for the steps to the house. "Let's call Lori and Hank and see if they can keep him while we take those babies out for a spin."

Debbie would rather have called Rachel. Andrew loved playing with Allison but Debbie didn't like showing off the toys to Hank and Lori. Debbie knew Hank and Lori weren't able to buy the kinds of things they would have, should have and wanted to. Debbie always felt like she and Mike were "rubbing it in" every time they showed up with something new.

"How about Rachel instead?" Debbie asked, following Mike.

"I think she was going to Hilton Head with Laura today." Mike opened the front door, motioning for Debbie to hurry it up.

"Damn." Debbie thought. "Ok. Hank and Lori it is." Debbie marched into the house. "You get Andy ready to go and I'll call Lori."

"Deal!" Mike shouted and headed into the living room where he tackled Andrew and initiated a tickle-fight.

As Debbie dialed she looked out the window at the Jet Ski's. "Damn, those are nice."

****

6:15PM

Rachel was not in Hilton Head. She sat in her assigned quarters at the station playing social games on Facebook and drinking the third beer out of the six she was allowed to have in her personal, government controlled habitat. Rachel made a big deal out of planning to go on excursions with her shipmates but rarely ever followed through. It wasn't that she didn't want to go. God only knew that she *needed* to go to maintain her sanity but, the fact was that she didn't want to spend the money. Even when shipmates offered to pay, Rachel's pride wouldn't allow her to accept the offer. So, here she sat.

It wasn't as if there was nothing for her to do and no social interaction to be had. Rachel owned a car, a 2000 Ford Focus that ran from point "A" to point "B", but was not the soul of dependability. Rachel chose to ride her bike everywhere. Frequently, Rachel would put on her bikini and cover-up, load a backpack, and bike to the beach on Tybee Island where she would spend the day baking in the sun listening to her "El-Cheap-O" MP3 player. Other times she would ride to Wilmington Island where she would have a soft-shell crab sandwich and a sweet tea on the deck of the Sailfish Bar and Grill. But, Rachel never invited shipmates because they would, invariably, want to turn the occasion into a bar-crawl. Most of Rachel's associates talked with her on Skype or through an IM frame on her Facebook page. Rachel didn't enjoy her frugal lifestyle and couldn't hide it from her shipmates if she associated with them. But, her on-line friends didn't and wouldn't know any better.

Rachel had been the benefactor of a partial athletic scholarship to Arizona State University. In Minnesota, in high school, Rachel was the captain of her softball team and a first-team, all-conference, pitcher. Her team had gone to the state semi-finals three of the four years she had played, only to come up short against schools from much bigger and better funded metropolitan areas. The partial scholarship was the result of never having won the big game. Apparently ASU didn't want to take too great a chance on a small town girl.

Her first year at ASU Rachel rode the bench along with several other freshmen while she took out FAFSA and non-government loans to cover the rest of her hefty tuition. In her second year Rachel earned a spot as a reliever for the team and had thirteen saves, which was pretty good and pretty promising for a sophomore. During the summer break, between her sophomore and junior years, Rachel blew out her ACL playing in an alumni reunion game at her high school. The scholarship went away and the bills piled up. Rachel's parent, a single mom, didn't have the means to help. So, repairs to the ACL complete, Rachel enlisted vowing to pay off her loans and make a new future.

In uniform Rachel was one of the guys. In her civilian clothes (even the baggy ones) Rachel was, as Gabriel Ortiz put it, "Smokin!" The years of athletics had given Rachel a lean, muscular build that worked nicely with a genetic inheritance, from her father's side, that dictated curves. There had been more than one Coastie from the Tarpon and the Aids to Navigation Team that had tried to gain her interest, but Rachel lived by the creed "If it's in blue, it's not for you." Dating a fellow service member was not an option for Rachel. There were too many eligible fish in the sea.

Rachel had discovered that having a nice body was a situation to deal with in and of itself. During her frequent, free tours through Fort Pulaksi, Terry Macomb would follow her around, leering. Terry always joked that Rachel knew every inch of the fort. Rachel assumed that by now Terry knew every inch of her. Terry creeped Rachel out. When Terry's cousin approached her about becoming a dancer at his titty-bar outside Savannah, Rachel's creeper-o-meter pegged. Since that time Rachel had limited her fort excursions.

Rachel exited Facebook, polished off her beer and clicked onto her bank's website. This was a time she dreaded. It was the middle of the month and time to pay bills.

"Ok Rache. How much don't we have?" Rachel said as she entered her password.

One thousand, one hundred seventy two dollars and twenty six cents in checking. Four hundred dollars in savings. "Wow…A banner payday." Rachel said as she clicked on "Pay My Bills" and started the process of doling out the greenbacks. Three hundred in student loan payments, seventy for insurance, two hundred to the pre-Coast Guard hospital bills, one-fifty for her Coast Guard chow-bill and fifty dollars sent off to savings.

"Great." Rachel sighed, "Looks like another two weeks of Redbox rentals, cheap beer and relative social solitude."

Rachel climbed off her bed and pulled another beer from the mini-fridge. "It's the way it is girlfriend." Rachel spoke to her reflection in the room's full-length mirror.

8:20PM

Ryan slipped another dollar bill into the blondes garter as she finished rubbing her breasts in his face. The wildly strong smell of her body lotion and perfume lingered on Ryan, filling his nose, as he pulled another dollar from the stack in his hand.

"I think she likes you!" Gabriel shouted over the thundering bass reverberations coming from the one-too-many speakers that surrounded the stage.

"She liked me the last time I was here too!" Ryan replied, placing the dollar in his teeth.

The blonde girl noticed the dollar and crawled seductively across the stage toward Ryan. When she reached him, she removed the dollar from his mouth with her breasts, gave them a good rub across Ryan's lips, then moved back across the stage toward another dollar bill in the hands of another spectator.

Ryan collapsed back into his chair next to Gabriel and grabbed his Jack and Coke, "Cheers, Gabe," Ryan offered up his glass. Gabriel obliged, clinking his drink against Ryan's.

"You need another one?" Ryan asked.

Gabe looked at his glass, nearly empty, then checked his pockets. He knew he only had ten bucks left, and he really needed to save it for the cab ride back to his apartment, "No, I'm ok bro."

"Bullshit!" Ryan exclaimed. "It's only eight-thirty man." Ryan flagged down the waitress, "Don't worry hombre. I got you covered."

"Ok man. Thanks." Gabe turned back toward the stage as the waitress came up. Gabe liked Ryan but, in a lot of ways, he pitied him.

Ryan Beck was a twenty-two year old player but only in his own mind. No one really envisioned Ryan as a popular guy. Ryan acted odd. He was overly concerned with his physical appearance. He worked-out almost as much as he partied, and he dressed to "the nines" no matter what he was doing. Even in the gym Ryan was wearing the latest, most expensive gear. Ryan drove a 2010 Mustang V6, that no one knew how he could afford, and was constantly bragging on his latest really expensive purchase. Most thought Ryan's lifestyle was funded by his wealthy parents in Miami. But, the reality was that Ryan's excessive behavior was a form of compensation.

In his sober, less self-absorbed hours, Ryan didn't regard himself as an attractive specimen. Barely over five-eight with an unkempt matt of dishwater blonde hair and a face besieged with acne scars, Ryan had very little luck with the ladies and his overbearing, braggart personality didn't endear him to anyone. The majority of Ryan's time was spent making people believe he was well-to-do because, in truth, Ryan believed that was the only way he could ever retain friends. Night after night, day after day, Ryan paraded himself around Savannah, crawling from bar to bar, party to party, trying desperately to use an overt disregard for the value of money to illicit female companionship or male respect. All of this had put Ryan into a hole with his parents who had started to tighten the valve on the money spicket. Ryan had had many arguments with his parents concerning money and his lifestyle, but despite what was good advice, Ryan chose to charge ahead with the life he had grown accustomed to. Increasingly, that lifestyle rested on the stack of credit cards Ryan had compiled.

The song ended. The blonde gathered what little clothing she had removed, blew a kiss to the crowd and snuck behind the curtain. Ryan and Gabriel applauded as the voice of the DJ echoed through the club.

"Gentlemen, let's give it up for the scintillating Diamond as she takes the stage"

"Shit yes!" Gabriel said.

"Diamond? Really?" Ryan scoffed, "She has a cesarean scar!"

Gabriel perched on his chair as the girl came on stage dressed like a nurse. She headed directly for Gabriel who was already digging in his pocket. "I got to go hit the ATM man!" Gabe said as he started to stand.

"To hell with it! Here!" Ryan handed Gabriel a few singles which Gabe gladly accepted, "To each his own," Ryan thought as he saw the blonde from before, Amber, come onto the floor to work men for table dances.

Ryan climbed from his chair as Gabe stuffed the first of the singles into Diamond's ample bosom. Ryan wanted a dance from Amber, probably more than one, and he wasn't opposed to asking for something more.

"When she's done have her come to the back booth man," Ryan nudged Gabe.

Gabe turned away from Diamond, "Dude. I aint got that kind of money."

Ryan looked away from Gabe, holding up a handful of twenties that caught Amber's eye.

"Dude!" Gabe exclaimed, seeing the cash. "Where'd you get that kind of cash?"

Ryan patted Gabe's back as Amber began stroking Ryan's chest. "Oh...I got money, Bro, and plenty of it. Enough to get us both laid."

Gabe watched Ryan disappear with Amber into a dimly lit corner as Diamond pulled off her shirt and tossed it over Gabe's head.

11

8:50PM

"Honey! It's going crooked. Turn the wheel to the left! The other left!" Mike yelled as he tried to direct Debbie down the ramp with the trailer in near total darkness.

They'd stayed out a little too long. Debbie dropped Andrew off at the Morgan's at four, along with Happy Meals for Andrew and Ally, a bottle of wine for Hank and Lori and a promise to be back to by eight. It was almost nine now, squarely after sunset (a violation of State and Federal Personal Watercraft operation) and, after a call to the Morgan's, Hank was on his way, bringing Andrew home. Mike figured they owed the Morgan's a favor. For now, they were just trying to get the damn Jet Skis on the trailer and return to their house before Hank arrived.

"Ok. Ok, babe. Stop there!" Mike shouted as Debbie pressed hard on the brakes. This was her third time trying to back the trailer down the ramp. She'd have to work on that particular skill-set. Debbie heard clanking, a little cursing, then the ratcheting of the watercraft into place on their bunks.

The driver's side door opened, startling Debbie. "I got it sweetheart. Scoot," Mike said with a smile, water dripping from his swimming trunks, squishing in his flip-flops as he hopped into the Tahoe.

"We need to hurry," Debbie said as she fastened her seatbelt. Mike was already motoring away from the ramp.

It had been fifteen minutes since Debbie had talked to Lori. Though Mike knew Hank drove like an old man, Hank had to be getting close to their house. Hank was going to be a little pissed off already. Mike didn't want to make it any worse.

"Honey..." Debbie said as Mike turned onto their street, "...I thought I left the lights on."

Mike pulled to a stop in front of the house and looked up at the darkness behind the front windows. When he and Debbie lived in San Diego, near Pacific Beach, leaving a light on and locking doors was a necessary part of your routine. Though Tybee Island could be sketchy sometimes, things were very peaceable.

"Maybe you didn't? We left in a rush, Babe."

"I'll go in and turn on the carport lights while you park this thing," Debbie said as she hopped out of the Tahoe and trotted off toward the house.

Mike pulled the Tahoe forward, ready to back into the drive.

Debbie reached the front door and searched for her keys in the dark. Finding them, Debbie opened the door wide and stepped into the living room, searching for the light switch. A big hand grabbed her and threw her from the front door to the couch.

"Mike!" Debbie screamed at the top of her lungs as the man jumped on top of her, placing a hand over her mouth as he struck her with a balled fist.

Debbie felt the concussion of the blow and her head spun with pain. As the man's fist rose again she heard an indiscernible shout from somewhere in the back of her home. It was another intruder. Debbie opened her mouth beneath the pressure of the covering hand then bit down with all her power as the next blow came from the balled fist. The assailant whooped in pain as Debbie felt his skin give way between her teeth. Blood trickled into Debbie's mouth. As the man's hand recoiled from her face, she screamed.

Mike backed the trailer slowly into the drive and toward the carport, wondering what was taking Debbie so long. The light switch for the carport was just inside the door, not two feet from where Debbie had entered.

"Damn, Deb," Mike said, throwing the Tahoe into park and hopping out. "I guess you must need help or some......." Mike said, frustrated. Then he heard Debbie scream.

Mike charged up the stairs and into the living room in a fit of adrenaline oblivion. As he came through the door he could make out Debbie lying on the couch. Next to Debbie a man was holding an apparently injured hand. The man didn't notice Mike, at first, and raised his foot, stomping down directly on Debbie's midsection. As Debbie uttered another wind deprived cry of anguish Mike leapt across the room grabbing the man by the arm and the back of the shirt. Mike dragged the intruder across the living room, hurling the man's head into the fireplace mantel. The man's head snapped back at the impact, his body crumpled to the floor.

"Debbie. Are you..." Mike turned around just in time to see the baseball bat racing toward him in the dark. The bat struck Mike in the side, sending him sprawling across the floor as Debbie fought for consciousness.

****

"Well..." Hank sighed as he approached the Harwood's darkened home. "At least they're home, Andy."

This wasn't the first time Hank had been forced to bring Andrew home from a night of babysitting. Mike and Debbie were frequently late for their pickup time and, in the interest of getting Allison to bed, Hank often volunteered his taxi service. Tonight was just like any other time. But, usually, Mike and Debbie would make a better show of the house, giving the illusion that they were home and waiting to receive their son.

Hank looked up at the front door of the house, noticing that it was open and that no lights had been turned on. "Mom and Dad must have just got here

Andy," Hank said to Andrew who had fallen asleep sometime along the way.

Hank climbed out of the truck, ready to unbuckle Andrew from his car seat, when he heard something break inside the house.

****

The lamp shattered against the bat as the intruder took another swing at Mike. Despite the pain, Mike managed to duck out of the way, feeling the wind rush past as the bat barely missed his head. Mike rolled across the floor, reaching for the poker in the brass bucket by the fireplace. He found nothing to grab as the bat found purchase, sinking into the bicep of his right arm.

"You rotten Bitch!" Mike heard the other man say as he rose to his feet and turned toward Debbie. "I'm gonna cut your tits off!" Mike saw a glint of metal, a knife blade, extending from the man's moonlit hand. The bat came down again. Mike flung his body to the left, causing the bat to slam against the floor, just shy of his skull. Then, the lights came on.

Hank stood at the front door of the house, staring. On the couch, the right side of Debbie's face was a bloody knot, her eye swollen shut. On the floor, Mike lay with his arm extended in an effort to block the next swing of the bat. Both intruders were masked, angry and at least one, aggressive.

Debbie's assailant shot toward Hank with the knife extended. Hank, immediately took a high-guard stance, ready to engage the aggressor.

"We need to go!" The other intruder screamed as he ran away from Mike, toward the back of the house. His friend didn't listen.

The man continued toward Hank with a deafening growl of anger. Five feet from Hank the man raised the knife. Four feet, three… and Hank delivered a snap-kick into the man's chest, sending him sprawling backwards onto the floor near the couch. Hank searched near the door for a weapon… anything he could use, finding nothing but a wicker basket full of dried reeds and flowers.

"Let's go!" The man at the back of the house howled as he ran out the back door and down the stairs, disappearing into the dark.

Hank bounced forward on his feet, moving from where he had been when he was initially attacked. The intruder on the floor rose to his feet quickly, staring at Hank, surprised by Hank's efficiency, gauging the result of another charge.

Lights on, Mike located the coal shovel for the fireplace amidst the mess of objects that littered his floor. Mike swung the shovel wildly, impacting the man's shin.

"Mother fucker!" The man shouted then bolted for the back door and the cover of darkness.

Mike crawled off the floor, reaching the couch. Debbie was bleeding from a cut on the side of her swollen face, drifting in and out of reality as her hands clasped over her injured stomach, "Debbie...baby."

Hank looked around the home, still on guard. The house was a disaster area. The intruders, the burglars... whatever they were, had destroyed the interior. Every piece of furniture was torn apart, every decoration shattered. Even the couch that Debbie lay on had its cushions torn to shreds. As his adrenaline level subsided, Hank raced out the front door, worried, peering into the back seat of his truck where Andrew remained, sleeping. The adrenaline disappeared.

With a shaking hand, Hank pulled his cell phone from his pocket and dialed, "Yes, yes, there has been a robbery here. People are hurt. We need police and an ambulance."

Hank looked inside, seeing Mike holding Debbie in his arms, using his shirt to stop Debbie's bleeding.

"Yes. Oh… 1522 Juniper Street. Tybee Island," Hank responded to the 911 dispatcher.

"We're on our way," Hank heard the woman respond as he saw a blue Chevy truck speed out of sight.

12

9:40PM

Hank sat on the bumper of the fire truck as an EMT placed a gauze bandage over his leg. The snap kick he'd delivered was fierce enough to rattle the intruder but not enough to prevent the knife from grazing Hank's left thigh. The wound was small, just a scratch, but it bled enough to turn Hank's jeans crimson red from the wound to his ankle. Hank hadn't noticed until Mike brought it to his attention. Even then, it didn't matter much.

"That's got it, Mr. Morgan," the EMT said as he stood, examining the bandage, "You don't really *need* to go to the hospital. It doesn't need stitches. But, I'd suggest a visit to the ER just the same... blood work, maybe tetanus."

Hank stood, taking his body weight on the wounded leg. "I think it'll be fine," Hank said. "Thank you."

Hank walked over to the back door of the ambulance where Debbie and Mike were both being attended to. The early prognosis was that Debbie had a slight concussion and, maybe, a broken rib. The side of her face was puffed up like a balloon and turning a shade of midnight blue. Mike lay on a gurney next to Debbie, ribs wrapped, arm in a sling. The Paramedic's were busy strapping them both down for the ride to Savannah General. To the side of the ambulance, Master Chief Braden stood talking to the police as his wife, Claire, held Andrew in her arms, stroking his hair as she wiped tears from his cheeks.

"Burglary?" Hank overheard Braden ask as he approached.

"Yes, sir," the young officer responded. "It appears the Harwood's entered the home while the burglary was in progress."

"What were they after?"

"We can't tell for sure. Probably electronics, jewelry, anything of value that could be pawned." The officer turned as a Chatham County Sheriffs SUV rolled up to the house.

Jeff, John and Mitch piled out of the SUV, taking note of the commotion. The neighbors had gathered around, along with a dozen or so half-tanked tourists from the nearby bars.

"Have a look inside, Mitch," Martin said as he pulled his badge from his front pocket and approached the Ambulance.

"Deputy, Agent Nguyen…." Master Chief greeted the pair.

"Master Chief." Jeff replied, shaking Braden's hand, "How are you, Petty Officer Morgan?" Jeff asked, patting Hank on the shoulder.

"I'm fine," Hank replied.

"What about them?" Martin looked into the back of the ambulance as the paramedics finished their work.

"They're beat up but they'll live," Braden responded as the Ambulance doors closed. "Damn scary stuff."

"They're lucky to be alive," Martin said as the ambulance rolled away. "And you're a hero," Martin looked at Hank.

Hank didn't see it that way. "I'm trained. That's all."

"Well…" Martin smiled, "Whatever you are… you showed up in the nick of time. Good job."

Lori's car screeched to a halt just down the block from the house and she flew out of the car, running toward Hank, "Hank!" Lori yelled as she threw her arms around his neck. "You're hurt?"

"I'm ok," Hank said as Lori released him and spotted his bloody pant leg.

"Like hell you are." Lori bent down, studying the bandage.

"Honey. Honey." Hank grabbed Lori's shoulders and brought her to eye level, "Baby, I'm ok. But, please, go help Mrs. Braden with Andrew."

Lori wiped a tear from her cheek as she looked over Hank's shoulder, seeing Andrew crying in Claire's arms. "Okay," Lori said as she stepped away. "Rachel is at our place with Ally. She came as soon as I called her."

"That's good, Babe," Hank responded, smiling, as he turned back to the gathered officers.

"Your wife?" Nguyen asked.

Hank nodded as he watched Lori rub Andrews back. In the ample time Lori had spent with Andrew the two had formed a bond. Andrew crawled out of Claire's arms and into Lori's, crying, but calming.

"Officer..." Martin studied the young man's nametag, "...Hickey here is going to let us have a look around the house, Gents."

This was news to the young officer who ruffled, "It's my crime scene, Deputy."

"It's a professional courtesy, Hickey. We'll be sure to let your supervisor know how cooperative and professional you are." Martin flashed a cheesy, patronizing grin.

"Bullshit," Hickey responded. "But, go ahead. The detectives from GSP won't get here for another thirty minutes...if they decide to come at all."

Hickey was right. The GSP didn't take too much interest in robberies, even when they resulted in an assault. Strained budgets meant the State Police Detectives had bigger fish to fry. If no one was dead then they usually wouldn't show up, unless the case connected to something else. The same was true with Chatham County. The County had equal difficulties with budgets and though, technically, they had a duty to check on this case... it would be ignored in favor of a more pressing criminal investigation. Despite its Southern Charm, Savannah had its share of violent crimes that kept the County and local police hopping.

Mitch appeared on the front deck of the home. Leaning on the railing he let loose a long string of tobacco juice. Wiping his chin, he motioned his head, indicating that Martin should come inside.

"Shall we?" Martin indicated to Jeff, Braden and Hank as he headed toward the stairs.

"Burglary?" Martin asked as he topped the stairs.

"Damned shitty one if you ask me," Mitch responded as he followed the group into Mike and Debbie's home.

The house was in complete disarray. There wasn't a single item that hadn't been turned over or tossed about. Every dish from every cupboard was on the floor. Pictures, posters, sconces... all on the floor. It seemed that no item was immune. Even Andrew's toy chest in the corner of the living room was upended. Wooden blocks, Hot Wheels and Star Wars action figures lay trampled.

"Didn't miss much did they?" Mitch said as he sighed.

"No." Jeff walked through the living room, considering the scene. "They didn't."

"What the hell would you rob from a toy chest?" Hank said as he bent over, picking up a Sponge Bob doll.

Martin raised his eyebrows, considering what Hank had said. He wasn't surprised. Neither was Mitch. Long before either of them entered the house they had wondered whether or not this "robbery" was related to the missing money. It was just way too coincidental that a member of the 942 crew had had their home sacked. True, people got robbed every day. Even touristy Tybee Island wasn't immune. But, this was coincidental nonetheless.

"Anything stand out to you Mitch?" Martin asked as he stepped over a pile of shattered china."

"About every damn thing stands out in some way or another," Mitch responded. "I see a lot that ought not to be here."

Master Chief Braden waded through the clutter, approaching the kitchen. "Such as…."

"Well…" Mitch spat into the sink, "For one thing, these folks look like they owned a whole lot of expensive stuff." Mitch motioned toward a hallway off the kitchen. "There's a drawer or two in the bedroom back there that's thrown out on the ground. There's jewelry on the floor, untouched. It's not that zirconium shit either. Why the hell wouldn't you take it if you were aiming to rob someone?"

"Good point," Jeff Nguyen said as he examined an "iPad" that was still plugged into its charger.

"You're saying those men were here looking for the missing money from the wreck?" Braden crossed his arms over his chest.

"Maybe." Mitch said.

"But not certain?" Hank dropped the doll and turned to Martin.

"No, not certain." Martin peered down the hallway. "But, it's a substantiated theory."

"Big words." Mitch rolled his eyes as he looked out the back door.

"What did they look like, Hank? What did you see?" Jeff asked.

"They wore masks."

"Black guys in masks? White guys? Aliens in masks?" Jeff pressed.

"Black," Hank responded.

"What else?" Martin asked, approaching Hank.

"I think they drove a blue Chevy truck. I saw one haul ass away from here. Does that make a difference?"

"Nope..." Martin said as he looked out the front window. "That doesn't narrow it down very well at all. Maybe later it will help."

"So..." Braden said through a furrowed brow. "You can't say for certain that this incident was a direct threat to a member of my crew," Braden raised an eyebrow. "You're speculating."

"Yes," Martin responded. "We are. But, don't discount anything."

"Do I need to request some kind of protection for these kids or what?" Braden was agitated. He wanted answers.

Jeff Nguyen decided it was time for him to seize control, at least as far as the Coast Guard side of this investigation was concerned. "Master Chief, we can't be certain that this incident was connected to our investigation. For now, it is only a possibility."

"That's comforting. I've got... we've got families," Hank responded.

Mitch spat another heap of tobacco juice into the sink then patted Hank on the shoulder as he walked by. "You know what the best protection against home invasion is, Hank?"

"What's that, Sir" Hank responded, frustrated.

"A dog," Mitch said.

Martin walked over to the couch, looking at the blood stained cushions. "Who did this?" he wondered to himself.

13

10:30PM

Robinson Anderson sat in a corner booth, watching his body guards make small talk with the too-young girl behind the counter. Sure, she was built like she was in her twenties, but it was apparent that she had yet to graduate from high school. Robinson, R.A., "Ra" as he had come to be known, really didn't give a shit whether one of his men banged the girl behind a dumpster later. As long as the two kept an eye on his ass, which they did pretty well, their private lives didn't mean a damn thing.

Ra took a swallow from his Dr. Pepper as he watched the pickup truck pull into the McDonald's parking lot. McDonald's or Wendy's, even Taco Bell, were his favorite places to meet for business. Ra couldn't recall the number of deals he'd made amidst the smell of fryer grease and charred beef. Fast food restaurants provided perfect cover. As long as he didn't push any product across the table, or under it, he and his posse appeared as just another group of hoodlums teetering on the brink of loitering. Usually, buying one item or another every few minutes kept the store manager off his ass and the cops from being called.

"T!" One of the men from the pickup exclaimed as he came through the side entrance. "Sup, Man?"

T, Tyrone, a bodyguard, turned away from the counter and approached the man. "Bitch! You got to keep shit quiet. I don't even know your name."

The man nervously lowered his head and voice as Tyrone squeezed down hard on his shoulder. Tyrone was huge, muscular, and his grip felt as though it could shatter the man's clavicle.

"I'm sorry T. I just wanted to…." the man responded.

"I don't give a shit brother. You got something to say to Ra?"

"Yeah, I do. Me and Byron did what Ra wanted us to do."

Byron limped in the side door, holding his chest, trying his best to make it look like this was his style of presenting himself. Tyrone, Ra and the other bodyguard, William, could tell the difference.

"What have you two mother fuckers done?" Tyrone said, grabbing the man, Roger, by the shirt and forcibly escorting him into a chair at Ra's table. Byron was seized by William, and tossed into a chair next to Roger.

Ra played with the straw in his drink, making it squeak as he worked it up and down in the plastic lid. He stared at Roger and Byron through a pair of Ray-Ban sunglasses, sizing them up, preventing them from doing the same. Ra had hired these two earlier in the day. He'd hired them to go look for his money, for the shit. Both of them were junkies, not meth, heroine. Both lived in Savannah and Ra knew these two pieces of shit would suck dick for a fix.

"What'd you find?" Ra asked, calmly.

Byron rubbed under his nose then across his forehead. He needed a fix. "We didn't find shit man. We trashed the mother fucker…everything. Didn't find shit." Byron grimaced uncomfortably, rubbing his torso as he shifted in his chair.

"What's wrong with your chest?" Ra asked.

"Them mother fuckers came home while we was in the house!" Roger replied. "We beat on those mother fuckers good, but some other white boy showed up." Roger threw up his hands.

"Mother fucker kicked me in the chest, man." Roger rubbed his chest. "I think he broke something."

Ra looked up, seeing Tyrone and William exchange disgusted glances. They had both advised him not to send these two to take care of the job... that they would handle it, but he didn't listen. He should have. Still, Ra knew these two were desperate, so desperate that they would turn the house into a junk yard to find what would reward them with a week's worth of product. In some ways, the fact that they had beat on the Coasties was a plus. It made things look more like a couple of junkies, rabid for money and drugs, had been responsible.

"You kill anyone?" Ra asked.

"Don't think so," Byron responded, then smiled. "Didn't have the time. But, I'd have cut that bitch." Byron held up his hand, showing off the bite marks.

"Get the fuck out of my sight," Ra said, motioning to William and Tyrone.

The bodyguards each grabbed a man by the shirt and neck and dragged them from their chairs, across the floor, toward the side entrance.

"Damn, man. We did what you wanted. Where's our shit?" Roger said as Tyrone banged him against a garbage can.

"Shut the fuck up," Tyrone said as he crushed down on Rogers arm.

William opened the door, tossing Byron out onto the pavement. Tyrone followed, heaving Roger a further distance. Roger and Byron scurried to their feet.

"That's fucked up!" Byron yelled as he headed to the driver's side of the truck.

"Bitch!" Tyrone reached into his jacket, feeling the hilt of his pistol. "You better get the fuck out of here!"

Roger and Byron flew into the truck, started the engine and squealed tires as they ran from Tyrone and William.

Ra walked up to the counter full of spectators and ordered an apple pie. The girl, the one the bodyguards had been talking with, filled the order silently. Ra handed the girl a ten then turned for the door before she could make change. "Have a good night," Ra said without looking back. So much for doing business at this McDonalds... there were many more.

"Crazy ass junkies," Tyrone said as William pulled up in the Mercedes.

Ra opened the back door. "They did a'ight," Ra said. "Least we know that country ass hadn't looked there yet."

"Still don't matter. Just cause the money wasn't in their house doesn't mean the fuckers aint got it."

"True," Ra said, facing Tyrone. "But this is a race, T. It's a process of elimination." Both men climbed into the car.

"One of them has it. They were the only mother fuckers that got near it." Ra closed his door then lit a cigarette. "Someone's gonna make it real apparent that they got bank, somehow, and we're gonna be there when they do."

William pulled the Mercedes out of the parking lot, down the street and onto Interstate 95, headed back to Charleston.

Thursday

14

6:30AM

Hank woke to the sound of laughter coming from the living room. It was squealing laughter, children's laughter... Ally and Andrew. Through sleep filled eyes Hank looked at the clock on the nightstand. It was six thirty. Even after a night of extreme duress, the kids were up and at play. Hank wished he could recover even half of the childhood resiliency he'd once had. Oh to be young. The smell of coffee reached his nose.

Rising from bed, Hank took a step down onto an angry leg. He'd forgotten the wound that was now grumbling at him from beneath the bandage. At the hospital, Hank *had* needed stitches, two to be exact, and a tetanus shot. He'd been sent home with a small quantity of Tylenol, non- prescription strength, and a day or two worth of bandages. Lori, of course, had run the nurses through the gamut, ascertaining exactly how to care for Hanks trauma. Hank just wanted to blow the whole thing off. At midnight, when they left the ER, Hank had talked to Braden. Despite Master Chief's contrary opinion, Hank insisted that he'd be at work for duty on Friday morning.

Debbie and Mike had been admitted to Savannah General for overnight observation. Debbie didn't have a concussion and Mike didn't have broken ribs. The blow's that each had absorbed had fallen short of the deliverer's intent. Though Debbie would sport a knot on the side of her face for the next week or two, it would heal. Knowing Debbie's prowess with makeup, no one would know she was injured. Mike would be on light duty for a few days. The injury to his arm was the most severe, a very deep bruise on his bicep. Mike could take the Officer of the Day position, which didn't involve driving boats or brandishing a sidearm, provided Braden allowed him to return to work before next week. The robbery and assault were a serious psychological event. Hank wondered if Debbie and Mike would snap back quickly. For now, until about noon today, Andrew was staying with Hank and Lori and, from the sounds of it, having a pretty good time.

"I thought I heard you rustling around," Lori said, entering the bedroom with a steaming cup of coffee. "Master Chief called earlier to see if you wanted to talk to a counselor about last night."

"What did you tell him?" Hank asked.

"That you'd let him know," Lori responded. "It might be helpful."

Outside the bedroom door, Rachel peeked in, not wanting to catch Hank parading around in his skivvies or birthday suit. Rachel had stayed the night on the couch after she, Hank and Lori had stayed up till the wee-hours re-hashing the night's events. Though shirtless, Hank was wearing long pajamas.

"It's okay Rachel," Hank said, accepting the coffee from Lori, sipping carefully as he hunted for a t-shirt.

"How's it feel?" Lori asked, bending down to look at the bandage.

"I don't know…stiff I guess."

"Sore?"

"And that," Hank said, grabbing a t-shirt from the dirty clothes bin in the closet.

"Rachel got a text from Debbie already," Lori said, taking the coffee mug from Hank.

"They'll be released by noon," Rachel said, reading over the text on her phone. "Debbie asked about Andrew. She wondered about the house. Mike complained about the food…"

Hank laughed.

"…and they wondered if I, you or we could come pick them up?"

"Sure can," Hank said as he took the mug back from Lori. "That ought to give the boys enough time to have gotten things kind-of picked up."

Hank referred to the "volunteer" work party that Master Chief said he would assemble in the morning. The all "volunteer" crew would sweep into Debbie and Mike's home, clean, repair and fix up as much of the damage as was possible prior to Debbie and Mike's return. It wasn't uncommon for Master Chief to direct the crew to help a shipmate. Once, Master Chief had sent the entire crew to build wheelchair ramps for an elderly member of the Coast Guard Auxiliary who'd had a stroke. Master Chief pulled the trigger on this kind of effort rarely and, every time, for good reason. Family, to Braden, was family.

Hank leaned into Lori, kissed her cheek, then limped from the bedroom into the living room. Ally and Andrew sat facing each other, throwing a stuffed "Big Bird" doll back and forth, breaking into a cackle every time someone missed the catch. It was good to see this. For all the insistence of the police, that the incident was just a B & E that had resulted in an assault, Hank couldn't let the skepticism of Martin, Nguyen and Dailey go. They couldn't, wouldn't, come right out and claim a connection to the money…but they didn't deny it either. It was no comfort to Hank and he was less than a day away from leaving his family, alone, for the weekend.

"More coffee anyone?" Rachel said as she went into the kitchen.

"Me," Lori responded.

"Me, too," Hank said, draining his mug.

Hank and Lori took seats at the dining room table as Rachel brought in the coffee pot, a hot pad, and the creamer… English toffee, Hank's favorite, but he'd never let the guys know that.

As Rachel poured, her face hardened. "I can't believe all this. You never think someone you know will be, you know, hurt."

Hank and Lori were silent. They agreed.

"Especially when you think about the other stuff that is going on." Rachel snapped her mouth closed. She'd screwed up. She knew it.

"Other stuff?" Lori asked. "What's up, Hank?" Lori's face turned stern. She'd been a military wife long enough to know when she was being left out of something important.

Hank didn't look at Rachel. He didn't shoot her the death needle's glare that he wanted to. That would have completely tipped Lori off.

"Hurricane stuff, Babe." Hank didn't exactly lie, but he wasn't about to be completely truthful. He didn't want Lori freaking out.

"Like?"

"Well…" Hank started, Rachel broke in.

"The local police told us there would be lots of crime in the aftermath of the storm." Rachel sat, clutching her mug. Hank let her continue, "Lots of folks taking advantage of the cops being strained for resources."

"It's more than a week later," Lori scoffed. "We barely got hit."

"Desperate people will do anything, Honey. If they think they can get away with it." Hank patted Lori's hand.

Lori sat silent, contemplating, not fully buying, but contemplating.

"I'm glad everyone's ok," Rachel said, breaking the quiet.

Lori sighed, "I love them both but... if Mike and Debbie weren't so over the top about having money...maybe they wouldn't have been a target. Take those new jet ski's for example..."

"New what?" Rachel asked.

Hank interjected, "Mike bought two new Jet Ski's yesterday. Nice ones."

Hank watched Rachel sink back in her chair, drifting into concerned thought. She babysat for Mike and Debbie often, and had mentioned seeing opened mail, bank statements, credit card bills, all lying out on the kitchen counter. Hank realized that Mike and Debbie had money but, thanks to Rachel's revelations, Hank realized that they also had bills to pay, lots of bills, enough to make a big purchase worse than frivolous...more like, destructive.

"Breakfast time guys." Lori said to Ally and Andrew as she rose from the table, "Captain Crunch or Life?"

"Life!" the kids shouted in unison as they scurried from the living room floor into the kitchen.

"Rachel, want some breakfast?" Lori asked.

Rachel was silent, thoughts streaming through her head.

"Rachel?" Hank asked.

Rachel's train of thought broke. "Life sounds good to me," she smiled. But, beneath the smile, all she could think of was a cell phone case.

15

10:52AM

Evan glanced over the legal document he'd taken from Paul Sulsky the day before. "Ryan Beck, USCG, Tybee, GA" appeared in bold print along with the names of several other Coastguardsmen. The document was amongst paperwork Paul Sulsky kept in his completely disorganized file cabinet at the Fish House. Searching through the files hadn't been Sulsky's idea. In fact, Sulsky went out of his way to talk down the possibility of discovering individual names amidst the crumpled mass of papers. But, Evan persisted, knowing that Sulsky had been to court on many occasions, fighting fines and violations issued by the Coast Guard and that Coastguardsmen had been there as witnesses. Henry Morgan, Michael Harwood, Gabriel Ortiz, Rachel Stone, Ryan Beck and Laura Hill were among the names listed and the only names linked to a current address in Savannah, one of which Evan now watched. Evan checked his watch. It was nearly eleven.

"Wonder if this kid will ever get up?" Evan said as he lit another cigarette.

Evan had been sitting outside Ryan Beck's apartment since midnight, waiting. The intent was to check the guy out, see where he lived, what he drove, what his habits were. Evan had learned plenty.

Beck returned home, finally, at three with a car full of girls and one other guy, a Latino, probably Ortiz. The entire troop staggered up the sidewalk, loudly, and into the building. At five, the girls, four of them, walked back out, clothes in disarray, bragging about their time with the "stupid ass rich kid," and about how much each of them had been paid even though both of the "dumb asses" passed out.

These weren't hookers. Not in the strictest sense of the word. Evan recognized one of the girls as a stripper from around town. The rest were probably her "titty-shaking" comrades. If Beck hired the four of them to come to his place for private dancing, the cost would have been exorbitant and they would have had a bouncer in tow. More than likely, the girls had been hired for sex. It happened occasionally. That meant hundreds of dollars... probably more like a grand. Evan knew military pay. Beck didn't have that kind of money. Evan's cell rang. It was Dennis.

"Boss."

"Anything?" Dennis asked, a hint of impatience in his voice.

"Other than the girls…nothing, yet."

"I talked to Joey at the Shangri-La. He told me the little bastard dropped over five hundred last night."

"Horny little shit," Evan interjected.

"Joey says Beck is in there all the time but he's never seen him spend that much. One or two dances, a couple of drinks, then he takes off."

"Looks like this guy's fortunes have changed. Or, maybe the other one, Ortiz."

"The little bastards are blowing my money on tits and ass!"

Dennis was getting worked up… too worked up. This was something that had been happening too much lately. Dennis always wanted fast results but, for the most part, was patient enough not to jump to conclusions. Evan supposed he understood the urgency. A quarter of a million dollars could get spent in a hurry.

Before too long there wouldn't be any money to get back. Still, "why not just write it off." Evan thought.

"Dennis, we don't know that for sure. Maybe he got a check from a rich relative?" Evan tried to calm Dennis. It didn't work.

"My ass, Evan!"

Evan sighed, "Ok then. What do you want me to do?"

"Make a statement!" Dennis shouted. "Let the little fucks know someone is watching them!"

"What…like a note on his windshield telling him to give it back?"

"I don't give a shit! Be creative! But make sure the little bastard is scared!"

As Dennis's voice howled through the phone Evan watched a silver Mazda pull up in front of Beck's apartment. Two African-Americans climbed out of the car, bending over near Beck's vehicle.

"Who are these guys?" Evan questioned as the two stood up, folding away knives. As Beck's car sank toward the pavement, the men walked up the sidewalk toward the apartment door.

"I'll call you back." Evan said, closing the phone over the sound of Dennis's voice.

****

The pounding on the door rang like thunder in Gabe's ears. "Who the hell would be at the door this early?" Gabe thought as he reached for his smart phone. The screen said it was eleven fifteen. Not so early after all.

The pounding came again, equally as annoying to Gabe's aching brain. Gabe definitely drank too much last night, and, he mixed liquor with beer. That was always a mistake. Gabe stumbled to his feet as Ryan shouted from the back bedroom.

"What the hell?" Ryan groaned.

The beating on the door came again, "Hold on!" Gabe shouted at the door as he walked from the couch. This was probably some jerk from work. It was probably that idiot Shawn wanting Ryan to go to the gym, "I'll kill that little…." Gabe said, opening the door.

The fist came out of nowhere, striking Gabe squarely in the left eye. Gabe grabbed his face as he stumbled backwards. The next thing he felt were massive arms wrapping around his upper body, holding him, then the next blow struck his midsection. Gabe threw up.

"Where the fuck you got it?" demanded the voice of the man holding Gabe as another punch struck Gabe's stomach.

Gabe couldn't breathe. He couldn't speak. He didn't know what the man was asking. Gabe didn't think the man cared about an answer as another fist connected with his face. The man threw Gabe to the ground, his head striking the edge of the couch. Just before he lost consciousness he heard a scream rise from the back of the apartment.

Ryan came down the hall carrying a hockey stick. As he approached the two men he swung the stick wildly, striking one of the men in the forearm as the other leaped from his feet, tackling Ryan to the ground. Before Ryan could react, his assailant was straddling him, delivering blows to his face. Blood spurted from Ryan's mouth as his lips exploded beneath the man's knuckles. Ryan was grabbed by the hair and dragged him into a sitting position.

"Where the fuck is our money, white boy?" the second man said as he closed the apartment door.

Ryan looked at the man through swollen eyes, still tasting the blood that flowed from open wounds. "What money? I don't have *your* money." Ryan spat, feeling a piece of tooth pass between his swollen lips. "I'm a Federal law enforcement officer. You're assaulting a Federal law enforcement officer!"

Both men laughed. "You aint shit, cracker," the man behind Ryan scoffed as the second man slapped Ryan across the face, hard.

The man who'd slapped Ryan, the biggest of the two, the one with the gold "T" hanging on the end of his necklace, knelt down. "You dropped a lot of cash to get your bean snapped last night, player. Where'd it come from? You don't make shit."

The man holding Ryan shook Ryan violently, "Talk, mother fucker."

Ryan could feel his thoughts becoming more scattered. He was hung over and he was beat to shit. Ryan wished he would just pass out. "I got my own money," Ryan labored to answer.

"I bet you do," T said, standing and producing a pistol from behind his back.

T walked to the couch grabbed Gabe by the shirt and placed the pistol at the back of Gabe's head. "I'm gonna blow this beaner's brains all over your floor, Mr. Federal Officer. You a lying bitch!"

"I don't know shit! I don't know what the fuck you're talking about!" Ryan spat.

"Maybe you don't. But, I bet one of your friends does. One of you mother fuckers got rich off our dime," the man holding Ryan said.

"I think we'll shoot Speedy Gonzales here. Then we'll see how fast someone coughs up our cash." T frowned, gritting his teeth as he moved the pistol to the base of Gabe's Skull.

"Don't!" Ryan shouted as he felt his bladder release.

T looked at Ryan and laughed. "He done pissed his pants."

The man behind Ryan laughed as well, releasing Ryan with a shove that sent Ryan crashing against the wall.

T walked over to Ryan, putting the barrel of the pistol against Ryan's forehead. "Now. Look." T took on a mocking, subtle tone. "You two mother fuckers got in a fight last night. You got your ass beat but, you can tell everyone you won." T reached into his shirt pocket, pulling out a piece of paper.

"See this?" T waved the paper in front of Ryan's swollen face. "You need to tell your friends that we want our money. And, you need to call this number when you're ready to give it back." T pushed on Ryan's head with the pistol then stood up, dropping the paper to the floor. T's partner was already at the door.

"We ain't gonna give you a lot of time, cracker. You don't want to see us again," T's partner said as he opened the apartment door.

"You say shit about this...other than what I told you to say... I'm'a cut off your balls." T walked out of the apartment, slamming the door behind him.

Ryan crawled across the floor to Gabe. Gabe was breathing, his eye was swollen and turning blue, but he was alive. Ryan leaned back against the couch, using his sleeve to wipe blood from his mouth. With a finger he felt the place where his front tooth used to be.

"How'm I gonna explain this to Master Chief?" Ryan

said as he heard Gabe groan.

****

Evan was outside the door and heard Beck being beaten. "Real bitch for that kid," Evan thought. Beck lived in a complex full of single working class folks. No one was around to hear him or Ortiz scream. Evan supposed, judging from the two black guys, that the Coasties had gotten the shit kicked out of them. Hopefully they weren't dead.

Evan followed the Mazda through Savannah and onto 95 North, headed toward South Carolina. This answered questions for Evan. These men were the other side of the bad deal. If Evan guessed right, they were after the same thing he was. Evan needed these two to answer the "w" questions. Evan needed to know what he was up against. Things were getting much more complicated and far more dangerous.

Evan pulled into the lane alongside the Mazda as his phone rang. Dennis, again, and once again Evan ignored the call. Dennis would be pissed, but Evan didn't have time to talk. Evan slammed down the gas pedal and came up even with the Mazda. As he did, Evan rolled down his passenger side window.

"Your back tire is flat!" Evan yelled at the driver.

T shot him a questioning look, "Wha

Evan rolled his finger through the air. Getting the message, T rolled his window down. Both cars slowed.

"Your back tire is almost flat! It looks like it's going to blow out!" Evan shouted.

T looked in the side mirror. The tire was almost flat. Evan had seen to it that the tire would be.

"Aight! Thanks man!" T shouted back.

Evan let off the gas and fell into the lane behind T as he turned the Mazda onto the next exit, coming to a stop on the side of the road. Evan fell in behind the Mazda, watching as T kept peering in the rear view mirror.

"He's probably wondering what the hell I'm doing," Evan told himself. "I better be quick."

Evan kept his silenced pistol raised as he leapt from his car and ran toward the Mazda. Evan's first shot went into the calf of the leg T had flung out the driver's side door, exactly as Evan intended. The second shot went through the back window of the Mazda and into Morris' neck. He'd meant for it to hit his head. Evan would have to work on his accuracy. Evan grabbed the driver's door and slammed it against T's bleeding leg. T let out a howl of pain, drawing the leg inside the car as Evan slammed the door.

"Don't!" Evan said, seeing T reach for his gun.

In the passenger's seat, Morris wasn't quite dead. Head lying against the side window; blood spewed from a gaping hole in the man's throat; Evan pulled the trigger again, burying a round in the side of Morris' skull.

"Poor bastard!" Evan said as he placed his pistol on T's temple.

"Who do you work for?" Evan asked as T bit his lip against the pain in his leg and the image of his slaughtered friend.

"Fuck you!" T replied, defiantly.

Evan moved the pistol quickly, shooting T in the left foot.

"God damnit!" T said, gripping his leg.

"I haven't got time for your tough- guy shit, boy!" Evan smacked T in the face with the barrel of the pistol. "Who?"

"I work for Ra damnit!" T replied.

"What'd you want with those boys back in Savannah?" Evan pressed the pistol to T's head.

"Mother fuckers took Ra's money."

Evan laughed. "Boy, that aint Ra's money." Evan stepped away from T, keeping the pistol trained on the man as he went to the passenger side of the Mazda.

Evan opened the door grabbing Morris's body and pushing it onto the floor board, "Roll down this fucking window!" Evan ordered T.

T rolled down the blood covered passenger side window as Evan slammed the door shut. Kneeling down, Evan pointed the pistol at T again.

"You drive your ass back to Ra and tell him to stay out of Savannah or I'll fill his house up with blood! You hear me?"

T shook his head yes, fighting back the pain.

Evan reached across the seat, grabbed T's pistol, ejected the magazine then tossed both back into the car. "Drive your fat ass home!" Evan commanded.

T started the Mazda and slammed on the accelerator, speeding away as Evan placed his pistol back in his belt. The phone rang again. It was Dennis. This time, Evan needed to talk.

16

1:20PM

"It's okay baby boy." Debbie held Andrew in her arms, squeezing him close, "Mommy is going to be just fine."

Hank helped Mike out of the car as Lori and Rachel lead Debbie toward the steps to the house with Ally in tow. Master Chief and BM1 Brooks stood at the top of the stairs. Braden's sweat-soaked shirt meant that he had been working hard to get the house put back into some form of order. Inside, Hank could hear music playing, some kind of rock, meaning that they had arrived a little before expected.

"How we doing?" Braden asked as Debbie and Mike mounted the stairs.

"Sore and unattractive," Debbie answered with her least painful smile.

"I'm doing alright, Master Chief," Mike said as a wince of pain betrayed his aching ribs.

"For a guy with busted ribs...I'd agree," Brooks said as she took Andrew from Debbie's arms.

A heavenly smell wafted from inside the house. It had to be something good... some kind of comfort food, meaning that Claire was in the kitchen.

"That smells fantastic," Mike said as the group walked inside.

The living room looked as if nothing had happened. The couch was in one piece, the cushions flipped over to the side that hadn't been slashed. The broken glass from the picture frames had been swept up and the carpet cleaned. The crew had worked hard. There was little doubt that the rest of the house looked just as good.

"Thank you," Debbie said, throwing her arms around Braden.

Braden uncomfortably returned the hug. What he and the crew had done was a very kind thing, but accepting the gratitude was never easy. Braden always tried to equate looking out for his crew to his "job." The truth was that he and Claire always leant a hand. But, it was never enough of a hand to satisfy the Bradens.

"I can't tell you how much this means to us, Master Chief," Mike said, tears forming in his eyes.

Braden patted Debbie on the back, "I'm pretty sweaty Debbie and I don't smell very good. You don't want that all over you."

Debbie snickered as she released Braden.

" Honey." Claire came from the kitchen and hugged Debbie.

"Thank you, Claire." Debbie said.

"It's the least I can do," Claire said warmly. "I had to be here to supervise these boys..." Claire looked at Brooks, "...and girls. They do a fine job of looking after a boat. But, a home...well...they're sailors," Claire brushed back Debbie's hair. "Tired?"

Debbie nodded then sat on the couch. The look of exhaustion in her face was evident.

"Time to wrap it up folks," Brooks shouted down the hallway.

Immediately the radio was switched off. Several of the crew meandered out of the back rooms carrying cleaning supplies and trash bags. As they passed by Debbie and Mike they shared hugs, pats on the back and the obligatory "hell-of-a way to get a day off" jibes.

"See you at work?" Laura Hill asked, ending the procession of Coasties.

"You bet. See you tomorrow," Mike replied as he sank slowly into the couch.

"Not likely," Braden raised an eyebrow toward Mike. "The Doc says you're SIQ for at least a week. You *will* take it easy."

Mike didn't like being out of commission, despite the fact that he really needed to stay still and recover. Coasties, like Mike, had a long "tough guy" tradition. Braden was having none of it.

"Ok then..." Claire pulled off her apron, folding it neatly and placing it on the kitchen counter, "...there is pot-roast in the oven, done, and on warm. There are rolls on the counter and a pitcher of tea in the fridge," Claire leaned over the couch, kissing Debbie on the forehead and ruffling Mike's hair. "We put a couple of those Swanson dinners in the freezer...use them." Claire's voice was motherly and comforting.

"Thanks again, Master Chief, Claire, XPO," Mike said as the party headed out the front door.

"Just get rested," Claire said as she walked out.

"Are you going to stick around a bit?" Braden asked Hank.

"For a while... yes."

"It might be kind of rough for them to be back in the house considering what happened," Braden spoke in a hushed tone.

"Yes." Hank glanced back at Mike and Debbie's exhausted faces. "We'll stay as long as it takes."

"Good," Braden said, patting Hank on the shoulder.

As Hank shut the front door he heard Debbie begin to sob. Hank couldn't imagine how violated she felt and her physical injury had to be adding to the emotional tempest. In all honesty, Hank couldn't believe that Debbie and Mike even wanted to come home. A home, to Hank, was supposed to be a sacred, safe place. No one in the room spoke. Andrew and Ally had already scooted off to Andrew's room where the sound of noisy toys and intermittent giggling could be heard. Lori sat on the arm of the couch rubbing Debbie's back as Rachel stood motionless in the kitchen, wondering what to, or not to, do.

"Why would anyone do this?" Debbie asked through gulping breaths.

Mike grabbed Debbie's hand and squeezed. "People can be crazy sweetheart. People can be desperate."

"But, why us?" Debbie's searched Mike's eyes for an answer. "There are people on this island with much more than we have. They could have gone after the Peter's house down the street. They're loaded. They flaunt it. And, they're out of town."

"I don't know sweetheart," Mike replied.

"I don't think bad stuff like this ever makes sense when it happens," Lori said, rising from the couch.

"They turned the house upside down. They could have been in and out of here with armloads of electronics in the time it took them to ruin my home," Debbie was agitated, questioning.

"But they weren't, Deb," Mike talked softly, trying to keep Debbie from a fit of rage. "And we can be thankful that we're all here, alive, and that what was broken can be replaced."

"It's like they were after something… like in movies," Debbie said, ignoring Mike.

"Deb…" Lori leaned over the back of the couch, "… don't get too wrapped up in why, sweetheart. Just worry about healing."

"Meanwhile…" Hank pulled out his keys, jingling them in the air. "I'm going to go buy a new deadbolt for your back door and a motion-sensor light for outside...front and back."

"Let me give you some cash for that, Hank," Mike said, reaching painfully for his wallet.

"No need, brother," Hank smiled. "I grabbed a twenty from you when you weren't looking."

"And, I'll get the Harwood family all settled in while you're gone," Lori gave Hank a peck on the cheek. "Let's get you to bed Debbie, Mike." Lori offered her hands to both.

Hank headed out the front door and started down the steps with Rachel following.

"Rachel?" Hank asked.

"I thought I'd ride along with you."

"What's on your mind? You've been very quiet."

Rachel looked at the Jet Skis under the carport then walked to the passenger side of Hanks car. "I don't know, Hank. I'm just... concerned about something."

17

2:00PM

Jeff had parted ways with John and Mitch after breakfast. It was growing increasingly difficult to keep his mandated investigative methods separate from the more liberal techniques his accomplices employed. Jeff had to admit there were times, lots of them, when he could have gotten much more accomplished if the Coast Guard allowed for more creative interpretation of the law. But, in the end he supposed the rigid formalities had helped him make "good," albeit petty, cases. This case didn't appear to be at all petty. Jeff couldn't quite understand why, but he had been uneasy and hyper-vigilant since leaving Benny's trailer.

It *was* entirely possible that Benny had been the one who stole the money from the wrecked boat. It *was* entirely possible that the assault on the Harwood's was the product of a random burglary gone wrong. It wasn't as if those types of things weren't occurring across the country every single day. Unfortunately, Savannah had some issues with crime which lent more credibility to both occurrences. But, John and Mitch were convinced there was a connection. They were convinced that someone, a Coastie, either had the money or that someone, a bad guy, thought they did. This was a hunch. Jeff had never dealt with hunches. He'd never been allowed the latitude. It was time for a little change.

Jeff came to a stop in front of building "H" of the Willow Wash apartment complex. This was the residence of Ryan Beck.

"Apartment 1A, first floor, right side," Jeff reminded himself with a quick look at his notes.

Beck struck Jeff as arrogant. At the interview, though Beck was obviously nervous, he'd still projected a haughty nature. Beck's service record supported Jeff's opinion. Beck had been given negative "administrative remarks" entries twice in his brief career, both for insubordinate conduct. Apparently he thought he was above tasks like cleaning the head, folding linen or scrubbing out garbage cans. As the one adverse entry had stated, Beck had a "lack of willingness combined with a very smart mouth."

"Tough shit kid," Jeff thought during his review. "Welcome to the military."

Jeff climbed out of his government sedan, grabbed his briefcase and headed toward Beck's apartment.

****

Through the pain, Ryan scrubbed at his carpet, trying desperately to remove the blood stains that marked the place where Gabe's head had come to rest. This wasn't the first spot he'd scrubbed. The place where he'd spat his tooth onto the floor had been completely saturated with blood. Try as he might, the stain wouldn't come out and probably never would. Once or twice, Ryan's head had swooned and he'd nearly passed out. It had been four hours since the two men had beaten on his head, and Gabe's. The pain and swelling were still intense.

Gabe lay on the couch, bags of ice covering his face. He was hurting pretty bad. The two brutes knew what they were doing when the beatings commenced. The blow to Gabe's head had been intentionally placed in a spot where no permanent damage would be done, only a week or so of ugly bruising and pain. The kick to Gabe's body had been enough to hurt, to linger, but not to shatter bone or explode organs. Ryan took the brunt of the lasting punishment in the form of the missing tooth. It was apparent to Ryan that he'd have to see an oral surgeon to get back his smile. Ryan's stomach hurt, he knew it would hurt for some time but the pain was concealable. It didn't really matter. Gabe and Ryan were both in deep shit when they told Master Chief.

"What were those guys after? I'm calling the cops, Ryan," Gabe said, adjusting the ice packs on his head.

"I don't know, man," Ryan said, slumping onto the floor, exhausted from scrubbing. "But if we call the cops they're gonna come back and kill us."

"Bull shit!"

"You don't think so?" Ryan responded in an agitated, worried tone. "Two huge guys just came in here and kicked the shit out of us, then promised to blow our heads off. You don't think they were serious?" Gabe glared at Ryan.

"I think we're better off saying something instead of sitting here. We're both going to get alcohol incidents, get sent off to screening, and get taken to Captain's Mast...if we don't say something!"

Ryan sighed in frustration.

"I'd rather have some protection. Even if it means I gotta live onboard the Station for a year," Gabe shot back. "Why the fuck don't you agree?"

Ryan stood, slowly, wincing as he rose. "I just don't like the thought of getting shot. If they found us here…if they want us dead, the fence at the station won't keep them from doing it."

"Better than your front door!"

The knock took them both by surprise, especially Ryan. Ryan didn't get too many visitors. Occasionally Shawn would come by wanting to go run or lift but no one else ever came by unless Ryan had offered up food or drink or some kind of party.

"It's two in the afternoon. Who the hell is this?" Ryan whispered.

"It might be those them again, man!" Gabe said, suddenly energized as he rose from the couch and grabbed the floor lamp as a weapon.

The knock came again. It wasn't strong. It was…normal. It didn't matter. Ryan grabbed his hockey stick.

"I'm going to open this thing on three," Ryan said. Gabe nodded, raising the floor lamp to the ready. Ryan held up one finger, then two, then three and swung the door open.

"Whoa guys! Holy shit!" Jeff said, jumping back from the door and reaching for his sidearm. "What the hell?"

Ryan and Gabe both looked at Jeff in shock, then at each other with fear and terror. They'd totally screwed up. They lowered their makeshift weapons.

"You don't have a peep hole?" Jeff asked, relaxing.

Ryan looked at his door, at the peep hole. "How stupid," Ryan thought.

"What the hell happened to you two?" Jeff said as he looked at Ryan and Gabe's swollen and blood streaked faces.

It was a moment of truth and decision. Ryan knew it. If he didn't say something first then Gabe would most certainly spill his guts. Ryan didn't want to lie but he didn't like the truth either. The truth meant telling everything. Ryan didn't want that.

"We got into a pretty bad fight last night," Ryan said as he shot a dagger filled glance at Gabe.

"From the looks of you...I'd say that was an understatement," Jeff said, walking into the apartment. "Where?"

Gabe's jaw tightened. The dagger stare shot back at Ryan with equal ferocity.

"At The Princess Club. We got into it with a couple of Army guys from Hunter," Ryan answered, doing his best to beat Gabe to any response, trying to force Gabe to comply.

"Who started it?" Jeff asked Gabe as he saw tension and angst racking the young man's face.

Gabe considered his answer. He looked at Ryan. Ryan's eyes pleaded... implored him to go along. "They did," Gabe replied.

"Who finished it?" Jeff stepped closer to Ryan, examining Ryan's face.

"We did." Ryan responded, trying to project pride and chutzpah.

"Tell the boss about this yet?"

"Not yet. Don't know how to," Ryan said as Gabe placed the lamp on the floor then sank onto the couch.

"It wouldn't be the first time different services have had disagreements. If I were you two I'd get on the phone to Master Chief pretty soon. He'll probably want to have a talk with the C.O. over at Hunter."

"Damn!" Ryan thought. He hadn't considered that.

"There wasn't a police report?" Jeff asked.

"No, Sir. The bar just kicked us all out and told us not to come back." Ryan couldn't meet Jeff's eyes as he answered.

"Really? That's how it was?" Jeff asked Gabe.

Gabe paused, looking at Ryan. "Yeah. That's how it went down," Gabe answered unconvincingly.

Jeff walked further into the apartment. "You know fellas, BM2 Harwood and his wife had their house broken into last night."

Ryan and Gabe shared shocked, concerned looks.

"They both got beat on pretty bad...had to go to the hospital."

"But, they'll be okay, right?" Gabe asked.

"They'll heal. But, they're pretty shook up."

Jeff stopped, staring down at the stained carpet. "Seems like trouble is following folks at your station right now." Jeff bent down, touching the scrubbed patch of carpet, "Spill some fruit punch here fella's?"

"Hawaiian Punch," Ryan answered a second too late to convince Jeff.

"Try vinegar." Jeff stood, examined Gabe's face, then sighed. "Anyhow… the reason I came to see you, Ryan, was to ask a couple of follow up questions."

"Sure. Anything," Ryan responded.

"Well…I don't think now is the appropriate time. You've had a pretty rough night… and day."

"That's for sure," Gabe offered.

"I think I'll just get out of your hair and maybe catch up with you at the Station tomorrow. You do have duty tomorrow, right?"

"Right," Ryan replied

Jeff headed toward the door. "A couple of suggestions…" Jeff stopped, "Use the peep hole and, if you're that worried about your safety, tell someone."

"We will, Sir," Ryan replied.

"Good," Jeff said. "Oh, what bar was it again? Where you had the fight?"

"The Shangri-La," Gabe responded.

"I'm glad I asked. I thought you said The Princess Club earlier?"

Ryan cringed. They were caught in a lie. He had to think quickly.

"Well, we went to both, actually," Ryan stated.

"Bar hopping?" Jeff smiled.

"Yeah," Gabe nodded.

"I remember those days." Jeff walked out swinging the door closed as he went, "By the way, Ryan, you've got some flat tires."

18

2:45PM

The car was ditched in a roadside swamp. Morris' body was left inside. Ra had called a physician's assistant he knew, a "speed freak" who became an addict during the long hours of residency, but T couldn't be helped. T died from blood loss in the back room of Ra's safe house on the outskirts of Beaufort. T had been Ra's friend since seventh grade. They'd grown up together. Ra didn't give a damn about Morris. People like Morris were a dime a dozen. But, T's death was a blade into Ra's heart. It burned.

"We got to think about what we're gonna do with T's body, Ra," William spoke softly.

"Just let him lie for a while. Just a little while...." Ra responded with a mixture of anger and understanding.

"A'ight," William answered, easing into a dining room chair.

Before he died, T had told Ra what happened. T told Ra about the Coast Guard guys and their alcohol and hooker spending spree. He told Ra about the beatings. But, most importantly, he told Ra about the man who'd shot him and delivered the man's message. To Ra, it all meant that he'd been right. It meant that when he'd guessed one of the Coasties had the money, he'd been correct. The fact that this other "Drug Lord" had his people looking the same direction confirmed it. But, it also made things much different, more urgent. Ra was in a race with his adversary now. There couldn't be any more subtlety. There wouldn't be any more giving people time to hand the money over. Ra had to get to the person who had the money and take it from them. Right now, that person could be any one of the Coasties that had been on that boat. And, somewhere along the line, T would be avenged!

William sighed, heavily, but said nothing.

"What?" Ra asked.

"Ra…" William was being deliberate, choosing his words carefully. "I loved T like a brother… like you."

"But?"

"But, I guess what I wanna say is, is the money worth it? I mean, people are getting dead and beat and it's the fed's we're messing with…."

"So you think I should just say to hell with it? Right?" Ra projected his irritation.

William leaned forward, hands on knees, "I just don't think it's worth anyone else getting killed. You make a shit load of bank, Ra. That cash aint really shit to you."

"It aint only about the money now!" Ra climbed out of his seat. "Your partner is lying in there dead and you're acting like a little scared bitch!"

William said nothing. He guessed this would be Ra's reaction. But, he had to let Ra know that doing nothing was an option.

"I don't want those mother fuckers thinking they can get away with ripping me off and I am damn sure not gonna let that fucker in Savannah get away with killing my people! This shit is personal and professional!"

"But mostly personal?" William asked.

"That ain't your business, mother fucker! You don't like this shit then head your scared ass out the door!"

"I aint about that," William replied, though escaping the coming madness had occurred to him.

Ra took a deep breath, fighting for composure amidst mental chaos, "Look. We got to think about what's happening here. Our people *are* getting killed, man, four in the past two weeks. And, our money is being taken."

William nodded in agreement.

"This kind of shit gets around. We let it go...we get a reputation. We get pushed around. We lose business...maybe, everything."

"So, what do you want?"

Ra paused, considering the question. "We got to make a statement... a loud one, a public one."

"End game?" William asked. "I mean... what's the final goal?"

"If nothing else... I want all of them dead! I don't want it cute either. I want it bad. I want it sick and I want it messy."

"Bet," William replied.

"Get some of our boys together. Get the crazy mother fuckers. I'll handle the rest." Ra's mouth creased in a menacing grin.

"I'm on it. How quick do they need to be ready?" William stood, retrieving his cell from his pocket.

"Real soon, this shit can't wait. We're gonna pay some people a visit, lots of people."

19

3:00PM

"Where do you want to go from here, Dennis?" Evan said as he lifted the beer to his lips.

They sat beneath an umbrella outside Mallory's Steakhouse, watching the Savannah River roll slowly past. River Street in Savannah was always a busy place, especially in late summer. Having so many people around made Dennis feel anonymous, despite the fact that he was easily identifiable in public circles. The beer at Mallory's was always the coldest in Savannah. Dennis supposed Evan could use one, or several, after the events of the afternoon.

"Thank you dear," Dennis smiled at the young waitress as she set another round of drinks on the table, smiled back, and walked away.

"Dennis?" Evan's impatience was evidenced in his tone.

"Enjoy your beer, Evan. Let me order you a very good, early dinner."

"That doesn't answer my question."

"I believe it begins my answer." Dennis looked at a menu. "How about steak?"

Evan hated this about Dennis. One minute, Dennis could be unimaginably spastic, demanding and not the least bit intelligent. The next minute, Dennis turned into a diabolical genius villain from some old time movie. "If...." Dennis thought, "...this guy wasn't bi-polar, no one was."

"Steak, sure, medium rare, potato, salad...all of it." Evan finished the beer in front of him and reached for the next.

"Good choice. Me too." Dennis took a deep drink from his beer as his eyes scanned for the waitress.

"What the hell makes you so calm now, when you were acting like a wild man earlier?" Evan eased back in his seat.

Dennis snickered, "That's easy, Evan."

"How?"

"Before today, I had doubts as to how urgent our situation was. Of course, I was extremely worried about the money being spent and I was even more worried about how to get it back without bloodshed. That's all changed now."

"You're going to have to explain this to me," Evan rolled his eyes.

"Oh, yes, two of the fillets. Make both medium rare, potatoes with the works, salad with house dressing," Dennis ordered as the waitress arrived, interrupting the conversation. "Anything else?" Dennis asked Evan.

"No. Thank you."

The waitress moved away leaving Evan feeling like an idiot. He could have ordered his own damn food!

"You were saying…" Evan encouraged Dennis.

"You see, our dumb assed friends from Charleston have opened a door for us. Knowing that they are dumb and knowing that they are prone to violence, we can do, quite literally, anything we want, any time we want and get away with it," Dennis exuded confidence.

"By blaming it on them," Evan stated.

"Blaming on and making it look as though," Dennis replied.

"So, it's full speed ahead?" Evan raised an eyebrow. "What does that look like, Dennis?"

Dennis laughed, "We go after them, all of them."

"Define all."

"All, Evan, all of those little Coast Guard pricks, their families, friends, all of them."

Evan's face fell, physically contorting to show his displeasure. This was wrong. Much as Evan really didn't give a shit about anyone, and didn't mind hurting anyone, what Dennis wanted was too big. Families... why?

"I don't think it needs to go that far."

"You don't think," Dennis responded angrily, "I don't pay you to think!"

Evan leaned forward, narrowing his eyes in an intimidating glare. "Tough shit, Dennis. I'm your muscle. I'm the one who does your dirty work. I don't give a shit about killing some ghetto prick on the side of the road but, when it gets this big, I am going to have a say."

Dennis didn't flinch," Are you, Evan?" Dennis leaned back, smiling confidently. "I can pick up this phone..." Dennis waved his cell in Evan's face, "...call my contact at Chatham, and have you jammed into a cell for the rest of your natural life."

Dennis knew everything Evan had ever done, every crime, every person Evan had ever beaten or killed. It was Dennis who had intervened on Evan's behalf, when Evan was implicated in a murder - which he'd committed. Evan didn't know how Dennis found him. He didn't know why Dennis cared about bailing him out of a jam, not until Dennis made Evan understand what his job would be, forever. There had been countless times that Evan wished he'd gone to prison rather than be a slave to someone so unpredictable.

"Shit!" Evan said, lighting a cigarette.

"Time is of the essence, Evan," Dennis continued calmly, as if voices had never been raised. "This Ra person is going to come back for the money and probably to kill you. We need to get the money before he does, and then we need to draw him to us. I'd like you to kill him as well." Dennis grabbed a cigarette from Evan's pack. "And, it appears as though this Ra is convinced that the Coast Guard has his money, firming up what I already knew."

"You don't know shit," Evan thought, dragging on his smoke.

"I want you to pick out a few of our boys to help you, Evan. Pick the ones you trust."

"I don't trust any of them," Evan thought as he grabbed his beer.

"I want you to go after family... up the pressure. Lay out ultimatums that involve pain."

"And the Coasties?"

"Them, too, but I'll be planning that approach. I'd hate to put that much pressure on you."

"They'll all be at their Station this weekend. They have..." Evan thought of the word, "...duty".

"Good," Dennis responded as the waitress arrived with their salads. "We'll have them in one place."

20

3:15PM

"You're bothered?" Hank asked, tossing a box of woodscrews into the shopping cart.

"Yes," Rachel responded.

The drive to Home Depot had been relatively silent. Hank waited for Rachel to initiate the conversation while Rachel sat in the passenger seat wondering what she should say. It wasn't every day that Rachel dealt with a subject as sensitive as accusing shipmates of gross wrongdoing. As a matter of fact, Rachel had never dealt with this subject. Rachel supposed that if it were someone else, not Mike, she could have spilled her guts without a second thought. But, Mike had always been a friend, a real good Coastie and a mentor. The fact that Mike and Hank were so close didn't make things any easier.

"It's Mike," Rachel said as Hank turned down the exterior lighting aisle.

Hank sighed. Hank guessed that Rachel was suspicious of Mike from her uneasy silence during their drive. Hank was suspicious too, though he wasn't going to be the first to initiate the conversation. "What about Mike?"

Rachel pushed her hair behind her ears. "Do you think, maybe, Mike would have taken the money?"

Hank stopped the cart, thought about looking surprised, but decided against it. Hank had to admit that, though Mike and Debbie flung money around recklessly, the timing of the Jet Ski purchase was far too coincidental. Hank didn't like to think of Mike as anything but an honest, squared away shipmate. But, given current circumstances, even if buying several thousand dollars worth of toys was an innocent act, Mike's timing was A-grade boneheaded.

"Maybe," Hank replied, looking Rachel in the eye.

"That's it? Just, maybe?"

Hank pushed the cart onward. "Maybe you took the money? Maybe I took the money? Maybe Ryan...."

"Do I look like I have a quarter million in my pocket?" Rachel responded, exasperated.

"Maybe you put it in a bank account in Switzerland?" Hank smiled the reply. He was by no means implicating Rachel.

"You know, Hank, I thought I could talk to you," Rachel folded her arms across her chest. "Just forget I said anything.

Rachel sped up her pace, trying to pass Hank. Hank turned the cart into her path, cutting her off.

"Rachel, wait, you can talk to me," Hank searched for the right words. "I just, really don't want to think any one of us could do it."

"You think I do?"

"No. No I don't," Hank responded softly.

"I sit for Mike and Debbie a lot, Hank. I know what kind of financial mess they live in. They're maxing out credit cards left and right."

"That's their decision. It may not be smart but lots of people do it."

Rachel rolled her eyes, "But, Hank, It's a crazy amount of money they pay every month. Debbie complains about it."

"I complain about my bills...every month," Hank responded. "It doesn't mean I can't pay them."

"Yeah, same here, but you don't see me running off spending *more*."

Hank swung the cart around and walked slowly ahead. "Maybe that's just their style. It's their life."

Rachel shook her head in disagreement. "Debbie isn't that way, Hank. She's smarter than that. So is Mike."

Hank thought about that point. He knew that Mike and Debbie were both very savvy when it came to juggling money. "Rachel, I admit it looks suspicious but, it's probably nothing."

"What if it's something, Hank? Those agents told us that people could come after us if they thought we stole. I'm not in the mood to be hunted. If Mike took it he needs to come clean."

"What, exactly, makes you so convinced that he did?"

Rachel stopped. "I didn't say anything before now. But, on the boat that day, when we got back into the cabin, the cell phones were all messed up."

"Messed up? How?"

"When I got my phone out, I knew where all the other phones were at in the box. When we got ready to go your phone was okay but, Mike and Ryan's had been moved."

"How?"

"The positions were swapped," Rachel looked into Hanks eyes. "One of them made a call while we weren't around, while we were on that boat."

Hank thought back to that day. He saw everyone's location. He traced every movement. Rachel was crawling around taking photos of dead people. He was standing on the deck of the wreck, looking at Rachel. Mike was standing on the bow of the 942 and Ryan was inside the....

"Ryan, Rachel, it had to be Ryan!" Hank exclaimed the conclusion a bit too loud, gathering looks from nearby customers.

"Why Ryan?"

"He was the only person that was ever alone in the cabin, after we found the money."

"Not Mike?"

"Mike was on the bow of the 942. He didn't go into the cabin until after you finished, after Ryan told us we had to leave."

Rachel studied her memory. She remembered things exactly the way Hank had described them. But, still, she wasn't convinced. "Maybe they did it together."

"Good God, Rachel... a conspiracy?" Hank flung his hands in the air.

"You never know?" Rachel said, and then reconsidered as Hank rolled his eyes in disbelief. "I just don't know, Hank. I just don't want any of us getting hurt anymore."

"You think that what happened to Debbie and Mike was directly related to this?"

Rachel didn't respond. She stopped, grabbing a roll of electrical tape from the shelf and tossing it into the cart.

"Me too," Hank said, squeezing Rachel's hand, reassuring her that she wasn't alone.

"We should say something. We should talk to Master Chief," Rachel responded.

Hank pushed the cart forward, Rachel following, rounding the end of the aisle.

"Look out, folks!" the voice rang out just as Hank's cart slammed into the side of a pallet full of plywood, two by fours, power tools and an assortment of other items.

"Oh shit," Hank said, pulling back on his cart. "I'm sorry, sir."

"No harm." Hank heard the voice, a familiar voice, coming from behind the plywood sheets. Paul Sulsky's round face appeared, smiling, recognizing Hank and Rachel.

"Mr. Sulsky?" Hank extended a hand to Paul. Odd as it was, as much as Sulsky was a nemesis, common courtesy had to prevail.

"Petty Officer..." Sulsky paused, as if thinking "...Morgan. Isn't it?"

"It is sir." Hank shook Sulsky's hand knowing damn well that Sulsky knew his name.

"Post Hurricane fix-up work, Sir?" Hank asked as he examined Sulsky's pending purchase

"This stuff, no," Sulsky smiled. "The fish house has needed some updating for a long time. This here represents part of my brand new lobby."

"Very nice," Rachel said.

"Thank you, young lady," Sulsky eyed Rachel up and down, the same way he did when she boarded his boat.

"DeWalt." Hank said

"Excuse me?" Paul raised an eyebrow.

"The tools you're getting…DeWalt. That's the good stuff… my favorite."

"Oh, yeah, they're good."

"Were you able to get the boats back in operation after Danelle? Any bad damage?" Rachel asked.

"When we saw you the day after the storm it looked like the Gina Marie was a little banged up?" Hank added.

Sulsky reached for the handle of his rolling pallet. "All of the boats are fixed up or getting there. I was catching shrimp on the Gina Marie this very morning."

"That's quick. I want the name of your insurance agency," Rachel commented with a smile.

Sulsky smiled back, a broken smile, a weak smile, "Well, sweetheart, that's privileged information. Kind of a fisherman's secret."

Hank and Rachel looked at each other with quizzical eyes. But, it was like Sulsky to act this way, to be elusive.

"Well, I better get going," Sulsky said as he pushed his cart toward the checkout line.

"Ok then," Hank said, Sulsky's back already turned.

"Nice talking to you," Rachel commented under her breath.

As Hank and Rachel headed for the next Aisle they heard Sulsky clear his throat. They turned.

"Are you guys doing okay?" Sulsky asked. "Is everything alright at the Station?"

Rachel whispered to Hank, "Why would he care?"

"Everything's alright, Mr. Sulsky. Thanks for asking," Hank responded.

Sulsky waived at the pair then turned to the cashier.

"Was that strange?" Rachel asked Hank.

Hank thought a moment, "Not for him. Not for Mr. Sulsky." Hank walked a few steps further, considering things. "Right now though... yeah, kinda."

21

6:30PM

At six thirty in the evening the sun wasn't about to set. But, the colors and feel of nighttime were making their presence known. As dusk fell, everything out here in the middle of nowhere South Carolina started to look forbidding, ugly. Though Mitch had been born and raised in the low country, there were still certain places and certain times that he didn't particularly enjoy. This place was going to go down as a "least favorite" as Mitch watched the wrecker wench lumber to pull the half submerged Mazda from the muck.

Mitch and John had overheard the call on their radio. A local, up near New Riverside, about fifteen miles from the state line, had watched two black guys show up around five thirty and send the Mazda into the drink. Really, it was pretty common for a car to go into the swamp. Drunks and idiots were doing it all the time. But, in this case, the car had been purposely dumped. "The damndest thing about it..." Mitch thought, was that the idiots did it in broad daylight and in a spot where the roof of the car would show at low tide. "Dumb."

Mitch had no idea why this call had caught John's fancy. This was a car... in the swamp... in South Carolina. It wasn't even their jurisdiction. Yet, here they were watching the car slowly rise from the water, standing next to one of the most god-awful, B.O. wreaking wrecker drivers in the world and two very suspicious South Carolina State Policemen.

"You're going to have to explain your interest in this case again, Deputy Martin," One of the officers asked.

"We're in the middle of an investigation into some drug related activity in Chatham County, Officer. This vehicle may have a connection," Martin responded.

"What the hell kind?" Mitch thought.

"Care to share some information, Deputy?" the officer asked, notebook poised.

"Well, I'm not sure if there is yet. But, if there is, I'll let you know," Martin smiled.

"We look like a couple of damn lookie-loo's John," Mitch whispered. "What the hell are we doing here?"

The officer turned away from John and Mitch as the car cleared the edge of the swamp and was dragged onto dry, flat, ground.

"I'm just curious, Mitch. There has been a ton of shit going on around here in the past forty eight hours and I'm not going to write off anything as irrelevant."

"So…" Mitch snickered, "… if some old woman gets a traffic ticket in Atlanta this afternoon we're gonna have a look?"

"Don't be an ass hole, Mitch," John scolded Mitch with his eyes. "Just have a little faith in my instincts."

The wrecker driver walked to the bumper of the Mazda and removed the wire tow cable.

"She's all yours, Officers," the near toothless man said.

"Body!" One of the officers said as he peered into the front seat of the car.

"I'll be damned," Mitch mumbled as John stepped forward.

"Gunshot wound to the head," the officer said as he leaned in the passenger side window, examining the body. "And to the neck."

A second officer moved around the Mazda in an efficient manner.

"Plates are removed," the officer remarked. "VIN removed as well. We need to get forensics out here."

John and Mitch walked up to the driver's side of the car and peered in at Morris's body.

"There's a bullet hole in the back window," Mitch said. "That's the neck shot, judging from the fact that the side of his head is blown off, left to right."

"He was double tapped," John said, looking around the interior of the vehicle. "Look here, Mitch." John pointed to the floorboard on the driver's side.

Mitch leaned into the window, cautious not to touch anything. The floorboard was wet from the brackish water of the swamp. But, even so, the dark stains in the carpet indicated blood. "Someone else got shot in here," Mitch said as he stood.

The officer standing by John and Mitch leaned in the window, examining the stains.

"Good eyes, Deputy." The officer stood and turned to John. "Are you ready to share that information now?"

"Nope," John said, stuffing his hands into his pockets. "This isn't the car we thought it was."

"You've got to be kidding me."

"No kidding, Officer," John shrugged his shoulders. "We were hoping this would be a pickup."

The officer's shoulders slumped as John pulled a business card from his pocket.

"Just in case your supervisor wonders who we were," John handed the card to the officer. "You can reach me at any time."

"We may," The officer responded, stuffing the card into the folds of his tablet.

"Okay then…" John turned and, along with Mitch, headed for their parked SUV.

"Why the hell did we drive up here?" Mitch asked as they climbed into the vehicle.

"Because…" John fastened his seatbelt. "It took two to tango when that drug deal was made after Danelle. That means two different people or two different groups of people may be after the same money."

"You know, John, other crimes do happen. Bad shit is terminal, everyday. I think you're out on a limb here," Mitch said as he stuffed chew into his bottom lip.

"You're right, Mitch. Bad shit does happen, everyday." John started the SUV and headed away from the scene. "Remember when Jeff called earlier...told us those boys got beat?"

"Yep," Mitch responded.

"Maybe this had something to do with it. Maybe it didn't."

Mitch rolled his eyes and sighed. "This is one of the most specific hunches you've ever had."

"I've got my reasons," John said as he sped off toward Savannah.

22

7:00PM

Jeff walked from the waning light of day into the dimly lit entry of the Shangri-La. He closed his eyes, hoping they would adjust to the cave-like lighting sooner rather than later. The smell of cigarette smoke was overwhelming, even though the club had opened scant few hours earlier. Mixed with the pungent smoke, the odor of generously applied perfume wafted through the air. All but the most "hell-bent on boobies" would have turned and exited the establishment at a run. Jeff wished he could. He hated strip clubs, period, even more when they possessed a "dive" quality.

"You got some I.D., mister?" the fat, non-muscular, bouncer at the door asked as Jeff blinked his vision into focus.

Jeff reached into his jacket pocket, pulling out his badge, "This good?"

The bouncer took the leather wallet holding the badge and Jeff's credentials, looked them over, then handed them back, "That's good for me. Can I help you?"

"Sure," Jeff responded as a half naked, portly woman walked past carrying a tray of drinks. "I need to talk to someone who was here last night, presumably late last night."

"That's not me," the bouncer responded. "I'm day shift."

"Day shift?" Jeff asked.

"We open at lunch. We get lots of business for lunch."

"You don't serve food," Jeff laughed.

"Man can't live by bread alone," the bouncer smiled the reply.

"Oh great. How utterly out of place," Jeff thought. "A Bible scholar in the midst of a flesh factory... perfect."

"One of the girls was probably here. Let me check the schedule." The bouncer left his stool, eased behind the bar and flipped through a clipboard of papers.

Jeff walked further into the club, noticing the collection of old letches gathered around the main stage, three young soldiers being ground upon by a busty blonde and a table full of businessmen being pawed by a collection of topless women. This was exactly what he remembered from his younger days. He was glad to be past it all… glad to be rooted and in a stable relationship.

"Amber was here. She worked late last night," the bouncer tapped Jeff on the shoulder as he delivered the news.

"Can I speak to her?"

"Sure, she's in back. I'll get her."

Jeff scouted around the club, finding a table under a vent that was a little less engulfed in smoke as a blonde appeared from the back room, escorted by the bouncer. They walked to the table as Jeff sat.

"This is Amber," the bouncer said, pulling out a chair, allowing Amber to sit.

"Good to meet you, Amber," Jeff said, half rising from his seat in a display of gentlemanly courtesy.

"You a cop?" Amber asked in a snarky tone, lighting a cigarette.

"No. I'm not a cop." Jeff replied as the bouncer moved away.

Amber leaned forward pushing her breasts into a voluminous crevice of cleavage, "You want a dance then?"

Jeff waved off Amber's advances with an open palm. "No, ma'am. I don't want a dance. I'm Special Agent Nguyen from Coast Guard Investigative Services. I'd like to ask you a couple of questions."

Amber fidgeted in her chair, nervous. Jeff struck a chord somewhere.

"You know some Coast Guard people, don't you?"

"We get all kinds of military in here," Amber replied.

"I'm sure you do. The guys I'm talking about were here last night, one white, one Hispanic, and pretty young." Jeff wished he had pictures of Gabe and Ryan. "You'd remember them. They were involved in a fight...bad one."

Amber became defensive and concerned. Her boyfriend had followed her after work on many occasions. When she and the other girls left the club with Ryan and Gabe last night she scanned the parking lot over and over again. Amber didn't think her boyfriend was around but she couldn't say for sure. In the past, when she'd decided to turn a trick for extra cash, her boyfriend had occasionally shown up. The results were usually bad and the Johns always got the worst of it. She hoped he hadn't put the guys from last night in the hospital, or worse.

"I remember two guys like that. I think they said they were Coast Guard. They were in pretty good shape the last time I saw them."

"That confirms that Beck and Ortiz were covering something up," Jeff thought as he waved away the portly waitress.

"They aren't in very good shape now," Jeff said.

Amber sank in her chair, worried that she was about to be implicated in something serious. "Crazy son of a bitch." she whispered under her breath.

"Excuse me?" Jeff asked, leaning forward.

Amber hesitated, puffing on her smoke. "My damn boyfriend…maybe he did it. Are they dead or something?"

This was more than Jeff expected. "Not yet. Tell me more."

"I didn't have anything to do with it, understand. Me and a couple of the girls went home with those guys last night. The white kid paid us each five hundred to come dance and suck him and his friend off. They passed out and we left."

"What time?"

"We left at around four in the morning. They were both asleep."

"Dumb shit kids!" Jeff thought. "They hired hookers."

"I just can't believe Matt would have been around then." Amber rubbed out her smoke.

"Matt, oh...the boyfriend. Why wouldn't he be around?" Jeff asked.

"He works midnights at the hospital. He's security."

"Last name?"

"Matt Baker. Tall, really built," Amber responded.

Jeff added Baker to his notepad. He'd check him out. "If it wasn't your boyfriend, Matt, can you think of anyone else?"

"A couple of big black guys came in here last night after closing." The waitress was back. She'd been eaves dropping from the table behind Jeff. "They were talking to Jesse, our owner, about those two kids," the waitress smiled. "I served the black guys drinks."

Jeff smiled back. "Did you hear their names? Is your owner here?"

"Jesse isn't here and I'd appreciate it if you didn't talk to him anyway. He'd fire me." The waitress nodded at Amber. "He'd fire us both for talking to a cop."

"I understand," Jeff replied. "Names for the black guys…did you hear any?"

The waitress pressed a finger to her temple, and then her eyes perked up, "One was named Morris. His friend kept saying, *'Damn Morris'*, every time Morris pinched my ass."

"And the other guy?"

"It was an alphabet name, you know, just a letter… "P" or "G" or something like that."

"What time did they leave here?" Jeff's notepad was out again. He wrote frantically.

"They left here at about four-thirty, maybe five."

Amber chimed in, "They've been in here a few times before. I think they deal."

Jeff's eyes went wide in a split second of realization, "That's a connection," he thought as he saw the bouncer approach the table.

The waitress scurried away as the bouncer arrived. "You got the stage next, Amber."

"Deal what?" Jeff asked Amber as she stood.

"Anything, everything…." Amber responded. "If you're not paying me then I need to go. I need money." Amber slid her hand over the top of her pants suggestively.

"I'm not paying, Amber, not for that." Jeff reached into his pocket, produced a twenty and handed it to Amber. "I might be in touch later," Jeff said as he stuffed the notepad in his pocket and headed for the door.

23

7:15PM

"And they are doing well, Master Chief?" Captain Lewis asked from the other end of the line at his Charleston home.

"They seem to be fine," Braden replied, accepting a glass of tea from Claire. "With all that's going on... I think the break-in had an exacerbated emotional impact. We're keeping tabs on them." Braden sipped the tea then placed it on the end table next to his chair. It had been a long day.

The call from the captain didn't surprise Braden. He'd expected it. It wasn't often that any Coast Guard unit got this deep into the muck all at once, and Braden didn't like it one bit. It was a hallmark of a "Braden Command" that the unit remained solid, steady and silent. All Braden wanted his unit known for was success and prosperity. In his career he'd had the normal bumps in the road. Personnel *would* get arrested for drinking and driving, they *would* wreck their motorcycles, and they *would* bounce checks. All this was just part of being in command and managing so many young, flawed, learning people.

Here and now, there was the possibility that a member of his crew was guilty of a serious theft; one of *Braden's* families had been beaten by thugs and two of his guys were reporting a bloody-knuckle brawl at a local bar. "Damnit...what next?" Braden thought, wishing Claire had added something stronger to his tea than ice.

"I don't have to tell you, Marc, we're all pretty concerned about things down there," the captain commented.

"Hell, Skipper, so am I," Braden replied as Claire reached over and squeezed his hand. Was the captain questioning his ability to command?

"Would you like me to send the Deputy Commander down... to help with things?" the captain voiced the comment as a request but, it smacked of impending action.

"I appreciate the offer, captain, but right now the deputy's presence would be counterproductive. The crew is going to be on edge as it is. Having the deputy around would just ratchet up the tension."

"I see," the captain responded.

"I've got Special Agent Nguyen in town still. He's doing a fine job and I plan on getting the most out of him while he's here." Braden squeezed back. Claire smiled and withdrew her hand. "I would like to have the Chaplain come down for a visit. I think the Harwood's could use it."

"He'll be there in the morning," the captain paused. "Anything else you need?"

"Sir, if I need anything you'll be the first to know," Braden replied as respectfully as his exhaustion would allow.

The doorbell rang sending Claire flying off the couch in response. She didn't want the kids screaming "Got it!" while Marc was on the phone.

"Ok then, Master Chief. Have a good night."

"You too, sir," Braden responded, then hung up the phone.

Braden looked to the front door where a completely drenched Jennifer Brooks stood dripping on the welcome mat. In the past thirty minutes the sky had clouded over and opened up in a serious downpour. During the summer months, late afternoon and early evening were prime time for rain and thunder. Any other time, Jennifer would have simply blown off the soaking. But, Braden could hear the muted curses coming from the foyer. His XPO was not in a cheery mood.

"And damnit, Claire, I just bought these flats Monday," Jennifer complained as she shook water from her shoes.

"I know, honey, I know. I had an outfit ruined running to the grocery to get ice during that hurricane stupidity." Claire patted Jennifer on the shoulder. "Come on in."

Jennifer walked through the foyer and into the living room where she stood still, sharing volumes of unspoken opinion with Braden. Braden reached over, grabbed his tea, then motioned for Jennifer to come have a seat on the couch.

"Would you like something to drink?" Claire asked Jennifer.

"Or a towel?" Braden added with a wry smile.

"Cute," Jennifer responded to Braden. "I'd love a drink-drink, Claire… if you have one?"

"How about a…"

"How about a nice, tall, Seagram's and Seven for all three of us?" Braden interrupted.

Claire paused, usually she and Marc didn't like drinking in front of the children but this time it could slide. "I'll be right back," Claire said, shuffling off to the kitchen.

Jennifer and Braden sat staring at each other for a moment. Both knew that the current situation was going to amount to one of the greatest tests of their careers. Commands came and went without coming near the level of drama and intrigue the two of them were enveloped in at this moment. Somewhere in the back of their minds they realized that things were far more serious than was presently apparent.

"What happened to them?" Braden asked.

"They got the shit beat out of them. That's for sure," Jennifer said as she pulled her pony tail over the front of her blouse, allowing it to drip on her lap instead of the sofa.

"At a bar?"

"At a bar called the Princess Club, but that's a bunch of horse shit. It happened in Beck's apartment. There's a blood stain the size of a bowling ball on his carpet."

"Do they need to go to the E.R.?" Braden asked. The mechanism of injury, for Braden, was subordinate to the immediate health needs of the crew.

"They might have wanted to. We may have wanted to send them a few hours ago. But, when I saw them they just looked like a couple of idiots who'd had their asses handed to them."

"Any chance they got drunk and fought each other?" Braden asked as Claire entered the room with the drinks.

"No way," Jennifer said as she took a glass from Claire and downed half the contents in a long swallow. "Both of the dorks have baby-smooth knuckles. The fight they were in was pretty one-sided." Jennifer finished as an audible belch escaped her throat.

Braden took a sip of his drink, taking the time to taste its contents, giving himself time to think. "Where are they now?"

"I ordered them both to report to the station."

Braden raised his eyebrows.

"Not for duty, for observation...in case their condition deteriorated." Jennifer winked at Braden. Neither Jennifer nor Braden had the legal authority to order Ryan and Gabe to duty based on what had transpired. Savvy as she was, Jennifer had tied the recall to a medical concern. It was a stretch but Braden agreed with the move.

"Have you been able to get hold of Nguyen?" Braden asked.

"I left a voicemail about half an hour ago. When I talked to him earlier, it seemed like he was more interested in what happened to the boys than he let on."

"How about Mike and his family?"

Jennifer downed another goodly portion of her drink, "I didn't talk to Mike but, I did talk to Hank. He, Lori and Rachel were just leaving Mike's house. Hank said he thought everything would be ok... tonight."

"I'm going to give Nguyen a call in a few minutes. I'd like to know what his concerns are."

"Don't make too much of it, Marc. Don't read into things," Claire reminded Braden.

Braden smiled and nodded at Claire. Somehow, she always kept him on an even keel, even in the most difficult situations. "I won't, Honey, and neither will Jennifer." Braden looked at Jennifer who rolled her eyes. It wasn't ever healthy to read into any situation. But when you didn't know much about what was happening, reading in helped fill in the blanks where your questions existed. Braden stared at his drink.

24

10:30PM

"Do you think they'll be ok, honey?" Lori asked as she finished brushing her teeth.

"Honestly…" Hank peeked over the top of his novel, "… I wouldn't be, so I don't expect they'll be any different." Hank went back to the novel.

Lori turned off the bathroom light then slipped under the covers. "I couldn't be. I don't think I could sleep in that house again."

Hank thought about what Lori said as Lori snuggled up beside him, placing her head in the crook of his arm, "Yeah, babe…" Hank kissed Lori's forehead. "It would be tough."

It was all Hank could do to convince Lori to let Allison sleep in her own room. The assault on the Harwood's eroded a person's securities. Lori spent the entire drive home talking about another deadbolt for the door, about paying the additional cost to have a dog in their apartment and even brought up the purchase of a handgun. In time, Hank knew Lori would regain her composure, but when he left tomorrow morning and was gone for seventy-two hours, Lori would be a mess. His cell phone would ring continuously, and he'd spend the weekend worried for her safety.

"Did you lock all the doors?" Lori asked.

"You watched me lock them, babe."

"How about the car?"

"And the car too, and I left a light on in the kitchen, and propped a chair against the doorknob." Hank kissed Lori's head again.

Lori stared at the ceiling as Hank went back to his novel. He'd read the same sentence four times already. The novel was a ruse. Hank couldn't concentrate on anything but his wife and daughter. But, he didn't want Lori to know that.

"I don't want you to go to work tomorrow," Lori said, brushing Hanks arm. "I don't want to be alone right now."

"Sweetheart…" Hank ran his fingers through Lori's hair, "… you are going to be fine. I've been standing duty for a long time now, and I've been gone for longer than three days before."

"I know but... this is different." Lori's voice cracked as her apprehension turned to tears.

Hank tossed his novel aside as he embraced Lori. "It only seems different sweetheart. You and Ally are safe. No one is going to come after you." Hank pulled Lori closer as a sob escaped her throat. "What happened to Debbie and Mike could have happened to anyone. It's horrible that things like that can happen to people, but they do."

"But they didn't take anything, Hank," Lori's responded, questioningly.

"What do you mean honey?"

"Debbie and I went through the house while you were at the store. Nothing was gone, not even her jewelry."

"Maybe they didn't have time. Maybe Mike and Debbie got home before they could."

"Hank, the whole house was trashed. That took time." Lori wiped her eyes. "It was like those men meant to hurt them. It was like they weren't there to rob anyone...like it wasn't random."

Hank had nothing to say. He'd been there when Mitch had expressed the same opinion of the scene. He didn't want to give into that line of thinking, if he did, if he accepted that Mike and Debbie were targeted then he had to accept that Lori and Ally could be in danger.

"There isn't anyone that you guys deal with that would want to hurt us, is there? There isn't some crazy drunk fisherman or drug runner that you've pissed off..."

Hank swallowed hard. The real answer was *yes* but he could never tell Lori the truth, not and expect her to keep calm. If Lori knew about the money and the bodies and what Jeff Nguyen had told him, she would never allow him to leave the house again. Maybe... maybe he should call Lori's father and ask him to buy tickets for Lori and Ally to come to Muncie for a few days. He'd call tomorrow, try to explain and then he'd talk to Lori. With any luck, she and Ally could be on a flight by Sunday morning.

"I can't think of anyone I've dealt with that would hate me that much," Hank said as he squeezed Lori tighter. "Maybe your Dad..." Hank smiled and laughed to lighten the mood.

"Maybe," Lori shared the laugh.

Hank leaned away from Lori, turning off his reading lamp. Light from a streetlamp streaked into the room as

Lori quieted and yawned, finding the strength to close her eyes.

"I love you, sweetheart... sleep well," Hank whispered.

"I love you," Lori whispered back as she tucked the blankets around her chin.

Hank smelled Lori's hair...touched her face. His ears reached out through the house, picking up the soft tones of Ally's mobile as it slowly wound down a lullaby. All became quiet, peaceful...still.

"Please keep them safe while I'm gone this weekend," Hank thought the prayer then reached under his pillow, feeling the foam handle of his expandable baton. It would be some time before Hank found sleep.

25

11:10PM

Paul Sulsky stood slowly. His knees were old and blaming their stiffness on high school football had long since ceased to be a good excuse. He'd been bending and crawling and hammering and mudding for most of the day. It took its toll on an aging body but the beer in the cooler was cold, the wife didn't give a shit when he got home and he wanted to get his new lobby built. It was going to be grand. There would be stainless steel counter tops, a tiled floor, tongue and groove paneling, a crab and lobster tank and a special-order neon sign in the window. For the first time in his life, Paul felt like a success.

"To my health!" Paul shouted as he tilted back on a beer.

"Burning the midnight oil, Paul?"

The voice came from the front door that Paul hadn't bothered to lock. Paul, startled, spilled beer down the front of his shirt and whirled around to meet Dennis's eyes.

"I'm sorry, Paul. I didn't mean to startle you like that." Dennis said.

Paul wiped at the front of his beer-soaked shirt. "Hell, Dennis, it's alright. This has gotta be washed anyway."

Dennis stepped forward, offering Paul a hand, "Making some changes?" Dennis said, looking around the room.

"A few," Paul replied, shaking Dennis's hand. "The old girl has needed a face lift for a long time now. I figured now was as good a time as any."

"A lobster tank?" Dennis released Paul's hand as he pointed.

"Yep, I think that'll make people believe the store is a little more… uppity," Paul said, digging into his cooler for a fresh drink. "Beer?"

"Oh…" Dennis waved a hand, "no thank you, Paul."

Paul withdrew a beer and popped the top as Dennis walked around and through the construction. The silence was awkward and nerve wracking. Most of the time, Evan was the only person Paul ever saw. Paul couldn't imagine what would bring Dennis here, personally, at this time of night.

"You're burning a little of that late-night oil yourself, Dennis."

Dennis laughed, "I am. I am indeed, aren't I?"

"I don't expect you came by just to have a visit, or to swing a hammer?" Paul's anxiety confounded his attempt at cordial humor.

"Visit, yes. Hammer, no," Dennis replied, brushing dust from his hands.

"Well, you know I always have time for you. How can I be of service?"

Dennis continued to examine the construction as he spoke. "I'm going to need a favor from you, Paul. I need to tap into your nautical knowledge."

"Sure thing," Paul replied.

"And, I'll need your boat," Dennis turned, staring at Paul.

Paul's Adam's apple swelled in his throat and he swallowed hard. Dennis's eyes were like lasers, burning into Paul's mind, reading every thought, every crease of his face or twitch of a muscle. Hiring- on convicts or hiding scoff-laws was one thing. Those things were normal. When the Coast Guard or the DNR found near-do-wells on your boat you could always play dumb. But, now, to have Dennis asking for the whole boat and for God knew what....

"I hope that isn't going to be an issue, Paul," Dennis smiled, "I could really use a hand with something."

This wasn't a request, Paul knew that much. He could tell Dennis "no," but the next morning some unfortunate accident would happen. Maybe the store would burn to the ground. Maybe one of his boats would sink. Maybe Paul, or his wife, would get in a real bad car accident. Paul didn't want to say yes, but he didn't have much choice.

"Well, I don't see much of a problem. You want to do some fishing?" Paul asked.

"Not exactly...." Dennis smirked. "I'm going to keep this very simple for you, because I know you are a simple man." Dennis grabbed Paul's shoulder. "Tomorrow, Friday evening, I need you to take some folks to Cockspur Island."

"Well, there's a bridge onto the island already. They can just take a car if that's what..."

"The bridge..." Dennis squeezed harder, "...isn't really an option, Paul. I need you to drop them off on the island...somewhere out of the way."

Paul fidgeted, taking a drink and wiping his mouth with his forearm. "It's awful shallow around Cockspur. There aint many places you could get a boat close."

"That, Paul, is why I'm coming to you," Dennis patted Paul's back. "You're smart about that area. You'll find a way to get a few men in."

"The best spot is near the Coast Guard Station," Paul said.

"Near there would be fine, Paul. Actually, that would be better than fine."

Paul's heart sank. "What do you want with those kids?" he thought as he considered Dennis' statement. Paul knew when he'd gone to the station with Evan that trouble was brewing. Paul couldn't imagine what any of the Coasties could have done to earn Dennis ire. Now, the extent of that ire was becoming clear. He wasn't being asked to put men on the Island for any reason other than bad. Paul didn't want to be a part of anyone getting hurt or killed.

"I sense a little apprehension on your part, Paul."

Paul decided to be bold. "Well, hell yes I'm apprehensive, Dennis. Evan came in here yesterday, drug me out to the Island, had me pointing kids out. And now you want me to drop your thugs off by boat. What the hell is going on?"

Dennis's eyes narrowed, menacingly. "I don't like being crossed, Paul, not by anyone." Dennis came up close, challenging Paul. "Being an acquaintance of mine, Paul, can be an extremely positive or extremely negative experience. I usually leave it up to the individual to decide which direction that goes in. Most of the time, I don't care either way. But, they should."

The threat rang clear. Paul could feel Dennis' anger seeping through his skin, causing his knees to shake.

"I wished I'd never met this bastard," Paul thought. But it was too late for that. Paul had no choice.

"What time tomorrow?" Paul asked, backing away from Dennis.

Dennis smiled, "They'll be here, at your dock, at dusk. Please, have the boat ready to go." Dennis turned and walked toward the front door as Paul gripped his beer with a quaking hand.

Dennis stopped. "It's going to look real nice in here, Paul."

The door swung shut behind Dennis as Paul placed his head in his hands.

Friday

26

12:08AM

The rain poured down in buckets and sheets. Jeff reached into the back seat of his sedan and pulled out his Seattle Mariners ball cap, always on hand when he traveled, as he contemplated the dash from the car to the interior of the Waffle House restaurant. He could see Mitch and John sitting in a corner booth, sipping coffee. Next to him, Marc Braden, obviously tired, tossed open the passenger side door then headed inside. Jeff followed suit, but at a gallop. When he was a member of the regular Coast Guard he rarely saw the exterior of a ship. He was a cook, the scullery was as wet as he ever got.

"Nasty night ya'll," a skin-on-bones waitress exclaimed as Jeff and Braden entered. "I'll get ya'll some hot coffee." She finished with a smile.

It was a nasty night. The weather was nasty. The circumstances were nasty and the smell of old grease, smoke and stale coffee was nasty. Why John insisted on this ramshackle diner was beyond Jeff's comprehension.

It was only midnight. There were, Jeff supposed, dozens of other places still open. Places that didn't reek. Places where you didn't have to worry about botulism or hepatitis when you picked up your fork.

"Ya'll want menus?" the waitress asked as she poured.

"Just the coffee is fine, ma'am," Braden responded.

From the corner booth, John waved, beckoning Jeff and Braden to come over.

"That coffee smells horrible," Braden whispered to Jeff. "But, I need the caffeine."

Braden looked like he needed the caffeine. When Jeff picked Braden up he could see the dark circles under Braden's eyes. Every move Braden made seemed an effort. Jeff knew that Braden had spent the majority of the day working at the Harwood's home, piecing together something like normal for that family. He knew that Braden had been on the phone with several members of the Sector Charleston Command, including the captain and he knew that Ryan and Gabe had come clean about their supposed fight. Still, despite any fatigue, Braden was here and insisting on involvement as things became more interesting.

"Master Chief, you look like hell," Mitch said as Braden approached.

"I'm at a greasy spoon at midnight. That's enough to make anyone look deathly," Braden responded as he sat.

The waitress cleared her throat over Braden's shoulder. It was obvious that she'd caught his comment but, as she handed over the coffee, her face wore a smile. Odds were that she felt the same way.

"This is gonna help," Braden said, smiling at the waitress.

"Honey, I'm just happy ya'll are here. This place can be a little spooky when it gets late." The waitress patted Braden's back then slipped off behind the counter.

"I can imagine," Jeff added as he sipped the scalding hot, highly potent, coffee.

"It's pretty late fella's. What's so urgent?"

Jeff looked at John, surprised at the directness of the question. So far, John Martin had been the sole of southern hospitality. Perhaps, the hour was getting to John as well.

"I needed to share some information with you, both." Jeff sipped his coffee again. "It's been an interesting day."

"Sounds about right..." Mitch replied. "That makes four of us."

"What did you two find out?" Jeff asked.

"You first," John insisted.

"Okay..." Jeff began. "I found two of our Coast Guard personnel beat to shit today. They claimed they were in a fight, but they lied."

"What happened to them?" Mitch asked.

"I made some contacts at a strip club. Come to find out, a couple of African-American drug dealers came into the place looking for our guys."

Mitch's eyebrows shot up immediately. "Hell, we were at the scene of a..."

John interrupted. "Go on Jeff."

"I've got a strong feeling that these two dealers represent the threat to our people that we thought may exist." Jeff responded confidently.

"And, the Harwood's were attacked by two African-Americans," Braden added. "Maybe the same two."

"So, what do you two know?" Braden stared at John and Mitch in turn.

"I think you're onto something, Jeff." John's face wore a satisfied grin, a relieved grin. "We have several

African-American gangs pushing drugs in this area. But, only a couple of them are capable of handling the kind of cash your people found."

"You've got names?" Braden asked.

"We'll have to take a look at our files to firm up a list of possibilities," John responded.

"What about the car today?" Mitch questioned John.

"Car?" Braden asked.

John gave Mitch a livid look that was obvious to Jeff and Braden. It was apparent that the two deputies from Chatham County were eager to get information from Jeff, but reciprocity wasn't their intention...at least not John's.

"We checked out a car in the swamp today," John began. "There was a dead black guy inside."

"Shot dead," Mitch added.

"Any I.D.?" Jeff asked

"We don't know, yet. We can get a copy of the report from the State Police tomorrow morning," John replied coolly.

"Do you think there's a connection?" Braden asked.

"I don't know. It's hard to say. We have a lot of crime around these parts. Chances are it's not related."

Mitch said nothing. Something was wrong with his partner, something significant. Earlier, when they'd crossed the state line to investigate the car, John insisted that "anything" could be related to their investigation. Now that there was a correlation, John was ready to dismiss the whole affair. Mitch knew better than to question his partner's integrity in public. But, once they got into the SUV, John would have some answering to do.

"I don't buy it," Braden said.

"Agreed," Jeff added.

"But it's not certain, fellas. You have got to remember that. What do you know for certain?" John questioned Jeff and Braden.

Braden's impatience rose to the surface. "Certain? I can tell you what's certain! I've got members of my crew who've been attacked. That's certain! Whether or not it's truly related to the drug money is completely irrelevant to me. I want to keep my people safe and all this guess work isn't doing that."

"Master Chief, I understand your frustration and I understand your duty," John offered.

"I don't think you do, Deputy. And, I don't understand your attitude change."

John's face hardened as Braden prepared to light into him. Mitch sat back, watching. He wouldn't go after his partner in public but that didn't mean someone else couldn't.

"My attitude?" John said, angered.

"Monday morning at the station you were sounding the alarm to my people. Last night at the Harwood's you were laying things out like Scarface was coming after us all. Tonight, all you want to do is down play. That's not very consistent." Braden's eyes locked with John's. "If you can't be consistent then I have to take matters in hand."

"What matters would you take *'in hand'*, Master Chief? You're no cop. You drive boats and drink coffee for a living. You don't have a clue about what's going on," John challenged Braden.

"Take it easy folks," Jeff said, purposely leaning as far over the table as he could, creating a barrier between John and Braden. "It's late and we're all tired."

The fire in John and Braden's eyes dimmed slightly as Jeff and Mitch shared a look of relief. Jeff knew Braden was hitting a soft spot in John's armor, so did Mitch. The fact that a soft spot existed concerned Jeff greatly. Moreover, the fact that John's response was a personal attack on Braden, resounded like an air-raid siren. Professional cops were trained to handle themselves under confrontational pressure. John was failing. The hour of the day was not a viable excuse. Something wasn't right.

"Let me put this a different way," Braden began. "The crewmembers involved in this mess are on duty this weekend. While they're at the unit I feel pretty good about their safety. But, if Monday comes and we don't have any clarity on the level of threat, I will have to move them out of harm's way."

"By Monday?" Mitch sighed. "Guess I better put my Braves tickets up on Ebay."

"I think we can have some resolution for you by then, Master Chief," John added.

"I hope so."

The bell on the door of the diner House rang as four young African-American men, dressed in gangsta attire stepped inside. The four attracted Mitch and Jeff's attention as they headed to a far corner table. There wasn't anything particularly uncommon about their entrance or their looks but the bling worn by one young man was eye catching. The brilliant gold and diamond "RA" hanging from his neck cast mirror ball reflections on the diner walls. The waitress looked at Braden with eyes that said "See what I mean," as she grabbed her order pad.

"That's serious jewelry," Mitch said, eyeing Ra.

"Very serious, if it's not fake," Braden responded.

"Ra, like the Egyptian god I suppose," Jeff noted as he finished the last sips of his coffee.

John dug into his jeans pocket, producing his cell phone. With a few touches of the screen he was ready. He held the phone up, aiming the camera at Ra.

"Why are you taking that clown's picture John?" Mitch asked as John pressed a button, the digital recording of a snapping camera filling the air.

Across the restaurant, Ra and his men heard the sound. Turning their heads toward the noise, one of the biggest of the men spoke.

"What the hell you snapping photos of cracker?" William bowed up as he started to walk toward John.

Jeff looked at William, then back to John. John wasn't nervous, neither was Mitch or Braden for that matter. But, Jeff had no desire to get into a fist fight.

"He's taking pictures of me," Jeff answered William.

"Is that right?" William stopped, not acknowledging Jeff, still staring at John.

Silence enveloped the room as the waitress quickly retreated behind the counter. It was a Mexican standoff of sorts, Jeff could feel it in the air. Across the table, Jeff could see Mitch tensing up. John calmly stuffed the cell back into his pocket, ignoring William then picked up his drink. Braden sat still, head down. Jeff tried to read Braden's thoughts. The Master Chief seemed to be focusing, working something over in his head.

"What's it to you?" Braden spoke clearly, authoritatively, but not to William. The question was directed at John.

"What the fuck'd you say nigger?" William took another step toward the table.

In one motion Braden rose, grabbed his chair, flinging it across the room and into Williams face.

William grabbed a bloody and broken nose as he stumbled backwards into a table. Braden sprang across the restaurant as Ra's men stood from their seats. Ra grabbed each man by their arms, restraining them.

"Call me nigger again!" Braden shouted as he landed a fist into William's mouth.

William fell across the table and onto the ground. Braden placed a knee on William's shoulder then wrestled his arm into a wrist lock. Braden manipulated William's wrist causing him to yell in pain. Jeff, Mitch and John stood, staring in awe and surprise as Braden humbled his much larger adversary. Ra didn't move.

"My friend told you whose picture was taken," Braden tweaked William's wrist again sending another spike of pain through William's arm. "That should have been good enough for you. Now you're on the ground, bleeding and embarrassed."

"Fuck you!" William yelled.

Braden applied pressure to William's shoulder, straining the rotator cuff, William howled. "Son. I'm in the mood to let you save some dignity and some time behind bars." Braden smiled at William. "My friend over there is Federal Law Enforcement..." Braden motioned toward Jeff. "If you apologize...he may not arrest your sorry ass."

Ra stood, leaning over the table to see William's face. "Apologize, dumb ass."

William looked at Ra then at Braden. "I'm sorry for the misunderstanding." William said bitterly.

Braden patted William on the shoulder then released his grip. "That's good son. That's good," Braden said, stepping away as William climbed to his feet.

"I want all of you out of here!" the night manager stormed out of the kitchen carrying a baseball bat. "Right now damnit, or I'm calling the police!" the manager held the bat at the ready, hoping for compliance.

"A'ight, a'ight," Ra said, leaving his table and heading for the door.

The manager turned to Braden, "Now!"

Braden ignored the man, as did Jeff, Mitch and John. They weren't about to leave until they knew Ra was gone.

Ra stopped at the door, William and the other men having already exited, and turned to Braden. "You got skill, brother. That's good to know," Ra smiled at Braden, slid out the door and into his waiting car.

"Now ya'll get going. The cops are on their way!" the manager nervously shouted.

Braden picked up the chairs that had toppled and arranged them neatly where they had been as Mitch walked calmly to towards the manager.

"We are the cops," Mitch said, offering his badge.

The manager lowered the bat. "Pretty aggressive for cops. Never seen that before… kind of refreshing."

"Those guys have been here before?" Jeff asked.

"A few times…" the waitress chimed in. "They never caused any trouble before but, that didn't mean they didn't make us nervous."

"Nervous? How?" Mitch asked.

"Lots of real unsavory folks, men and women, would come in here when they were around," The waitress responded. "Most of them looked real bad… like junkies do. I never saw anything change hands but I always thought something was going on."

Jeff pulled out his notepad, hurriedly recording what the waitress was saying. "That explains John's interest," Jeff commented under his breath.

"Where'd he go anyway?" Mitch looked around…no sign of John, or Braden.

****

"Couldn't hold it?" Braden asked, standing in the door of the restroom, staring at John as John stuffed his cell phone into his pocket.

"The excitement's over. Might as well answer nature's call," John turned to the sink.

Braden let the door close behind him. "Call huh? Who *were* you calling?"

John turned off the water. "I was texting my wife, Braden... not that it's any of your business." John's eyes narrowed as he toweled off his hands.

"She must be a good woman... staying up this late?"

John turned from the sink, "She's the best."

"I bet." Braden stared John down.

John walked to the door, brushing Braden's shoulder as he passed, "I'll give you some privacy."

"False alarm." Braden replied, following John out the door.

****

John walked through the restaurant, tapping Mitch on the shoulder as he headed to the door, "Let's go. It's late." John walked outside.

"That's pretty abrupt." Jeff's eyes followed John.

"It is," Mitch replied. "But he gets that way now and again."

"I don't trust him." everyone fell silent as Braden uttered the words. Mitch and Jeff may have had uneasy feelings but, leave it to a Master Chief to be direct.

"Watch your ass." Braden's gaze met Mitch's eyes.

Mitch didn't know how to respond. Braden had just forced Mitch's ill feelings to the forefront and Mitch couldn't shake his concern. John had never behaved this way, not in the twelve years they worked together. They'd been shot at, chased, stalked... just about anything you could imagine that would make you want to take a desk job. Mitch trusted John with his life, without question... until today. What the hell was happening?

"Master Chief..." Mitch started. "I always watch my ass and, for years John has watched my ass, too." Mitch headed toward the door. "We'll let you know what we come up with."

"Nice to know all ya'll get along so well," the waitress said, watching Mitch exit.

Braden said nothing as he pulled two tens from his wallet and handed them to the manager. With a smile,

Braden headed to the door, leaving Jeff alone in the restaurant.

"It's been a long day folks. I hope your night gets...better," Jeff said with a smile as he made for the exit.

"The coffees were only five dollars. It's better already," the waitress said, snatching the bills from the manager's hand.

27

12:32AM

"What the hell is going on, John?" Mitch asked as a bolt of lightning ushered in another downpour.

John was headed toward the sheriff's department, anxious to check out for the day and anxious to be alone. The phone call he'd received this afternoon had turned everything upside down. His role was supposed to be very clandestine but, now, he'd been impressed into very overt service. He had no idea how to shed Mitch, which was what he *needed* to do. The longer Mitch remained present, the more difficult it would become to explain away the interest in occurrences that seemed "outside" the investigation. There was no way John could put off Dennis' calls and there was no way, yet, to shake Mitch.

"I can tell you what's going on," John shouted angrily. "We're working too close with a Boat Jockey and a part time Coast Guard cop. Neither one of them knows jack shit about real police work and we're letting them play our game."

Mitch considered John's statement. In a way, John was right. Braden and Nguyen were both outside their element. But, Mitch had watched John work with outside agencies before and it had never been this confrontational. Then again, John had never acted this strange before.

"They're concerned about their folks. They have every right to be."

"Then they need to just hunker down on that and let us do the rest. They're in the way," John replied, frustrated.

"In the way of what? We spent most of our day chasing dead bodies in another state. We haven't done a damn thing that helped make heads or tails of what those Coast Guard folks are up against," Mitch's tone intensified.

"That's because we don't know if anything that's happened is tied to the drug money."

"Like hell!" Mitch exclaimed. "We've had cases like this before, with a lot less call for concern, and we've put people under police protection."

John didn't have an answer. His mind raced, thinking of options. He knew the plan. He knew what was going to happen Friday night. He knew Mitch was right. "Damnit…" John thought, "…shut up, Mitch".

"Why'd you take that boy's picture?"

John scoffed and shook his head.

"What was it that interested you about him?" Mitch pressed the question. "He wasn't familiar to me. Do you know him?"

"You don't think a gang of blacks wearing a few thousand dollars worth of bling, in that place, at midnight, doesn't warrant interest? Come on, Mitch. We've made entire cases starting with less than that."

Mitch considered John's statement. John was right. The situation at the restaurant wasn't normal and definitely raised an eyebrow. But, it all seemed too coincidental.

"You're right," Mitch said, turning to look out his rain splattered window. "It's just been a damn long couple of days." Mitch rubbed his face, the five-o-clock shadow turning into a stubbly beard.

"Braden and Nguyen are just up against something they aren't familiar with. Everything is suspicious to them right now. I don't blame them," John said bringing the SUV to a stop at a red light.

"Let me see that picture," Mitch held out his hand.

John hesitated. But if he wanted Mitch to believe that all the upheaval was a product of uncertainty, he had to hand Mitch his phone.

"Here," John said, handing Mitch the cell.

As the light turned green Mitch tapped at buttons on the Smart Phone. John did his best to watch Mitch from the corner of his eye but the pouring rain and road glare demanded focus. "Just push the camera icon," John said.

"I know what to push," Mitch said, holding the phone up in front of his face, cocked to the side, blocking John's view.

Mitch scrolled through John's recent calls, incoming and outgoing. He didn't give a damn about the picture. He wanted to see who John had been talking too. Throughout the day there had been numerous calls. Several were from Jeff Nguyen, one text from John's wife, about picking up dog food, and ten or more calls and texts from someone named Dennis.

"You're gonna stare a hole through my screen. What are you doing?" John said nervously as the lights of the Sheriff's Department building came into view.

"Just taking a good look… the big fella looks like a guy I pulled over once," Mitch smiled as he punched up the latest of John's text messages. It was a message to Dennis, the picture was attached and the message read, "Ra's in Savannah. What do you want me to do?"

"Rain's letting up," John said as he pulled into the department's parking lot, coming to a stop near Mitch's truck. "Curbside delivery." John smiled at Mitch as he held out his hand for the phone.

Mitch punched buttons on the phone quickly. The screen went black. "Well, he's one ugly S.O.B. no matter who he is."

"Most bad guys are," John said, stuffing the phone back in his pocket as Mitch made his exit, "See you in the morning."

"You bet," Mitch opened his truck door. "Good night buddy."

John drove the SUV through the parking lot to its assigned space. Turning off the ignition, John watched Mitch turn out of the lot then punched the face of his phone. The outgoing text message folder appeared. Mitch hadn't been too slick after all.

"That dumb ass redneck," John said as he leapt from the SUV, raced across the lot and jumped into his jeep. "Damnit Mitch!"

28

12:45AM

"Where does he live?" Dennis asked calmly, trying to temper a frantic John Martin.

"I don't want him hurt. I'll handle it. I just wanted you to know that there *might* be a problem," John said nervously, desperately.

Dennis looked across the room to where Evan sat sipping a glass of Makers Mark next to the fireplace. Evan made no moves, betrayed no emotion as John's voice echoed over the speaker phone.

"Mitch is just a dumb ass redneck, " John offered a half hearted laugh.

Dennis cleared his throat then leaned forward toward the speaker, "Deputy Martin, you wouldn't be calling if you believed that."

The line was silent save for the sound of the rain whipping across John's windshield.

"We're in a very tense situation here, Deputy. Ra obviously isn't heeding Evan's warning which means we need to act fast. And now, you're telling me your position in my organization may be compromised?"

"No, Dennis…" the apprehension in John's voice became tactile as he continued, "… I don't believe that's the case. I can and will get Mitch under control."

Across the room, Evan snorted a laugh.

"You're a law man, Deputy." Dennis tapped the speaker with his forefinger. "It's not in your nature to see things from my point of view." Dennis rose from his seat. "You and your partner have made a few enemies in the past haven't you?"

There was a pause before John answered, "Yes."

"Would you say that a few of them may wish you some physical harm?"

"What are you getting at? Where are you going with this?" John demanded.

Dennis paused. "I want you to give me an address, Deputy. Then, I want you to go home and get some sleep."

"Fuck that, Dennis!" John shouted.

"Need I remind you of how very much you have to lose if, say, your wife or your superiors found out about our arrangement?"

"You're a bastard!" John railed.

"In my line of work... it's a prerequisite." Dennis smiled across the room at Evan, "The address, now!"

John stuttered. Dennis could hear him breaking down on the other end of the line. Evan rose from his chair and slipped on a jacket to cover his shoulder holster.

****

Jeff watched Braden enter the house. "What a damn day. I need to sleep," Jeff said aloud as he pulled away from the curb. The Ramada was five minutes away. The thought of a hot shower and a few hours between crisp sheets had never caused Jeff such, exhausted as he was, excitement.

"Note to self..." Jeff said to no one in particular. "Do not piss off the Master Chief." Jeff laughed. "Damned if he didn't kick that guy's ass." Jeff laughed alone, as he drove. He was getting slap-happy. His cell phone rang.

"What now?" Jeff asked the air as he looked at the phone's display. It was Mitch.

"Please tell me he's calling to say goodnight," Jeff said as he pulled the phone to his ear and pressed the talk button. "Mitch. What's up?"

"I'm about to my house, Jeff. Can you meet me here?" Mitch said, a hint of excitement and dismay tinting his southern drawl.

Jeff looked at his watch, "It's one fifteen in the morning, Mitch."

"Can't wait," Mitch replied. "I'm gonna text my address so you can plug it into your GPS. See you in a few." Mitch hung up.

"Son of a…" Jeff slammed a fist onto the steering wheel. "It better be damned important."

Jeff's phone rang again, the "incoming text" ringtone.

"Ok, Mitch, I'm on my way."

29

1:30AM

Rachel couldn't sleep. She knew she'd be lucky to see the inside of her eyelids before the first hints of daylight broke the eastern horizon. It had been a long day and, stubbornly, her racing mind wouldn't allow it to end. She'd had two cups of chamomile tea, a lavender soak in the tub and watched four episodes of "Ancient Aliens". If that combo didn't force sleep on you, you were in deep trouble. Finally, Rachel figured she'd have to beat herself to sleep, so off she went, jogging - no - running into the pitch black of Cockspur Island in the wee hours. Stupid scary... yes, effective... she hoped so. At least it wasn't raining, at the moment.

Rachel had checked out with the mid-watch before she left. Danny, the young kid, had nearly jumped out of his skin when she popped into the watch-room at such a late hour. At least Danny knew where she was going and where to start looking if she didn't make it back. Rachel didn't put it past the island to house a bear, or some rabid stray dog, or any number of ghastly beings. But, she was very fast. They'd have to catch her before they could harm her and if they had genitals... advantage Rachel and her muscular, kicking, legs.

As she flew past the pines that lined the narrow island roadway, the moon broke through the clouds sending brilliant light into the steamy night. Ahead, Rachel saw a form dart out of the woods and across the road.

"Shit!" Rachel screamed as she came to a dead stop.

The white tail stood frozen by Rachel's scream. After a flick of its tongue and a sniff of the air, the deer snorted and bounded off.

"Okay then."

Rachel regained her composure and continued on her run. She'd run to the parking lot of the Fort then back to the Station. That was about a mile round trip and at a sprint, Rachel hoped it would be enough to collapse her body into sleep. Headlights appeared down the road.

"Party hounds," Rachel said through heavy breaths.

At this time of night, any moving car on the island would undoubtedly belong to one of her fellow crewmen returning from a night of debauchery in downtown Savannah. They would stop. She would stop. They would tell her she was crazy and she would gag from the smell of cigarette smoke and stale beer escaping from their vehicle. After a brief conversation she'd either give up her plans and ride back with them or she'd keep going. She kept her options open as the car grew closer.

"Which idiot are you?" Rachel asked as she peered hard through the night, the car coming into focus.

It wasn't one of her crewmates. The car was official. The car had a light-rack on top. It was Terry Macomb.

Rachel tensed as she stopped, "What the hell is he doing out this late?" Rachel considered turning tail and running, full speed, back to the station. "Damn."

The spotlight on Terry's cruiser came on, drowning Rachel in blinding white light. Rachel put a hand to her face against the brilliance as Terry let the car creep forward. The cruiser's window drew up next to Rachel.

"Awful late for a workout," Terry stated as he switched off the spotlight and eyed Rachel up and down.

"Creep," Rachel thought, wishing it had been one of her friends. "Awful late for a patrol." Rachel said, fake smiling.

"Well…" Terry stiffened in his seat, trying to look authoritative and masculine, "… every so often I like to make a late night of it. It's all a part of keeping the park secure…anti-vandalism and so forth."

"My ass," Rachel thought. More than likely Terry was trying to nab a Coastie speeding on the island after hours. Better yet, he probably wanted to bust an inebriated Coastie. That would have made his entire decade.

"Well…." Rachel didn't know what to say. "I hope things stay quiet for you."

"You're the most excitement I've had all night." Terry remarked.

"Well that's good, I suppose?" Rachel replied.

"Yes. Yes it's really good."

"For God's sake I'm going to hurl," Rachel thought as she suffered Terry's leering gaze and creepy smile.

"Why don't you climb in and let me run you back to the Station," Terry said, patting the passenger seat.

Through the trees Rachel caught the gleam of a set of headlights. The car was at the front gate of the island, the lights no more than pinpoints piercing the dark.

"I'd love to, Terry, but I think you have some police work to do," Rachel pointed toward the headlights at the gate.

Terry leaned out his window, catching sight of the headlights. As Terry slumped back into the cruiser it was obvious that he was debating which activity he was more interested in undertaking... driving Rachel or catching the bad guys. Rachel had to think fast.

"I'll let you get to it. Besides, I am a sweaty, stinky mess. My pits are atrocious. I'd smell up the whole cruiser." Rachel smiled and slapped the top of the car. "I guess if I shaved them it would be better."

A look of disgust came over Terry's face. He wouldn't give up trying to get into Rachel's pants, but the "hairy pits" had worked their magic for now.

"You just get on back to the station, Ma'am," Terry said as he put the cruiser in reverse. "It aint safe out here at night. Not for a girl like you."

"I'll take that as a compliment," Rachel said as Terry whipped the cruiser around and headed for the front gate.

****

Ra stepped out of the car following William and two other nameless goons William had brought along for the ride. Ra didn't care what their names were. One was called, maybe, Jamal and the other was some creative handle like Big-H or Little-Q. Ra didn't care. All he wanted was a group of mean bastards who weren't opposed to spilling blood. Judging from the looks of these guys that wasn't going to be a problem.

"They aint real big on keeping people out of here," William stated as he examined the park gate.

The swinging gate spanned the paved road leading onto Cockspur Island. Made of aluminum rails and stanchions the gate was attached to a cement pole with a sturdy hunk of chain and a hefty-looking padlock. To each side of the gate, "decorative" boulders were put in place to keep vehicles from cutting through the grass and onto the road. The boulders were a problem. But, the gate wasn't going to be much of an issue.

"Can we cut it?" Ra asked as he watched William mess with the chain.

"We don't need to cut it. I can pick that old ass lock with a screwdriver. It aint a problem."

Ra looked up and down highway 80. The gate was about one hundred yards off the highway and partially hidden by tall grass and sporadic small pines. So far, not a single car had transited the highway. It was two in the morning. All the beach goers and party hounds were in bed. The over stretched Chatham County Sheriffs barely patrolled this area in the early hours of the morning and the State Police virtually ignored the area altogether. Getting onto the island was going to be easy.

"So let's go!" One of the nameless goons exclaimed, working the slide on his Beretta.

"Just shut up," Ra shot the man a disgusted look. "Try the lock, bro."

William bent down examining the lock, then pulled a small pouch from his jacket pocket. William opened the pouch and selected the appropriate picking tool.

"One minute," William said, holding a penlight in his mouth and working at the locks tumblers. Then, the headlights appeared.

"Shit!" William said as he stood, stuffing the tools back into his jacket. The car was close.

****

Terry had turned off his lights after leaving Rachel. Any opportunity for excitement sent Terry into "ninja" mode. He punched the sedan's accelerator, building his speed up to fifty miles per hour then dropped the car into neutral, coasting over the bridge, stealthily approaching the front gate. The "perps" never heard him coming.

"Oh…I got ya boys!" Terry talked to himself as he reached for the headlight switch.

Terry could see someone large working on the gate's lock. Three others stood watching. This wasn't the first time people had tried to get into the park. Most of the time it was a group of students from Savannah State performing some ridiculous fraternity pledge requirement. The pranks never involved anything overly malicious. The students showed tremendous respect for the fort. The usual requirement was to place a Savannah State banner on the flagpole in front of the fort or to skinny-dip in the fort's mote. Terry would just scare them a little and send them on their way. When the lights came on, Terry knew immediately that these weren't college kids. He reached for his shotgun and turned on his blue lights.

"Let's see some hands gentlemen," Terry said, stepping out of the squad.

Ra couldn't see Terry. The squads headlights were blinding and the occulting blue lights provided only a fragmented silhouette. It was possible that another cop sat in the passenger seat, calling for backup. Then again, he could be alone. A Sheriff's deputy wouldn't be on the island, behind a locked gate and it certainly wasn't a state cop.

"Okay, alright, officer," Ra spoke. "We don't want trouble."

"Sure you don't," Terry responded sarcastically. "That's why you were messing with my gate in the middle of the night."

"It ain't like that player," William said, side stepping until he was silhouetted by his own cars lights. "My sister left her purse out here today. She needs it back."

"And she didn't realize that until now?" Terry laughed. "Every one of ya'll, turn around and place your hands on the hood of your car. Do it slow. Keep your hands where I can see them at all times."

Ra, William and the goons all turned around slowly. Facing the car; they bent at the waist, placing their hands on the hood.

"This ain't no good, Ra. We're all packing," William whispered.

"Take it easy. This is just some stupid fucking rent-a-cop."

Terry worked the shotgun in his hands. Terry's nerves were peaked, the tension was palatable. He always went around fantasizing about being the lone lawman in the face of incredible odds. In the fantasies, Terry took things in hand, saved the day and got the girl. In this case the girl would be Rachel. A story about busting four guys, single handedly, could be just what he needed to get Rachel into his bedroom.

Terry looked back into the squad, looked at his radio. Procedure dictated that he call for backup or at least report what was happening. But, Terry was working tonight without anyone knowing. He'd been told to "lay off" the Coast Guard by his supervisor and that meant not laying traps for them on the island after the park was closed. Terry thought that was stupid. Terry wanted to bust people, everyone, not just the Coasties, but they were his only available target. Taking down these punks would make his night forays legitimate. His boss would never question him again. Terry would call in when he got these guys secured.

Terry racked a round in the shotgun as he stepped out from behind the squad's door, "Ya'll got some identification on you?"

"He's alone," One of the goons commented.

"He's a park cop. I saw the symbol on his door," the other goon chimed in.

Ra considered his options. He damn sure wasn't going to let this hillbilly cop take him to jail.

"What do you want?" William asked.

"We have to make it quiet," Ra responded as he saw Terry climb over the gate, shotgun at the ready. This was not what Ra wanted. Things were getting way too complicated... too late to go back now. It was all or nothing.

Terry strolled up on the group, wary, looking the men over, deciding who the biggest threat would be. Only one of the four was skinny. The rest were pretty well built, kind of stocky. Terry knew there had to be a weapon somewhere, but with their hands on the hood Terry could blow a hole in anyone who reached. Terry stopped behind William, a plan formulating in his head.

"You!" Terry poked William in the back with the barrel of the shotgun. "Stand up! Hands up! Turn around slowly till I tell you to stop!"

Terry took a cautious step back as William gathered his full height. At six feet three inches tall, William towered over Terry. He turned in a circle as Terry examined his belt line, and his pants...no weapon could be seen. Terry reached into his belt, producing a set of handcuffs which he tossed at William.

"Take those..." William caught the cuffs. "Put them on your buddy there." Terry motioned toward Ra.

"Aint that your job?" William replied, smart assed.

"Just do it. I aint asking!" Terry leaned into the shotgun.

Ra watched. The cop's hands were unsteady. His breathing was fast. This guy was out of his element... some kind of rouge redneck looking for his "Rambo" moment.

"You 'bout to shit your pants, cracker?" Ra asked, mockingly.

"I think this mother fucker might," William laughed.

"Just let me beat this cracker's ass!" One of the goons shouted, rising from the hood.

Terry didn't know what to do. He shifted his aim back and forth between the men as they laughed at his expense. "You lean back down!" Terry yelled at the goon. "Put those damn cuffs on that guy now!" Terry screamed into Williams face.

Ra stood up...all of them were standing now, facing Terry. "You a scared ass cop wannabe. You need to get your ass beat."

"I'll blow your goddamn face off if you come a step toward me!" Terry shifted his aim constantly, back and forth. He was over his head.

Ra, William and the goons all laughed. "That right?" Ra asked Terry. "You aint even got the safety off," Ra lied, but it worked.

In the second Terry took to look at the shotgun's safety, William grabbed the barrel of the gun and hefted it to the sky. Terry squeezed the trigger and a cone of flame and smoke belched from the gun. The sound of the shot echoed across the marsh. William yanked hard on the shotgun, pulling it free from Terry's hands. With a shove, William sent Terry sprawling onto the pavement. Terry fumbled with his holster, trying to produce his pistol, trying to get control.

"Don't!"

Terry looked up to see Ra standing over him, pointing a .22 pistol at the space between his eyes. His hands dropped. "Don't kill me," Terry plead as he felt a warm spot growing in his pants.

William pointed at Terry's crotch, laughing as he turned away. The goons joined in, high fiving each other, exchanging fist bumps and hand slaps.

Ra didn't laugh. He bent down over Terry, pressing the barrel of the pistol against Terry's forehead. "Well, officer, what should I do with you now?" Ra smiled.

"You're in a shit load of trouble young man," Terry tried to sound official. "You're going to go to jail for this."

"Police man, aint no one gonna know I ever did anything wrong," Ra snickered as he unsnapped Terry's holster and removed the pistol. "William!" Ra yelled.

William regained his composure, coming up to Ra. "What's up?"

"Drag him out onto the bridge."

Terry struggled as William pulled him to his feet. William slapped Terry in the side of the head with an open palm then wrapped a beefy arm around Terry's neck.

"You two dumb asses!" Ra yelled at the goons. "Move the cops car to the center of the bridge. Real close to the edge."

Terry went into complete panic as William dragged him backwards onto the bridge that spanned between the mainland gate and Cockspur Island. Terry saw his squad peel off in reverse, blue light turned off, headlights off. He heard the squeal of the tires as the brakes were slammed. He looked at Ra who followed. Ra's face looked demonic and Terry wondered what evil was in the man's mind. Terry started to cry.

"Don't do this, man," Terry's voice squeaked past Williams grip. "I can forget you. I can forget you!" the tears streamed down Terry's face.

At center-span William moved Terry to the edge of the bridge. Terry twisted back and forth but his efforts were useless. William was far too strong. Ra approached, examining Terry's pistol, admiring the polished look. Ra held the pistol up, allowing the barrel to glint in the moonlight.

"Show me his fucking hand!" Ra told the nearest goon.

"No!" Terry screamed as the big man grabbed his arm, extending it out.

Terry fought at Williams grip with his free hand. The second goon grabbed the arm, twisting it behind Terry's back.

Ra approached Terry. "I think you're sick of your job, cracker." Ra's face betrayed a devil as he looked into Terry's eyes. "I think you're sick of everything."

"What are you doing?" Terry's scream was muffled as William tightened on Terry's throat.

"Hold his shit," Ra said as he grabbed Terry's hand, placing the pistol in Terry's palm. Ra forced Terry's hand and arm upward placing the barrel of the pistol under Terry's chin.

"No! No!" Terry couldn't fight hard enough to break free. "Please, no!"

Ra placed Terry's finger on the trigger, covered by his own, as William and the goons turned Terry around, back facing the bridge.

Terry twisted hard, trying desperately to break free. He lost his footing, slipped, and the pistol reported across the night air. The back of Terry's skull heaved into the night sky, pieces hitting the river below with the sound of thrown pebbles. William pushed the body over the side of the bridge, into the uncaring water.

Ra tossed the pistol over the bridge. Terry's body had disappeared below the surface immediately and the hollow "splunk" sound of the pistol seemed to accentuate the end of Terry's life. Ra didn't care. There were streaks of blood on the bridge…a couple of pieces of flesh. Ra didn't care. This was just the first.

"Boss…" One of the goons smiled victoriously at Ra.

"What?"

The goon held up a small ring of three keys. "One of them says front gate."

Ra snatched the keys, "Wipe down the car."

30

2:05AM

Mitch finished the beer in three tremendous gulps as he cracked open a second that sat on the table by his front window. Mitch wasn't playing around. He intended to get drunk, late as it was, before he even considered going to bed. Beauregard, Mitch's aged Golden Retriever, stood at his side, looking out the front window. Mitch expected the headlights of Jeff's car to enter the driveway at any moment.

Mitch poured some beer onto the tile floor. "It's been a damn shitty day Beau!" Mitch said as Beauregard licked up the beer. "Crazy shit happens, right?" Beauregard looked up at Mitch, cocked his head then went back to the beer. "Good idea boy," Mitch said as he tore into his second beer.

Mitch didn't want to believe what seemed apparent. He'd been friends with John for years and had never had reason to take his partner for anything other than a good cop. Now, it appeared the good cop was a ruse. Every case, every lead, every conviction were all by design... masks that assured some other deal. The second beer was gone. Mitch crushed the can in his hands then reached for a third as headlights appeared at the head of his driveway.

"I can't believe he found the drive in the dark," Mitch told Beauregard then headed for the front door.

Mitch's home was tucked back off the main road about a quarter of a mile. The home had been in Mitch's family for years. It had belonged to Mitch's grandparents who made the original purchase in 1922. Even then, the house was old. The gravel driveway wound past a shed, then past a massive willow tree that had stood since before the home was first built. It would take a minute for Jeff Nguyen to navigate the drive. Mitch hefted the remains of his six-pack and proceeded onto his front porch. He was sure Jeff could use a beer as well. Beauregard followed.

"Be good," Mitch rubbed Beauregard's head. If Beau didn't know folks he had a tendency to bark like a mad dog. Beau was way too skittish to go after someone but his throaty bark was usually sufficient to get their attention. As the car drew closer, Beau plopped down on the porch next to Mitch's feet. Mitch didn't register the occurrence as the shape of the vehicle became clear. It wasn't Jeff. It was John.

"What the hell is he doing here, Beau?" Mitch asked as John stomped on the brakes, skidding to a stop on the gravel.

"And in such a hurry?"

John sprang out of his truck. "You dumb son of a bitch!" John yelled as he walked toward the porch.

Mitch was taken aback. John had discovered his snooping, maybe. "Good to see you, too." Mitch replied calmly.

John stopped at the foot of the steps to the porch, angry, hands on hips. "Don't play stupid, Mitch! I know you looked through my phone and I know you saw some stuff that…"

Mitch interrupted, "That makes it look like you're crooked?"

John looked at the ground, searching for words. "Yep, crooked as hell!"

"Are you?" Mitch tilted his third beer, reaching out with his nerves to acknowledge the presence of the handgun tucked into the back of his pants. It was there.

John sighed, "I don't have the time to tell you why, bubba." John's eyes were apologetic but the moment passed in haste. "You need to get your shit and get the hell out of here right now!"

John was frantic. Mitch could see that in his posture, hear it in his voice. "What the hell is going on?" Mitch dropped his half-full beer onto the porch as Beauregard uttered a low snarl. "Is someone coming after me?"

"Hell yes! He's a bad son of a bitch, Mitch. He'll shoot you dead!" John stepped onto the porch. "And me too if he finds me here warning you!"

Mitch reached out, grabbing John by the collar, pulling John into an oncoming uppercut. "God damnit, John!" Mitch yelled tossing John to the porch as Beauregard began to bark.

John wiped a trickle of blood from his mouth. He'd bitten his tongue hard when the punch landed. "You can beat the shit out of me later, buddy. We need to leave!"

Beauregard moved off the porch, snarling and barking, looking toward the shed. Beau paced back and forth, head never leaving a single spot in the darkness, just outside the reach of the shed's lights.

"Beau?" Mitch said, reaching for his handgun as the first shot rang out.

The bullet hissed in the air before it slammed into John's torso. Blood and bone from a gaping exit wound splashed against the side of the house as John's body slumped, lifeless, onto the porch. Mitch dove for cover behind an old oak barrel next to the front door. A second round pierced the night, punching through the barrel and exploding into the siding next to Mitch's leg.

"Come on you son of a bitch!" Mitch screamed as he stuck his pistol over the barrel, firing several shots toward the shed.

Another report rang out. This time the bullet cut through the barrel, grazing Mitch's left leg below the knee. As Mitch yelled in pain, Beauregard charged away from the porch, toward the shed. Beau was wild. Mitch hadn't seen this out of the dog for ages.

"Thanks buddy. I love you, Beau." Mitch said, knowing that Beau was going to be just enough of a distraction for Mitch to get inside the house. Inside the house, if the shooter chased him in, things were going to be much different. The playing field would tilt hard in Mitch's favor.

Mitch stood, carrying the barrel to cover his movements toward the door, as he heard Beau tear into something. Beau's growls were muffled. It was the same sound Beau made when he was younger, when Mitch played tug of war with Beau. "God damnit!" Mitch heard someone yell in the darkness... then a single shot. It was a handgun this time, not a rifle like before. Beau yelped and was silent.

Mitch dove inside the door, smashing his hand across the light switches that controlled the porch lights and the overhead lights in the foyer and living room. The house was bathed in darkness and Mitch army-crawled across the floor to the end table where he'd laid his cell phone.

Mitch fumbled his hand across the top of the table. "Where the hell is it?" It wasn't on the table.

"Figures," Mitch thought to himself as he heard a creaking come from the front porch, from the lowest step, the one that had always creaked. "Thank God for old houses," Mitch thought as he switched magazines in his handgun then crawled to cover behind his grandmother's ancient china cabinet.

Mitch trained his pistol on the front door of the home. With any luck, the shooter would be dumb enough to enter through the door, silhouetting himself in the dim light provided by the Georgia moon. This was a stretch and Mitch knew it. If this guy was a good as John said he was… he'd never make that mistake. Mitch waited, silently. The house was so completely quiet… even Mitch's breath sounded loud. Mitch wondered if he could actually "think" quieter.

A squeak came from the porch, not near the door but from the side porch. The shooter was trying to find another way into the house. There was only one other way in and that was through the rear door in the kitchen. Either way, front or rear, Mitch would have the guy dead to rights… game, set and match. Suddenly, the Charlie Daniels Band filled the air. It was "The Devil went down to Georgia" it was loud and it was Mitch's ringtone.

"Shit!" Mitch thought to himself, realizing the phone had been in his back pocket the entire time. Mitch yanked out the phone and touched the screen. It was a text message from Jeff Nguyen. It read "Found the driveway. Be right there."

"Oh no," Mitch said, realizing his advantage was gone.

****

Jeff came up the driveway slowly. Not a single light was on at the main house, only the lights around a small shed illuminated the path. He'd already had a near miss with an opossum and two raccoons on the drive out here and sure as hell didn't want to hit a goat or a cow or whatever else may be strolling around in the middle of the country. It was after three in the morning. He was dead tired and he knew it wouldn't be long before tired eyes started playing tricks on him.

"John's here too?" Jeff said to himself as he reached the expanse of gravel in front of the home. "Must be some real juicy news."

Jeff stopped the car and crawled out, stretching tired muscles. He looked around, bewildered by the lack of greeting… the lack of light. On the front porch he saw a tipped over barrel near the front door. Next to that he could see a few beer cans scattered about and off to the side, obscured by the railings, he saw a body.

"What the hell is..." Jeff started to ask as he reached for his weapon. Mitch exploded out the front door.

"Hit the damn deck!" Mitch yelled as Evan Gregory rounded the corner of the porch.

Jeff threw himself to the ground as Evan opened fire. The bullet passed through the windshield of Jeff's car. Jeff buckled as the round struck him in the shoulder, spinning him around and throwing him face-first into the gravel. Blood coursed out of the wound as Jeff fumbled to grab his pistol with his functioning arm.

Mitch fired at Evan, sending a round into the siding and a shower of wooden fragments into Evan's face. Evan reeled back into cover as the first hints of fluid reached his eyes from the splinter imbedded in his forehead. He was pissed. He felt sloppy. Cops weren't this good. These bastards were just lucky. Evan popped back out, firing again as Mitch threw himself off the porch, diving for a stand of low bushes not six feet from Jeff's car. Jeff heard the round strike Mitch with a wet thud. Mitch hit the ground and rolled close to Jeff, blood escaping from a hole in Mitch's side.

"Damn that bastard," Mitch said, coughing blood.

Jeff pulled up his weapon as he heard Evan step from cover and race across the porch to get another shot at Mitch. Jeff fought to work the slide and, as he did, realized that the pistol wasn't loaded. He never kept it loaded. He'd never had to worry about it being loaded. All those months in an office, all those months of doing nothing of any significance... he was complacent and now, more than likely, he and Mitch would both pay the price.

Mitch rolled over, bringing up his handgun as Evan came around the hood of the car. Mitch squeezed the trigger, aiming through fading vision, sending a bullet through Evans left thigh. Evan collapsed to his knees as he raised his gun. His shot struck Mitch in the chest and Mitch fell silent. Jeff did nothing. He lay there. He played dead as he heard Evan limp around the car.

"Redneck son of a bitch!" Evan shot Mitch again, twice more in the chest then turned his attention to Jeff.

Jeff remained still, trying not to breath. He had to be ready when his chance came… if a chance came. The guy was shot in the leg. The guy had been firing, at least five rounds that Jeff had counted and maybe more before he arrived. Maybe the guy was losing blood, a lot of blood.

"And who the hell are you, gook?" Evan said as he leaned against Jeff's open door, "You're a long way from sushi out here." Evan bent down, placing the barrel of his pistol on Jeff's forehead.

With a fluid motion Jeff reached, grabbed Evans arm and drove it into the door. The pistol went off, sending a bullet ricocheting off the door and into the vehicles interior. Jeff maintained his grip on Evan's arm as he swung a leg around, kicking Evan in the back of the leg, bringing Evan to his knees on the rough gravel. Evan pulled back violently on his arm, breaking free of Jeff's grip but sending his pistol flying across the driveway in the process. Gritting his teeth against the pain, Jeff delivered a blow to the side of Evan's head with his injured arm, the force of the punch knocking Evan sideways and fully onto the ground.

Jeff didn't know how. He had no idea where his strength was coming from, but suddenly he was on his feet, standing over Evan. With ferocity outside his ability, Jeff delivered an open palm thrust into Evan's throat causing Evan to cough and gag, struggling to find purchase on precious air. Evan backed away from Jeff, over the top of Mitch's lifeless body and, as he did, placed his hand on Mitch's pistol. Evan raised the pistol swiftly, pulling the trigger through the motion. The bullet entered Jeff's arm, just below the already injured shoulder.

Jeff spun around from the force of the bullets impact as pain washed across his body. Evan pulled the trigger again, a second bullet passing millimeters from Jeff's face as Jeff grabbed Evan's arm, twisting hard, stretching sinew, snapping cartilage, breaking bone. Evan wailed in pain as Jeff wrestled the pistol from his grasp, Evans useless arm falling onto Mitch's body.

Jeff leveled the pistol on Evan. "Who the hell are you?" Jeff demanded.

"Fuck you rice eater!" Evan shouted in reply.

Jeff pointed the pistol at Evan's knee and fired a single round. Evan's kneecap shattered and blood sprayed across the ground. Jeff didn't care about procedure, he didn't care about handcuffs or interrogation rooms. Adrenaline had taken over and he was losing blood. He had to get something from Evan now.

Jeff knelt down, striking Evan on the face with the pistol. "I said...who are you?" Evan didn't respond, only roiled in pain from his wounds as Jeff buried his knee in Evan's chest, pressing down on his solar plexus.

Jeff looked over his shoulder, at the wound to Evan's thigh. The shot Mitch had managed to get had struck Evan's femoral artery. Blood flowed from the hole in Evans pants in spurts and fits. The wound was fatal without immediate attention. Jeff rifled through Evans pockets finding his wallet and cell phone.

"Evan Gregory, that's who you are," Jeff said, looking at Evan's drivers license. "Who sent you, Evan? Why did they send you, Evan?" Jeff pressed the pistol under Evans chin.

"You're all dead," Evan sputtered, losing strength. "We're going to kill all of you." Evan finished, weak, soft...fading.

"Who's *we*?" Jeff asked, pulling his knee from Evan's chest, hoping to give the man a few more seconds of breath. "Whose going to die?"

Evan's dimming eyes locked on Jeff. A look of defiance, a menacing, devilish smile crept across Evan's face. "Semper Paratus," Evan chuckled then faded into death.

Jeff let the pistol fall from his hands as he gathered in the carnage. Blood pooled on the gravel, soaking the ground, saturating Jeff's clothing. He pressed buttons on Evans cell, pulling up records of old calls and texts. There was something about tomorrow night, a boat, some men… Cockspur Island.

"My God," Jeff said, realizing the meaning behind what he was seeing. "I've got to warn them." Jeff struggled to his feet. His mind was drifting. His head felt light. Looking down his sleeve, Jeff could see that he had lost a lot of blood. Shock was setting in. He had to get help.

Jeff reached for his car door, tried to brace himself… then fell to the ground. As darkness poured in around the periphery of his vision he punched numbers into Evan's phone. Nine... One..., "No," Jeff said as he succumbed to blackness.

31

5:50AM

Hank had set the alarm for five-thirty this morning. Usually, he set the alarm for six thirty. But, today Hank wanted to spend time with Lori and Ally before he went to work for the weekend. The past few days had been stressful. The next few days would be too. Hank understood Lori's apprehensions about being alone in the apartment and he shared them equally. Later today, after speaking to Lori's father and making the flight arrangements, he'd feel better. Hank supposed sending them away for a week, maybe two, was a good idea. Lori would still spend her time worrying about him but, he wouldn't have to worry about her.

The smell of coffee and toast wafted from the kitchen as Hank packed. Four pairs of underwear, four pairs of socks, two towels, spit-kit, two complete uniforms and an issue of Field and Stream that he had never gotten around to reading. Another weekend's worth of stuff... another weekend away from his family. Before *this* weekend, packing up had been so easy. It wasn't that way today. Hank wondered if it ever would be again.

Ally burst through the bedroom door at a full sprint, giggling, flinging herself onto Hank and Lori's bed like a circus performer.

"Hi baby," Hank said, holding out his arms, catching Ally in a bear hug as she launched herself off the bed. "Good morning." Hank planted a wet kiss on Ally's cheek as she did the same.

"Mommy says breakfast is ready for us, Daddy," Ally pulled away, smiling as she spoke.

"What is breakfast today, honey?"

Ally considered the question for a second. "Bread and megs and juice," Ally replied. Megs were eggs. She always called eggs, megs.

"That sounds great!" Hank said, hoisting Ally in the air, pecking her on the cheek then turning her loose to run to the kitchen. Hank smiled as she ran out the door, giggling and cackling.

Hank grabbed his gear bag, zipped it closed then headed out of the bedroom with a sigh. His thoughts turned to the worries that wracked his family, to the separation that was coming and the reasons for the same. "Is it really worth it?" Hank shut off the bedroom light.

****

Rachel toweled off, the steam from the cramped shower rolling out the door and fogging up her barracks' room mirror. She'd managed to fall asleep at four but the sleep had been tenuous. Dreams dominated her slumber. In her dreams she was being chased by someone. As she was chased, she passed the shadowy forms of her friends all urging her on towards a dark building, toward a feeling of safety and escape. She woke before the dreams ended, she never knew if she reached safety or not. She would remember this dream, though she didn't want to. She hated remembering *these* dreams.

"Why couldn't it have been about getting a massage from Sam Worthington?" Rachel said as she wrapped her hair and grabbed her toothbrush.

The smell of the galley crept into her nose. It was after six which meant the cooks had been preparing breakfast for the past half an hour at least. Rachel smelled bacon, she thought she smelled fried potatoes and she definitely smelled coffee. She would require a huge volume of coffee this morning and, despite the fact that it was a heart attack on a plate, she would eat everything the cooks had to offer. Tired bodies craved carbs and Rachel planned a full surrender.

"You've got your work cut out for you today," Rachel told her tube of whitening toothpaste. "Coffee, ketchup... and I might even steal a smoke from someone if I get too riled up." Rachel popped the brush into her mouth, scrubbing vigorously as she hummed a Beach Boys' song. When she reached the chorus she flung an arm out to her side for emphasis, striking the ironing board that hung by the sink, sending it onto the floor with an abusive bang as it struck the tile.

Rachel froze. The sound jolted a memory from last night. She remembered sounds she heard as she climbed, exhausted, under her sheets. It may have been a gunshot, maybe two. It was loud but it was distant. Maybe it was the mid-watch throwing trash out. The lid of the dumpster sounded like a gunshot every time it slammed down. "That was it," Rachel thought, then spit into the sink.

****

Mike pulled the covers back slowly. Debbie was still asleep but she hadn't been for long. She'd sat vigil over the house until four in the morning, clinging to a baseball bat and her cell phone. Every noise sent her into hyper-alert. Several times she had sprung from the couch, holding the bat at the ready. Mike had had to talk her down each time. Debbie dissolved into whimpering tears after each startle. Hopefully, today, something could happen to make her feel a little safer, maybe.

The sun was over the horizon already. From the front window Mike could see the reds and yellows of dawn giving way to the full light of day. His face hurt. His arm hurt. He was stiff as a board. Moving to the kitchen took a lot of effort and Mike couldn't imagine what it would feel like to reach up into the cabinet for the coffee and filters. The adrenaline dump after the attack and the prescribed Demerol from the hospital had done their jobs masking the pain, but this morning both had worn off and Mike wasn't about to take another Demerol. He hated high-grade pain meds.

"Ouch," Mike said as he grabbed the coffee. "Glad I'm not in a bowling league."

Mike got the coffee going and the smell immediately perked up his senses. He was enormously glad they owned a Bunn coffee maker. In just a few short minutes he'd be sipping on "liquid alert" as Debbie called it. Coffee in the morning was normal. Mike liked normal, especially amidst all the abnormal that plagued his life at the moment. The television in the living room came to life, the sound of Little Einstein's on Nickelodeon filling the house.

"Hey sport," Mike said, finding Andrew on the couch, wrapped in a blanket.

"Hi, Daddy." Andrew responded without moving. "Mommy is still in bed. Is she alive?"

Mike's face sunk at the comment. "Of course little man. Why?"

"I didn't know if the bad men had come last night. I was worried." Andrew pulled the blanket up around his chin as Mike sat on the couch next to him.

"They aren't going to come back, Andy...not ever." Mike ran his fingers through Andrew's hair.

"What has this done to my son?" Mike asked himself as he crawled under the blanket with Andrew.

****

Marc Braden brought his car to a stop near the swarm of police vehicles crowding the bridge to Cockspur Island. It was six thirty in the morning. The gathering of police, Park, State and County Law Enforcement was so thick he couldn't decipher what had occurred. If it had been a bridge-jumper, he'd have received a call from the station telling him a small boat had responded. Apparently, this wasn't a jumper...at least not one that could be saved.

"What else? What now?" Marc said, rubbing his head, still sleepy.

Marc threw his car into park. Exiting the vehicle he caught sight of Alice Strong, the park director, arms crossed, eyes red and swollen from tears. A few cars ahead he saw members of his crew waiting to make it past the scene, necks craned in an effort of discovery.

"Head into work," Marc said, slapping the side of Hanks F-150.

Hank jumped in his seat, startled. "What do you think happened, Master Chief?"

"I'll find out, Hank. Just get to work and get folks going. I'll be there in a few minutes." Marc walked past Hank, coming up next to Alice as Hank rolled slowly past.

Noticing Marc, Alice turned, "Hello, Master Chief."

Marc stuffed his hands in his pockets, not sure what to do with them. "What happened, Alice? Is it something we can help with?"

Alice grabbed Marc's arm, squeezing a thank you. "We found Terry's car out here early this morning, abandoned. We think he committed suicide."

Marc stepped forward and peered over the hood of an ambulance to see Terry's abandoned vehicle and the nearly dried blood that covered the railing of the bridge. "Good Lord," Marc said, eyes dropping.

"We aren't sure. But, the Paramedic's found skull fragments, brain tissue and a .9mm shell casing. Terry carried a .9mm," Alice wiped her eyes. "The County Dive Team is on the way. They're going to dive… and drag for the body."

"When?" Marc asked. "When did this happen?"

"During the night or early morning," Alice replied. "We don't know. He wasn't authorized to be here last night."

"My God." Marc could feel another measure of energy escape his body. He didn't like Terry Macomb but this was tragic. There had been so much tragedy in such a short period of time, so much emotion, sorrow... anxiety.

"Will you let me know what happens?" Marc asked Alice, clutching her shoulder, "If there is anything we can do then..."

"Of course, Marc," Alice replied, patting Marc's hand.

Marc pulled his hand from Alice's shoulder slowly, letting her know that he was with her physically and spiritually. No leader, no supervisor was ever equipped to deal with situations like this. Marc, thank God, had never had to deal with the death of a crewman and had no idea how he would...if that time ever came. God willing, it wouldn't.

32

6:50AM

Chaplain Gary Carmichael sipped his coffee as he stared at the morning news broadcast. Another anonymous blonde reporter with over emphasized breasts was delivering headlines that no one, at least not the young men on the Station Tybee crew, paid any attention to. Gary heard several of the crew discussing the reporter's visit to the station earlier in the week and how "hot" she was. Gary wondered if the Coasties would ever realize that chaplains weren't immune to hearing about "hot" females, or, from the females, "hot" males. As Gary watched the reporter end her segment, he found himself agreeing with the crew.

Gary was relatively new to the Coast Guard and, as a group, found Coasties much more reserved and reverent than the other military services. Imbedded with Marines in Afghanistan, Gary's religious and spiritual background was offered no quarter. The Marines were brash and brazen and Gary supposed they had every right to be. In a span of seconds, Marines could go from the most earnest prayer to a string of obscenities that would make a hooker blush. Under fire, even Gary found himself uttering a few choice words from time to time. Afghanistan was so different, so intense, even the most reserved of men came to adopt a rugged, roughshod demeanor. For Gary, a tour with the Coast Guard was meant to be a break that returned him to the normal world.

As another sip passed Gary's lips the cook announced that morning chow had ended. The crew scurried from their seats, placing cups and plates on the counter and exiting the galley with a chorus of "See ya later Chaps," and, "Have a good day, Reverend." Gary, as always, responded jovially. The crew didn't realize that he was aboard for the weekend. Those were his orders. Gary just hoped Master Chief Braden didn't mind. Tybee had been going through a very rough time. The Sector Commander was concerned, but Gary didn't want to seem like a spy.

"Good morning Chaps," Jennifer Brooks announced her entrance into the galley, smiling at Gary as she proceeded to the coffee pot carrying two mugs.

"Double fisting this morning?" Gary smiled.

Jennifer looked at the mugs, snickered, then reached for the fullest carafe, "No… not yet anyway. One of these is for Master Chief."

Gary rose from his seat and walked to Jennifer's side. He was ready for a second cup of coffee, "He's in then?"

Jennifer topped off the mugs then filled Gary's cup. "He's in his office, wondering if you might join us for a chat?"

Gary dumped a creamer into his mug. "I most certainly will."

"Good…." Jennifer paused, sighed, and then smiled genuinely at Gary. "We're glad you're here."

"That's always nice to hear," Gary smiled back as Jennifer hefted the mugs and headed down the hall toward Marc's office.

Striding down the hall, Gary was again greeted by a string of "Good morning, Sir's," and "Hey…Chaps," from the crew. It was a duty relief day so the full bulk of the station's company was on hand. Gary knew quite a few of the faces but, regrettably, not many names. But at the door to the Communications Center Hank Morgan's face was readily identifiable.

"Petty Officer Morgan… how are you?" Gary patted Hank on the back.

"Chaplain, Sir, I'm fine. How are you?" Hank wheeled around with a warm greeting.

Gary had spent some time talking to Hank after Hank's father was diagnosed. Their conversations weren't overly complicated. Hank needed someone to talk to so he'd reached out to Gary. For Gary, that was the best part of his job… being there for someone in need. In Afghanistan he talked to Marines every day and about anything. Since he came to the Coast Guard the only real interaction he'd gotten came when something traumatic was happening in an individual's life. Other than that, Gary was a bit of a social pariah in this military branch.

"Hank, I'm doing great." Gary shot back. "Talk to you later?"

"Sure," Hank responded as Gary reached the Master Chief's office door, paused as Jennifer stepped out of the way, then accepted Jennifer's military courtesy by entering the office first.

****

Marc Braden rose from his desk, shooting a sharp glance toward Ryan and Gabriel who immediately leapt from their seats and snapped to attention.

"Good morning, Chaplain," Marc said, extending a hand to Gary. A brisk shake was followed by Marc accepting his mug of coffee from Jennifer. "Please have a seat," Marc motioned to a comfortable looking couch.

"It's great to be here, Master Chief," Gary said as he placed his coffee on an end-table and took a seat.

"I'm sorry there isn't time to be more cordial, Chaplain, but I need to speak with Seaman Beck and Fireman Ortiz about some important items."

Marc noticed Ryan and Gabriel exchanging worried glances. Both of them sported obvious bruises and their faces grimaced with a host of aches when they sat or stood. In many ways, Marc was glad that Jennifer had ordered the young men to the Station last night. Despite the ass-whipping they'd received, both looked well rested and somewhat recovered from the emotional torrent of the last two days. Marc wished he felt the same.

"Oh, please, don't amend your schedule for me, Master Chief," Gary replied.

Jennifer took a seat on the couch next to Gary as Marc plopped back into his chair. Everyone in the room could tell that Marc was exhausted. Marc's eyes seemed receded into his skull and the dark circles beneath them were undeniable. The truth was that, under almost any other circumstances, Marc would never have come to work in this condition, opting for a few extra hours of sleep or a "Chief's prerogative" day off. Neither was an option.

"Chaplain…" Marc began after a swig of coffee, "… you're here to help. Right now I think you might be able to."

"Fair enough…." Gary replied then assumed a quite position of observation.

Marc turned to Ryan and Gabe. "You two look like hell warmed over. What did the doc say?"

Gabriel nudged Ryan's arm, electing him the official spokesman. "We have some bumps and bruises and the doc said we should take it easy for a couple of days," Ryan replied.

"Light duty?" Marc asked.

"Two days light duty…no underway time." Jennifer responded for Ryan.

"I see." Marc leaned back in his chair examining Ryan and Gabe's faces, noting the bruises and the bandage Gabe wore above his left eye. "Explanation time boys."

Ryan looked at the floor considering his options. He could lie. It was the easiest thing to do. To Ryan it didn't matter that one lie could lead to another and another. He was used to fabricating. Fabrication had helped him maintain the reputation he desired. But last night, as he watched Gabe struggle into bed, the lies lost their importance. Not twenty-four hours earlier he and his best friend had nearly been killed by men Ryan didn't know and for a reason Ryan accepted as his personal responsibility. It was time to be honest… even if it hurt.

"Master Chief…" Ryan began, regret and guilt flooding over his face, "I am pretty sure that I am the reason this happened."

Marc rubbed his forehead with both hands. "Please don't say this Beck. Please don't tell me you took that dirty drug money."

Ryan fumbled with words, not sure how to respond.

"Go on," Jennifer prodded Ryan.

"I spend a lot of money. I spend a lot of money that I don't really have," Ryan held his head steady though his voice betrayed his nerves.

"We've noticed, Ryan." Marc responded, dreading the next few words to come from Ryan's mouth.

"I especially like to gamble, Master Chief. I bet a lot on sports and I don't do very well. I'm in the hole pretty deep. I think that's the money the guys who beat us up were after."

Marc was relieved, so much so that a momentary smile crept across his face. Marc regained his stone center. "You don't think it had anything to do with the drug money?"

"I don't know, Master Chief, maybe. But, I don't have that money. None of us has that money."

"I believe you," Marc replied with cautious relief. "But, they weren't there about your gambling." Marc turned to Jennifer as Ryan's faced locked in a surprised, frightened, pose. "Jennifer, get Rachel and Hank in here."

****

Rachel stepped off the 41683 holding two empty Pepsi bottles and a candy wrapper. As usual, the "other" duty section had left their trash on the boat, expecting Rachel and her section to clean up.

"There is no way I'm accepting this boat!" Rachel shot a pissed-off look at the off-going Officer of the Day, Petty Officer Manuel. "You guys need to clean this shit up!"

"Damn, Rachel, who pissed in your cereal this morning?" Manuel responded.

"I'm not your maid!" Rachel said, slamming the bottles and wrapper into Manuel's chest as she walked past and up the gangway to the main dock.

"You're in a good mood this morning," Laura said, catching up to Rachel.

"I'm just tired of Manuel's guys always leaving crap for us to take care of," Rachel stormed up the gangway. "It's ridiculous!"

"I agree."

Rachel stopped, looking up to see Hank staring at her with a smile.

"Don't patronize me this morning, Hank," Rachel responded.

"You need to calm down," Hank gathered himself into his best, official stance, "Are you okay this morning?"

"She's tired," Laura chimed in.

Rachel heaved a sigh. "I may be tired but that doesn't make me wrong."

"No one said that," Hank answered then looked past Rachel to where the 41683 was docked. "Manuel!" Hank yelled.

"We'll take care of it!" Manuel yelled back as he and two other crewmen climbed onto the boat, cleaning supplies in hand.

Hank turned to Rachel. "Why so tired?"

"I had a hard time getting to sleep," Rachel answered.

"Who didn't?" Hank thought.

"She went jogging in the middle of the night," Laura added.

"When?" Hank's tone intensified.

Rachel looked at Hank quizzically. "Around three or so. It sucked. I ran into Terry Macomb on one of his secret missions. I hate that guy."

"You saw Terry last night?" Hank asked urgently.

"Yeah…why?" Rachel responded.

"We need to go see Master Chief right now," Hank took Rachel by the arm and started up the dock toward the main building.

****

"Just the people I was looking for," Jennifer said as Hank and Rachel came down the hallway toward Marc's office. "How fortunate."

"We need to see Master Chief, XPO. It's important," Hank said, coming up short of Marc's office door with Rachel in tow.

"And he wants to see you too." Jennifer extended an arm, ushering them toward the office. "Come on."

Inside the office, Hank saw Ryan and Gabriel standing at attention facing Master Chief Braden's desk. Chaplain Carmichael sat on the couch, a look of curiosity and concern crossing his features. Master Chief's face was drawn, desperate.

"Hank, Rachel, come on in," Marc invited. "XPO, please shut the door."

Jennifer turned and closed the door with a dull thud that advertised "Do not disturb" to anyone nearby.

"I need to talk to all of you," Marc began. "Gabe, like it or not you're involved."

Gabriel rolled his eyes as if to say, "Great, just perfect."

"I'm never, ever hanging out with you again," Gabe whispered as he leaned close to Ryan.

"What is it, Master Chief?" Rachel asked, concerned.

Marc leaned forward, elbows on his desk. "Yesterday, these two..." Marc indicated Ryan and Gabriel, "... were assaulted by two African- American men."

"Ouch..." escaped from Hank's mouth as he surveyed Ryan and Gabe for the first time.

"These men..." Marc continued, "...demanded that Ryan and Gabe return their money."

"Drug money?" Rachel spat out.

"Yes, Rachel, drug money," Marc answered.

"I knew it. I knew it!" Rachel exclaimed, eyes focused on Ryan. "You son of a bitch!"

"Wait a minute!" Ryan screamed back at Rachel as tensions flared.

"Quiet!" Marc rose from his chair in full throat. "Ryan doesn't have the money, Petty Officer Stone! I am convinced that none of you took it. I always believed that."

Rachel turned to Ryan. "What about your phone Ryan? I know you used your phone when we were on scene with that boat."

Ryan's anger turned to embarrassment, "I used my phone to…"

"To what?" Jennifer asked.

"To call in some bets," Ryan responded, eyes sinking to the floor. "I had to. I needed to get ahead. I didn't think it could wait."

"You've got to be kidding me?" Jennifer spat out in disgust.

"I'm glad to hear it," Marc eased back into his seat as the entire room stared at him in disbelief. "I'm not glad that you have a gambling problem, Ryan, don't get me wrong. And…" Marc turned a scolding eye to Rachel

"...I'm not glad that you kept this information a secret, young lady. It could have made a huge difference early on. Don't ever hold back on me again!"

Marc let the moment rest, allowing Rachel and Ryan to process the chastisement. "I am glad, Ryan, that you admitted this to me. I'm glad that, now, we can get you some help. And, I'm glad that your shipmates..." Marc motioned toward Rachel and Hank, "... can lay their suspicions to rest. But, as relieving as this all is, I think we have good reason to stay alert, cautious and very vigilant."

"You know something?" Hank asked.

Marc took a drink of coffee. "Last night I was called by Agent Nguyen. We met and we spoke. Nguyen informed me that he had investigated what happened to Ryan and Gabe and he discovered that the men who attacked them were drug dealers. It had nothing to do with gambling money."

"Damn..." the word snuck out of Gabriel's mouth. "Oh... sorry, Chaplain."

"It's alright Gabe. That's actually a good choice of words." Gary sat on the edge of the couch now, wondering whether or not he wanted to hear any more.

But, if he was going to be any help, he needed to know as much as he could.

"There's more," Marc examined everyone's eyes. "These men were African-Americans."

"Is that significant?" Gary asked.

"Petty Officer Harwood and his wife were attacked by two African-American males," Hank answered Gary.

"And…" Marc continued, "…Nguyen and I met up with Deputy Martin and his partner last night. Come to find out, Martin had, without any good reason, gone to a homicide scene in South Carolina yesterday, to see the body of a dead black man."

"You think there's a connection?" Jennifer asked.

"I do. While we were together last night a group of blacks came into the restaurant. Agent Martin went out of his way to photograph them… and they did seem suspicious."

"Martin knows something," Hank said.

"I think he knows more than *something*. I think Martin is involved, somehow." Marc looked at Gabriel as Gabe shook his head back and forth. "Go ahead, Gabe."

"Damn," Gabe whispered.

"Yeah, damn," Gary added.

Hank let his mind wander as the room grew quiet, each person considering the implications of what Marc had offered. Marc's inference that John Martin was a "dirty cop" was suggestive of something from a Hollywood movie script. Drug lords, dead bodies, cops on the take... Hank could think of dozens of Coasties he'd met who would be salivating over this situation, eager to be "action heroes." Hank didn't want any of it but right now, he didn't have a choice.

"So, they know who we are. They know where we live. They think we have their money and they're willing to use violence to get it back." Hank crossed his arms, anxiety ramping up. "Do you think what happened to Terry Macomb had anything to do with this?"

"What happened to Terry?" Rachel asked excitedly.

Hank had forgotten why he was headed to Marc's office in the first place. Rachel, quite possibly, had been the last person to see Terry Macomb alive. "He's dead," Hank answered.

"What? I just saw him last night. When...?" Rachel couldn't believe what she was hearing.

"They think Officer Macomb committed suicide last night...sometime after three. His car was found, running, at the center span of the bridge and there was blood on the…" Marc cut short on the details as tears welled up in Rachel's eye's, "…they think it was suicide."

"What was he doing on the island that late?" Ryan chimed in.

"I was jogging last night, really late," Rachel stuttered. "He pulled up and told me he was protecting the island from vandalism."

"What else, Rachel?" Jennifer rose from the couch and patted Rachel on the back.

"He offered me a ride back to the station. But, then, a car pulled up at the front gate and he went to check it out." Rachel looked at Marc, sorrow and guilt clouding her eyes. "I didn't think he was suicidal. He didn't act it."

"It's alright, Rachel," Marc replied.

"I thought I heard gunshots last night, right before I fell asleep. But, I guessed it was the dumpster lid closing. It could have been Terry killing himself." Rachel was enveloped in self-blame and Jennifer eased her onto the couch where Gary reached out and clasped her hand.

"You said shot's, Rachel?" Hank asked.

"Yes. I think," Rachel replied in sobs.

"He shot himself twice?" Hank turned to Marc.

Marc met Hank's gaze, understanding Hank's point.

"Rachel," Marc climbed from his chair then bent down, coming eye to eye, "I want you to talk to Alice Strong." Marc reached out, delivering a reassuring squeeze to Rachel's knee. "I want you to tell her what you've told us."

Rachel nodded as Marc rose. "Ryan, Gabe…can you guys take Rachel outside?"

"Sure…sure thing, Master Chief." Ryan took Rachel's hand as he and Gabe lead her out of Marc's office.

"What a mess," Jennifer said as the door closed behind Ryan. "What the hell do we do now?"

Hank helped himself to a chair across from Marc's desk. "We don't know anything for certain. With all due respect, Master Chief, all you have is a hunch."

"You're right, Hank," Marc replied. "I can talk this up to anyone I want, but the fact of the matter is that I can't prove what I'm thinking."

"It's a pretty damn good hunch if you ask me," Jennifer interjected. "What does Nguyen think?"

"I believe he agrees with me…senses what's going on, but he's a purest. He likes knowing for sure." Marc turned and looked out the window. "I need to make sure this crew stays as safe as I can keep them, without looking like I'm suffering from total paranoia."

"I don't think you're paranoid, Master Chief," Gary offered. "I've been neck deep in some pretty scary stuff before and gut feelings kept people from becoming casualties."

"We can lock the gates down...post a guard, keep extra bodies awake at night making rounds," Jennifer pulled out a small pad of paper, ready to take notes.

"That sounds good. Make it happen," Marc agreed.

"What about Mike and Debbie? What about family members?" Hank asked, concern for Lori and Ally bleeding through.

"You were going to the Harwood's for dinner tonight, right, Chaps?" Marc asked Gary.

"That's the plan," Gary responded.

"I think there's safety in numbers. I'm going to send Ryan and Gabe with you Chaps and..." Marc turned to Hank, "I think Lori should show up too."

"What about your family?" Hank asked Marc.

"I'm sending them to Atlanta for the weekend."

"Why not have all the families get the hell out of dodge?" Jennifer asked.

"I can't order that. How long would they need to stay away? Could they afford it?"

"Lori is going back to Indiana sometime tomorrow." Hank interjected.

"It's their choice, XPO. But, for tonight we can keep everyone close-in," Marc nodded, agreeing with his own decisions.

"Our mission set is pretty light today. We have an escort tonight at eight. But, even with Ryan and Gabe gone and the extra watch, we'll have enough bodies to cover things." Hank said, relaying what he read on the operations calendar.

"Should we keep the off-going section on duty?" Jennifer asked.

"No. I don't want to go that far, yet. That may be something I do later but I need to talk to Nguyen," Marc scanned the grim looking group. "Get things going folks."

"Aye, aye...." Jennifer said as she headed for the office door. "Come on, Hank."

Hank rose from his seat, deep in contemplation. "Aye, aye, Master Chief," Hank said as he followed Jennifer out of the room.

"Chaplain?"

Gary turned to Marc.

"I know your background, Chaps. I know you've been in the shit before," Marc's eyes searched Gary. "Don't be afraid to act, if you need to."

"I won't, Marc," Gary headed for the door. "What are you going to do?"

Marc picked up his cell phone, waving it at Gary. "I haven't been able to reach this guy all morning," Marc sighed. "I need to find Jeff Nguyen."

33

6:30PM

Hank had no idea where the day had gone. The gates to the station had been locked since early this morning and not a single tourist had come by to gawk or to solicit a tour. The closed gates made the station feel like a penitentiary, like some gulag tucked into the depths of the Siberian wilderness. No one went in or out. No one wanted to unless they had good reason, not with all that was going on. Alice Strong had come by to speak to Rachel for a few minutes an hour earlier but she had been the only visitor.

"It might have been this way at the Fort," Hank thought aloud. "They were isolated and in danger too." Hank sighed. The atmosphere of the station was overwhelmingly tense. The anxiety level of the crew was peaked, and the secrecy of "need to know" disclosure had torn at the fabric of morale.

At nearly seven in the evening Hank stood on the pier jigging a fishing pole up and down. He didn't care if he caught anything but it would be nice if he did. A tug on the line and the ensuing struggle would offer a brief respite from the turmoil that, in the past five days, had become his life. Hank jigged, wondered if he still had any shrimp left on the hook, then laid the pole on the pier.

Lori and Ally were headed to Indiana in the morning. Early tomorrow, they were going to hitch a ride with Master Chief's wife and son then board a plane at Hartsfield-Jackson in Atlanta. By five-o-clock tomorrow afternoon they would be in Muncie on Lori's mom and dad's back porch. It was much better this way. But, for tonight, Lori and Ally would be at Mike and Debbie's for dinner and an extended, if not overnight, visit.

Master Chief left the station at two in the afternoon, setting out to find Jeff Nguyen who hadn't been reachable... hadn't checked in. The look on Braden's face was dire as he pulled out of the gate. Either from stress, worry, lack of sleep or a combination of all three, Braden looked like a walking skeleton. Hank had never seen Braden so weak...so unsure. The last thing Braden told Hank was to keep the armory safe unlocked. Braden wanted the firearms to be accessible. This scared Hank more than anything.

After lunch, while walking the grounds, Jennifer Brooks told Hank about Marc's conversation with the Sector Commander, a conversation to which she had been privy. As Marc spelled out some of his concerns, the captain had been almost amused. Braden, it appeared to Jennifer, was thought to be paranoid, inept and over reacting by his superiors.

"I don't give a shit if he is," Jennifer had said. "I'd rather do that than perfume this crazy shit up to the point where I could sleep well."

Jennifer was still at the station, sitting in her office pretending to go over the unit budget. Hank had been in her office twice in the past hour and, neither time, had the image on her computer changed. Hank's phone buzzed.

"Leaving for Debbie's...LY." The text from Lori read.

"I should be there," Hank spoke in a whisper as he read the words.

"They'll be okay, Hank," The soft voice drug Hank from his melancholy. It was Rachel.

In return for Rachel's assurances, Hank offered a half-hearted smile, void of any certainty. Rachel's true feelings were, unfortunately, the same. Of the four who'd found the wreck in Romerly Creek, Hank and Rachel were the only two to be spared persecution at the hands of strangers. In their hearts, both wished more that they had been, would be, confronted. The waiting and uncertainty wore heavily on them both.

Perhaps, Hank thought, it was some innate military trait, this desire to face up, boldly, to danger. All he knew for certain was that fear was the abyss on which his wits teetered.

"Alice just called the watchstander," Rachel spoke. "The park gate is locked for the evening."

Hank sighed. "Did they find Terry's body?"

"No." Rachel kicked at a pebble. "They're going to try again tomorrow."

"Are you okay?"

Rachel shrugged her shoulders, "I have to be."

Hank couldn't argue. He didn't want to argue. Rachel was right. She had to be ok…for now.

"Laura wants to know when you want her to take the 942 out for the escort."

Hank rubbed his eyes, feeling the strain of *one more* decision bearing down, "It's going to be a long one. Tell her to have the boat ready to go by seven-thirty."

"Sure thing," Rachel said then headed for the building.

****

Dennis marched out of his house, tossing a leather bag into the back seat of his BMW. The clank of metal on metal resounded as the weapons in the bag bounced against each other and amidst the ample boxes of ammunition Dennis had packed. His watch read six forty five, far too early to head for his rendezvous with Paul Sulsky and the thugs he'd hired the day before. But, more than enough time to take a swing through the city in hopes of locating Evan. Dennis wasn't too worried but he was concerned.

It wasn't unusual for Evan to go off the grid after a particularly nasty job. In the past, after a hit, Evan had disappeared for days. When he returned Evan always told Dennis it was "necessary." Dennis didn't question Evan's motivations. Evan was a professional and had the record to prove it. In the few years Dennis had been associated with him, Evan had "taken care" of at least a dozen people, male and female, and the police had never come close to sniffing out his involvement. In the back of his mind, Dennis believed Evan went M.I.A. in order to drown what little guilt he felt in bourbon. Now was a really inopportune time for Evan to be drunk in some backwater hotel. Dennis knew Evan would show up, eventually, tonight, or Evan would pay a hefty price.

****

Ra drank the last of his soda and tossed the can across the room, just missing the trash can. William and the goons hovered around the remaining few slices of delivery pizza wiping pepperoni grease from their mouths, listening to rap music from William's smart phone. The small arsenal, a pistol for each man and two shotguns, lay on an empty queen-size bed gleaming with fresh gun-oil, ready for tonight's assault.

"Assault…" Ra thought the word. That's what it was. It was like some Special Forces mission from "Call of Duty." Ra and William would head for the Coast Guard Station while the thugs went to the Harwood's home. The money had to be in one of those places and Ra intended to find it. This was going to be Ra's rite of passage. After tonight, he wouldn't be just another small-time dealer. A hit on a federal installation, a clean hit, would make him respected, maybe even a god. He'd be referred to in the same breath with the big Mexican Cartel's and their powerful leaders. If the "cracker-ass" dealer from Savannah happened to get in his way... all the better. One less competitor was never bad.

"A quarter million is a lot of cash, man," One of the goons spoke, breaking Ra from thought. "But, is it worth what we're doing?"

"Having second thoughts?" Ra asked the man, leaning back in his chair, staring at the hotel room ceiling.

No one spoke.

"Let me tell you the difference between a quarter million dollars and a quarter million dollars worth of drugs," Ra's focused in on the goon. "I can make or I can grow a quarter million dollars worth of drugs for less money than I've spent feeding your fat asses today."

Ra had the men's attention.

"You see all these cops on the news, smiling about the street value of the shit they seize...that's a bunch of bullshit they're talking. Drugs aint got shit for value until they get sold. Why the hell you think the Mexicans toss that shit in the water out their boats? Why the hell you think the runners just give up so easy?"

"Cause they're scared as hell," one of the goons offered.

"No," Ra sat up. "It aint that. It's because every one pound of product they lose can be immediately replaced with another thousand. It doesn't cost them shit to make more. It doesn't cost them shit to lose boats or men or planes. All that shit is nothing... it's economics, you simple ass."

William nodded his understanding as the goons stared blankly, pondering.

"A quarter of a million dollars is equal to millions and millions of plants and pills, that can make you tens of millions. The money is always more important than the product. If we lose that money we lose a hell of a lot more. We need to scare mother fuckers off our money. We need to make sure they don't want to play in our yard!"

"And the killing don't matter." William added.

Ra smiled at William, "No. It doesn't matter. Fuck them. They'll get a nice burial. They'll be heroes."

"And if we don't find the money?" a goon asked.

"We're gonna get paid...one way or another." Ra answered.

It was ten after seven and the sun was starting to set.

****

"Hope you're hungry," Gary Carmichael stepped through the door holding two huge bags filled with Kentucky Fried Chicken and all the fixings. "I told you I was bringing diner."

"Thank you, Chaplain," Debbie replied with a smile as she took one of the bags from Gary. "You didn't have to."

"My pleasure..." Gary shook a hand offered by Mike. "Besides, we're a little late tonight."

"Not for us," Mike replied warmly. "Seven is dinner time around here."

"Hey, Mike," Ryan said, following Gary in the door.

"Hey, Boats," Gabe added.

"Ryan? Gabe?" Mike raised an eyebrow. "What are ya'll doing here?"

Gary turned to Ryan and Gabe. "I invited them along…hope you don't mind."

"We don't," Debbie shouted from the kitchen. "They look worse than we do." Debbie added, indicating the bruises and cuts on Ryan and Gabe's faces.

"That's true," Mike said as he shut and locked the door.

"Who do we have here?" Gary walked across the room, holding out a hand to Lori who rose and accepted gladly.

"I'm Lori. I'm Petty Officer Morgan's wife."

"Yes, Lori, Hank has told me about you…" Gary smiled, "… and all good." Gary chuckled. "Who are these two?"

"That is my daughter, Ally, and that is Mike and Debbie's son, Andrew," Lori pointed out the children who were transfixed by the coloring books and crayons spread out across the floor. "They're deep in their artwork." Lori added.

Gary leaned over, peering at the coloring. "Looks good. We shouldn't interrupt them."

"Want to sit?" Mike asked Gary.

"And Ryan and Gabe can help get this on the table," Debbie directed.

Gary found a comfortable position in a chair next to the front window. It was a perfect vantage point to monitor the front of the home. Ryan and Gabe went into the kitchen. As Ryan helped Debbie, Gabe checked the back door and flicked on the back porch lights. A quick scan of the yard and back alley showed nothing unusual.

It had been a different, intense day in the company of Chaplain Carmichael. After addressing the crew at morning quarters, the chaplain packed Ryan and Gabe into his government vehicle and set out for the Harwood's home. Unbeknownst to Mike and Debbie, the chaplain had cased their home and their neighborhood looking for ways in and out, formulating a plan...just in case.

"You really think we're in danger, don't you, Chaps?" Gabe had asked.

"I think an ounce of prevention is worth a pound of cure," Gary had responded.

Late in the afternoon, Mike had snuck out of the house to the Seven-Eleven down the street, where he'd met up with Gary, Ryan and Gabe to discuss things. Gary made Mike aware of the danger that might exist, and Mike hadn't argued. Everyone agreed to try to keep Debbie, Lori and the children as at ease as possible, though the tension of the time was evident. It hung in the air like fog.

"Thanks for coming over, Chaps," Mike said as he found a seat on the couch next to Lori. "And, thanks for the dinner."

"Like I said... it's my pleasure. Shoot, I'm a single guy and being a man of the cloth... a Friday spent in the company of some good folks, at a fantastic home, is about as wild as I get," Gary smiled the reply.

"Lori..." Gary began, "... I understand you're taking a vacation to Indiana?"

"To see my Grammy and Papa," Ally responded from the floor, not looking up from her coloring.

"I don't call it a vacation," Lori replied. "Hank thinks its better that we are..." Lori paused, searching for the right words, "...somewhere else for a while."

"When are you heading out?"

"Tomorrow morning. We're going to get a ride with the Braden's to Atlanta. Our flight leaves in the afternoon."

"I understand." Gary looked into Lori's face, letting her know that he understood it *all*... that he knew the *why's*.

"I wish I did," Lori replied, staring at her hands.

"Boat's, where's the bathroom?" Gabe came from the kitchen and tapped Mike on the shoulder.

"Down the hall..." Mike pointed, "...second door on the left.

Gabe headed down the hall quietly as Gary looked at the clock on the wall behind Mike. Gabe was doing his job. Every few minutes, he or Ryan were to make a round of the home, looking out the windows in the back rooms, hopefully not getting caught. It was Gary and Mike's job to distract the attention of Debbie and Lori through conversation.

"What happens later, when people want to leave or go to bed?" Gary thought to himself. He hadn't figured that part out yet but, there was still time.

"Everything's ready," Debbie called from the kitchen. "Let's eat."

34

8:10PM

Marc Braden had been looking for Jeff Nguyen since before noon. Every phone call had gone immediately to voicemail. A quick call to the CGIS office in Charleston let Marc know that Jeff hadn't been in touch with them either. Jeff hadn't been to the Sherriff's Department, he wasn't at his hotel...Marc had checked. It was eight thirty in the evening, the sun was gone and Marc was grasping at straws.

"What was that guy's name?" Marc asked himself as he searched his mind.

Marc had somehow managed to locate John Martin's residence and had spoken to Martin's wife. She had no idea where John was and didn't seem overly concerned. For her, she said, the less she knew about John's job the better off she was. She knew he did a lot of undercover work and that this "wouldn't be the first time" he hadn't come home. The smell of alcohol on the woman was unmistakable. Marc knew his fair share of military spouses who'd found comfort in a bottle. Marc supposed that drinking somehow countered the nights alone and the not knowing. Marc left her with a "thank you" and whispered a prayer for her as he backed out of the driveway.

The Sherriff's department had been little- to- no help. Given the nature of John and Mitch's work, the department stopped just short of denying their existence. Getting an address or a phone number was out of the question and, once again, undercover deputies didn't work a monitored schedule so their whereabouts weren't readily known. Mark only hoped that after he left, someone from the department would try to contact John or Mitch. Marc hoped that their lack of alarm was a façade.

"What was his name?" Marc said aloud, slamming a fist against the steering wheel.

"Mitch, what?" Marc fought with his sleep-deprived mind. He had heard Mitch's name at least once. Jeff Nguyen had said it. It was when they were in the car headed for the diner. "I need coffee." Marc thought as he whipped into the parking lot of an unnamed convenience store.

The coffee smell was overwhelming which meant the coffee Marc was about to purchase had been steeping in a pot for more than a few hours. There was no amount of creamer that could make the java taste anything unlike hot asphalt so Marc didn't bother.

"One dollar, Sir," the pimple faced teen behind the counter said vacantly, not bothering to look up from his magazine.

Marc dug in his pocket, produced a dollar bill and tossed it on the counter.

"And…" the teen looked up at Marc with half closed eyes, "… would you like to purchase a lottery ticket? The daily drawing for tomorrow is more than a hundred thousand dollars."

Marc sighed, "I don't think so, son."

The teen returned to his reading as Marc walked for the door, then froze in place.

"What did you just say?" Marc turned to the teen. "Which drawing?"

"The daily, Sir. Would you like a ticket?"

"I just won the lottery," Marc said as he charged out the door to his car.

Marc fumbled with the cell phone as he plopped into the vehicle. "Hello, Rachel."

"Master Chief? How are you?" Rachel asked.

"No time for conversation, Rachel. I need you to get on the computer in the watch room and I need you to find me an address for a man named Mitch Dailey. I need it fast!"

****

At ten in the morning, maybe, Jeff had found a sliver of consciousness. Again and again there was a feeling of wetness on his face. Through slits of eyes he saw Beauregard standing by him, felt the dog licking his face… hoped the dog wasn't tasting him. At least he wasn't dead. The waked moments didn't last long. Jeff tried to move and the exertion sent him back into blackness.

In the late afternoon, Jeff guessed, he'd been roused by the sound of a vehicle and screams and chatter. It was a school bus unloading children on the main road near the entrance to Mitch's driveway. The bus and children may as well have been a million miles away. Jeff didn't have enough energy to cry out. Beauregard was lying next to Mitch's body, diligently guarding his master, waiting for Mitch to wake up. Jeff could see dried blood on the dog's coat. The dog had been hurt. Jeff passed out again.

Now, Jeff woke to darkness and the sound of the gravel driveway rumbling under the wheels of an approaching vehicle. Beauregard was on his feet, standing over Mitch's body, barking at the top of his lungs and illuminated by the approaching headlights. Jeff had to move. He prayed he could find the strength. God only knew who was coming up the drive. It could be salvation or it could be someone coming to finish the job Evan had started.

As the vehicle skidded to a stop, Jeff's hand found purchase on the grip of a pistol. He didn't know whose. He didn't care. Beauregard's barking was so loud, so intense. Struggling to a sitting position; Jeff raised the pistol as a car door opened.

"Easy, boy... easy." The voice was familiar and Jeff lowered the pistol.

"Marc!" Jeff found the wind to scream the name, then slumped against the side of his car.

Marc heard the desperate call and ran to the sound of the voice. In the moonlight, Marc could see the body laid out on the front porch of the house and the dried blood spattered against the home siding.

"My God! What's happened here?" Marc said as he rounded the rear of Jeff's car.

Beauregard continued to bark as Marc took in the horrific scene. Mitch Dailey lay on the ground, stiff and already bloating amidst a pool of dried blood. Next to Mitch, the body of some other man lay covered in blood, contorted in rigor mortis. And then there was Jeff Nguyen. Jeff was propped up against the open driver's side door of his car, right arm dangling at his side, covered in dried blood. Jeff's breathing was shallow, his eyes narrow slivers of white, looking up at Marc. Beauregard quieted as Marc knelt at Jeff's side.

"You're alive," Marc said as he felt Jeff's pulse and visually examined the wounds.

"I feel dead," Jeff responded, reaching out, grasping Marc's arm. "I'm glad to see you," Jeff whispered. "What day is it, Marc? What time is it?"

Marc removed his sweatshirt, ripping off a sleeve to use as a bandage for Jeff's arm. The wounds weren't bleeding but, if Jeff became active, they could easily start again.

"That doesn't matter right now," Marc answered as he put pressure on the wounds, "We have to get you to a hospital."

"It does matter!" Jeff insisted, mustering the best shout he could.

Marc stopped, shocked, and looked at his watch, "Its Friday, Jeff. It's getting close to nine."

"Oh my God," Jeff said.

"What is it, Jeff? What's wrong?"

"The crew... their families, they're all in danger, Marc."

Marc froze, terror filled his face.

"I found information. They are coming after the money tonight, Marc. They may already be there. You've got to call the police. They're coming on a boat."

Marc fumbled for his cell. Opening the face, he shook as he dialed 9-1-1. The phone was silent as Marc waited for what seemed an eternity then it beeped. Marc pulled the phone away from his ear, staring at the screen.

"No service! Damnit! This phone is a piece of shit!" Marc moved the phone around over his head.

"Try mine. I had service out here." Jeff pointed to the phone lying on the ground by the car.

Marc grabbed the phone. "No battery!"

"Just go, Marc!" Jeff pushed Marc away with his good arm, "Just go and call for help when you get a signal. I'll be okay. The dog will look after me."

Marc stood, "Stay alive!" he ordered Jeff.

Jeff tried a smile then held out his pistol to Marc, "Take it! Go fast!" Jeff ordered in return.

Marc grabbed the pistol then ran for his car. He didn't know how far he'd have to go to get a signal but, he knew he was thirty minutes away from the station.

"God help us," Marc said as he flew out of the driveway.

35

"942 – Station, op's and position," Rachel transmitted. Laura and her crew had been underway for escort duty since seven- thirty and Rachel had dutifully checked their status, as required, every thirty minutes.

"Station - 942, operations as before, nearing Elba Island Cut, 942 out," Laura responded.

The vessel to be escorted, a relatively small liquid natural gas (LNG) hauler, had been late to the rendezvous point at the Savannah Sea Buoy. This was a common occurrence. It wasn't often that the unit was tasked with escorting ships, this function was more a show of willingness, operational alertness and vigilance, designed to keep any possible terrorists guessing and concerned. As Master Chief said, it was "deterrence," the best form of protection the Coast Guard could offer. Still, for the poor sap that had to man the bow-mounted M240 machine gun, the ride was a salt water spray-soaked test of endurance. Though they carried ammo, they never loaded the gun for LNG escorts. One errant tracer round could, maybe, cause the LNG tanker to explode, thereby reducing the city of Savannah to cinders. The bow gunner was strictly for show.

"She sounds frustrated," Hank said as he poked away at the keyboard of the watch room computer.

"She has a right. They were an hour late," Rachel said as she finished recording her conversation with the 942 in the radio log. "Is she still here?"

"She is," Hank responded, referring to Jennifer Brooks. "She is making a round. She's just as tense as the rest of us."

Rachel grabbed a microphone, "Portable One – Station."

"Station – Portable One," Jennifer Brooks responded.

"Just checking in," Rachel transmitted.

"Station – Portable One, everything's quiet. I'm checking the shop buildings then the gate… will let you know when complete. Portable One, out."

"She's got guts," Rachel commented as Hank pushed away from the computer.

"We all do. We have too," Hank stood. "But, I wish I had more."

Hank looked out the windows at the piers, noticing the stillness of the tide. It was five after nine and, right on schedule, the Savannah River had reached slack tide, waiting patiently to start its ebb of water back into the Atlantic. "Did Master Chief say anything about why he needed that address?"

"No," Rachel responded. "He just said he was amazed that I found it at all...then he hung up." Rachel stood, joining Hank at the windows. "He sounded so...urgent."

"I hope he's alright," Hank sighed.

"How's Lori?"

"She texted me a few minutes ago... said Ally was getting tired but that she didn't want to go home," Hank sighed.

"Ally didn't want to go home, or Lori?"

"Lori," Hank replied softly. "I'm going to get some water. You need anything?"

"I'm okay," Rachel replied as she returned to her chair.

Hank exited the watch room and walked down the main hallway toward the galley. He, Rachel and Jennifer were the only people at the Station and, combined with a feeling of impending doom, the quiet was even more disconcerting. Hank paused at the door to the main office, looking toward Jennifer Brook's computer screen. The same page was still displayed... some random piece of a manual. The lights went out, the hallway went black.

"Hank!" Rachel yelled from the watch room as the emergency lights came on.

"Where's Jennifer?" Hank thought to himself as he heard the emergency generator in the next building begin to fire up. The machine whined and barked and chugged, then fell silent.

****

Jennifer came out of the shop building, flashlight and radio in hand, headed for the front gate. She couldn't concentrate on anything other than the possibility of some miscreants descending on the station to inflict indescribable bodily harm on the crew. She was tired, the hyper-vigilance and stress were taking their toll on her body. She couldn't imagine what Master Chief and the rest of the crew who were directly affected were feeling.

Jennifer had spoken with Alice Strong earlier in the afternoon. She explained the safety concerns and Alice, still roiling from Terry's alleged suicide, eagerly promised to make sure the front gate was monitored throughout the night. For this reason, Jennifer had decided to forego carrying a firearm on her round. The only way on or off the island was through the front gate. That gate was guarded. They were safe…more or less, but the unease was hard to shake. Jennifer didn't suppose she would sleep tonight.

She heard the rustling behind her just in time to turn around and take the full force of the shotguns butt in her forehead. Her head spun as she hit the ground in a daze, the pain shooting through her skull like white-hot blades.

She reached for her radio and a massive, booted foot swung down into her forearm, sending the radio tumbling across the lawn. In a flash of movement the large man fell on her, placing a rough hand over her mouth and his knee in her stomach. Others, other men, scrambled past. One headed for the shop building. One headed for the power panel on the side of the main structure.

"I want my money." Dennis crouched down, looking into Jennifer's face as she tried to fight against the man who held her. "You may have it. You may know where it is, or one of your friends does."

The station's lights flickered out as Dennis grabbed Jennifer by the hair, yanking her face toward his. "I'm going to get it back, get repaid, one way or another."

Jennifer heard the emergency generator try to start. It didn't. The other man had sabotaged the machine. She thought about Hank and Rachel, wished she had brought a sidearm with her, then found a way to bite the big man's hand, drawing blood, tearing flesh.

As the man withdrew his hand in pain, Jennifer screamed. "Hank! Rachel! Run!"

Dennis pulled a pistol from behind his back.

The shot echoed across the stillness of the island.

****

Paul Sulsky sat in the pilothouse of the Gina Marie, watching the pines, looking for movement. He'd done what he had to do. Dennis and his three hired hands had shown up at his dock early, at eight forty. The lines were cast off by eight forty five and they arrived here at Cockspur Island at five after nine. Evan wasn't with Dennis. Evan didn't show up at all, but Dennis hadn't seemed to care. Dennis only said "Fuck him" and then ordered Paul to get moving. There were a lot of guns on Paul's boat. Dennis and his men had brought a lot of guns.

The trip to the island had been a nervous one. Thanks to radar, Paul had detected the smaller Coast Guard boat traveling up the river, escorting the LNG tanker. Paul immediately illuminated his deck lights, stepped away from the helm, told Dennis to stay out of sight, and pretended to wash his decks as the Coasties powered by. They paid him no mind. The Gina Marie looked like a shrimp boat at the end of the day, cleaning up, getting ready to head home. When Paul reentered the pilot house he saw one of the hired hands leaning over a high-powered rifle, taking aim at the person behind the machine gun of the Coast Guard boat.

"Is that what they intend to do?" Paul thought as he slowly crept toward Cockspur, guilt weighing heavier on his conscience.

"Maybe they just mean to scare them," Paul told himself. "Sure… just to make them nervous or something." He concluded in silence as the upstream tip of Cockspur came onto his radar. In the next few minutes he would be at the spot where he could nose the Gina Marie into the soft mud and allow Dennis and his thugs to debark.

Now, several minutes or eternities later, Paul sat on the Gina Marie watching. Dennis and his men had crawled down a rope ladder rigged over the bow and had scampered into the tree-line. After that, Paul didn't see a thing, just the dark outlines of pines and beyond that, the faint glow of the Coast Guard Station's lights. Those lights went out.

"What the hell are those boys doing?" Paul said.

"What am I doing?" Paul asked himself.

This was all about money. People were getting hurt over money. Innocent people were being harmed because of what Paul was doing. Paul heard the report of a pistol and his heart sank in his chest.

Paul grabbed the Gina Marie's throttles and slammed them down hard in reverse. The boat grumbled off the mud bottom. Paul could hear the sound of oyster shells being blown into the hull, see the mud swirling up around the stern of his boat, and then the Gina Marie was free. Paul wheeled into deeper water as he slammed the throttles into forward gear.

"Not because of me God Damnit!" Paul yelled as he headed toward the Coast Guard Station's piers. "Not because of me!" The Gina Marie lurched forward as the pilothouse radio came to life.

"Coast Guard Station Tybee, Coast Guard Station Tybee, this is Sector Charleston on channel sixteen," The voice was urgent, the message repeated again. No one answered.

36

9:10PM

"And so, for a grand total of thirty chocolate bars, ten MRE's and a Beyonce CD, the guy let us use the showers in his house," Gary laughed out the end of his story.

"That's an expensive shower," Debbie remarked as she sipped at her soda.

"It was a bargain," Gary stated confidently. "After two weeks marching through the Afghanistan summer the Taliban could smell us coming."

The room chuckled. Gary had been regaling the room with stories of his time in Afghanistan for the past hour. At this point, Gary was forcing conversation in an effort to keep everyone awake, interested and, hopefully, from the desire to leave. For the most part, everyone had that "I wish he would shut up" look on their faces, everyone except for Lori who desperately insisted that Gary continue. Lori didn't want Gary, Ryan, or Gabe to leave. More than that, Lori didn't want to go home.

It was still early, only ten after nine, but to the people in this house, in their current mental and physical state, it felt like the wee hours of the morning. Gary wished, in hindsight, that he'd brought anything but carb-laden comfort food for dinner. Everyone had a belly full of fried chicken, biscuits and mashed potatoes. The children had already succumbed to the meal and were sacked out under blankets on the floor, in front of muted episodes of Phineas and Ferb.

"I need to hit the toilet," Ryan said as he stood from his chair.

"Again?" Debbie asked.

"I have a weak bladder. I can't help it," Ryan replied as he scurried off.

Between the two of them, Ryan and Gabe had made ten trips to the bathroom in the past two hours, both claiming to have bladder control issues. Gary wished the boys had been a little less overt, for fear of raising suspicion, but so far Debbie and Lori didn't seem concerned. Gary watched as Ryan entered the hallway, looked over his shoulder, then ducked into Andrew's bedroom.

"May I have some more tea?" Gary asked Gabe.

"I can get it for you," Lori said, grabbing Gary's glass and heading for the kitchen.

Gabe sprang from his chair. He knew Gary wanted him to check the back door.

Earlier, Debbie had insisted that everyone take a seat in the living room and Gabe was forced to comply. As such, the back of the house had only been checked twice in the past hour. Mike and Gary had been able to keep a passive vigil over the front. The trips to the bathroom were adequate to check the sides but the back of the house....

"Let me help," Gabe said.

"It's tea, Gabriel," Lori said. "I think I can handle it." Lori pushed past Gabe and into the kitchen. Gabriel turned to Gary and Mike, shrugging with a look that said, "I tried."

Gary gave Gabe an "It's okay" look as Gabe, looking over his shoulder at Lori, returned to his seat. "How about you, Mike?" Gary asked, turning to Mike. "Any good stories to share?"

"Oh, no. Don't get him started," Debbie rolled her eyes.

Mike didn't hear anything. He was staring out the front window, noticing a car that had parked halfway down the block. Mike watched as two men exited the car, went to the trunk, then disappeared from view behind fences and trees. The hair on Mike's neck stood up. He craned his neck this way and that, trying to find the men again.

"Mike?" Gary asked, leaning forward in his chair, following Mike's line of sight out the window.

From the corner of his eye Gary caught a flash of motion on the porch stairs, saw the man's form come to the top, saw the shotgun rise from the man's side.

"Get down!" Gary shouted, diving from his chair, grabbing Mike as he went.

The shot came through the front window, shattering it, sending a shower of broken glass across the floor and onto the children who sprang up at the sound. Gabe flew forward, tackling Debbie to the ground as Ryan ran from the back bedroom.

"Lori!" Gary yelled as a blast blew open the back door of the house, bits of shattered wood spraying onto

Lori as she screamed and fell to the floor.

****

Ra and William pulled up to the main gate of Cockspur Island seeing the squad car parked at the top of the bridge.

"Damn!" Ra slapped the dashboard as the squad's lights came on, blue beams occulting through the darkness.

"What now?" William asked.

Ra considered the situation. He would not be denied his moment of infamy, the moment he became something more than he was. "Flash our lights at them and then get out and wave," he directed William.

"What?"

"I'm sick. I'm hurt. You need them to help... to call an ambulance," Ra instructed William.

"And when they get close? When they see you aren't sick?"

"Then I'm gonna shoot the mother fucker!" the rage in Ra's voice pierced the air.

William flashed the headlights repeatedly.

"Now, get out!" Ra pushed William.

William climbed out of the car and began waving his arms frantically toward the squad.

****

Alice watched the headlights flash, watched as the big man climbed from the car and waved. Maybe they needed help? Maybe they had seen her from the highway, parked atop the bridge? This wouldn't be the first time people had needed help and had come to the gate to get it. Over the years countless numbers of people had come to the park for help. The park was the only real structure between Wilmington Island and Tybee Island. Alice and her staff had dealt with everything from "out of gas" to "my wife's in labor." Still, given what she had heard from Jennifer Brooks, caution was called for.

"Dispatch – PD 334," Alice spoke into her radio's microphone.

"334 – Dispatch," a voice replied.

"I have a 10-37, suspicious vehicle. I am moving to investigate," Alice informed the voice.

"10-4," the voice responded.

Alice put the squad in drive and rolled slowly toward the waving stranger. At least someone knew she was here…what she was doing.

"They're coming." William said as Alice drew closer.

Ra tucked his pistol into the folds of his hoodie then lay back in the seat, feinting illness.

****

"They can't reach them," Laura barked at the crew of the 942. "Sector is trying to raise the station and they can't."

"Maybe Rachel went to pee?" Shawn Jones yelled through the front hatch of the 942 from his position on the bow gun.

"It's possible," Petty Officer Lyle.

Laura paused, considering the circumstance, as yet another call to the Station, from the Sector, came over the radio.

"I don't like it!" Laura brought the 942 to neutral. Inside the cell phone box, a ringing was heard.

"Open it," Laura reached across her seat, snatching the box from Lyle, flinging the lid open and grabbing her ringing phone just before it went to voicemail. "Petty Officer Hill," Laura answered.

The voice on the other end of the line was frantic, "Laura! It's Master Chief! I need you to give me your full attention."

"Is something happening?" Laura asked. "What's going on?"

"Laura, the crew back at the Station is in trouble. It may be on their doorstep already."

Laura waved her hand at the 942 crew, demanding they be quiet.

Marc continued, "You need to drop the escort and head back. When you get there, I want you to get everyone on the 942 and stay away from the unit. Head for Hilton Head."

"I can do that, Master Chief," Laura engaged the engines and started her turn back toward the Station.

"Be on the lookout for a boat, Laura, a shrimp boat. The bad guys were going to use a shrimp boat to get onto the island."

Laura's heart sank, "We passed a shrimp boat a few minutes ago. It was close to the Station but it wasn't…."

"That may have been them," Marc said as he swerved around and past a slower vehicle. "You may be headed for a fight, Laura. I'm authorizing you to do whatever it takes to meet any threat."

"Understood," Laura responded, grim determination settling over her psyche.

"I'm not too far away from the island," Marc's voice softened, trying to bring calm to the mind of his subordinate amidst the most difficult of situations. "Be safe, Boatswain's Mate."

The call ended and Laura gathered herself. The crew inside the cabin had overheard the conversation. The aft gunner was digging into his ammunition pouch, loading slugs into the Remington shotgun. Shawn was crouched down, peering in through the forward hatch, waiting.

"Go to full load on the 240 and hang on!" Laura

screamed at Shawn as she slammed the throttles full-forward.

****

The gunshot was loud, passing through the walls, echoing down the darkened corridors of the building. At the sound, Hank dropped to the floor and army-crawled to the armory door as Rachel called to him from the watch room.

"Get down and be quiet!" Hank yelled through the dark.

Hank reached up to the doorknob of the armory. "Son of a bitch," Hank whispered to himself. The armory door had an electronic lock. Hank fumbled with the cumbersome rings of keys attached to his belt loop, one of the two held the actual key to the armory. Motion in the corner of Hank's vision startled him to a defensive position.

"It's just me." Rachel crawled into the main office space, coming up next to Hank, holding a portable VHF-FM radio and the keys to the unit's government vehicle. "What happened to Jennifer? Was that a gunshot?"

Hank didn't answer as he managed to grab the armory key-ring from his belt. In the dim light Hank found the lock then slowly, quietly, opened the armory door. A sound came from the side door of the station, the doors Master Chief had told the crew to keep locked…thank God.

"My God, Hank. What's happening?" Rachel remained on the ground as Hank swung open the door to the armory safe, grabbing two pistols and four magazines of ammunition.

"Here," Hank handed a pistol and ammunition to Rachel.

Rachel knew, now, what was happening. They had all been denying the possibility that danger this great could become a reality. But, here it was. Rachel never expected it, not like this. Even after what had happened to Mike and Debbie, even after Ryan and Gabe and the death of Terry Macomb… she didn't believe. Rachel's hands shook as she loaded the weapon… worked the slide. Jennifer Brooks might be dead. Rachel and Hank might be next. Rachel began to hyperventilate.

"Look at me," Hank knelt, his face in front of Rachel's. "You have to find a way to get very deliberate right now." Hank's tone was firm, authoritative. "You need to get in touch with every last bit of your training and a damn good bit of common sense. I need that,

Petty Officer Stone!" Glass shattered somewhere on the main floor of the building.

Hank reached back into the armory safe, grabbing body armor for both of them, "We're going to use our defensive tactics training," Hank said as he velcro'd his body armor in place. "We need to move and we need to get out of the building."

Rachel nodded, "What about the radio?" Rachel indicated the portable she'd brought from the watch room as she donned her armor.

Hank found a roll of scotch tape atop a nearby desk. Hank turned the radio on to channel sixteen, the distress and hailing frequency, then taped the transmit button down. Everyone would hear them and what was occurring, but Hank didn't want a response that would give his position away.

"This is Coast Guard Station Tybee," Hank whispered into the radio. "We are being attacked by an unknown number of persons. Shots have been fired. We require immediate assistance." Hank clipped the radio to his belt as the sound of footsteps could be heard coming from the galley.

"We go now. I've got the lead. We're going to try to get out through the floor hatch in the watch room." Hank waited for Rachel to nod a response. The watch room was no more than twenty feet away. In the floor, behind the radio console, was a hatch that dropped down into the station's crawl space. If they made it there then maybe, maybe they could sneak their way to the far side of the property and head into the woods. Rachel nodded.

Hank crab walked to the office door then took a quick peek into the main hallway as Rachel positioned herself behind him. In the moment he looked down the hall, Hank could see a flashlight beam probing the galley. The bad guys were threatening but they weren't professionals. They hadn't taken the time to, if she was dead, search Jennifer's body where they would have discovered a master key for the unit, and they were using flashlights. Flashlights, Hank had been trained, were a "Here I am! Blow my head off!" signal. Shoot the light and you'll probably kill what's behind it. For what it was worth, Hank knew he and Rachel had some advantage.

It was all hand signals now. Hank pointed to the corridor, to the near wall. He would exit the room first. Rachel would follow. Hank took another quick peek, no one in the hall yet, then silently moved out of the office, taking up a position, six inches off the wall, sighting in on the far, exterior doorway. Rachel slid out of the office, facing the galley until she felt her back bump Hank's. They crept along the wall toward the watch room as a flashlight beam came through the far doorway's window.

"Shit!" Hank thought. They were at the doorway to the watch room. They just needed a few seconds.

A flashlight illuminated Hank and Rachel. It was the intruder in the galley. Rachel fired.

****

Lori screamed and rolled herself out the back door of the kitchen and into the hallway just as the man burst into the house. The man caught sight of her as she ducked into the hall and fired a shotgun blast that barely missed Lori's legs, sending a shower of drywall and wood in all directions.

Gabe grabbed Andrew and Ally, shoving them into the fireplace for cover as another shotgun blast tore through the front window. The shot ricocheted off the hearth, one of the lead pellets grazing Gabe's leg as he hit the ground rolling toward a frantic Debbie.

"Stay down!" Mike yelled as he crawled to the wall under the shattered picture window.

Gary flung his back up against the wall next to the front door. The man who had entered through the kitchen hadn't noticed him yet but, if he did, Gary was an easy target. Gary reached above his head and flipped off the overhead lights in the living room.

Gary remembered this scene. It had happened in Afghanistan, in a small village where he and a Navy corpsman attached to the Marine unit were helping an elderly woman who'd stepped on a landmine. The Taliban entered through the door of the cramped home. The children in the home ran screaming as the AK47's chattered death. The old man, the husband, sank to the ground, face reduced to a smear of goo. Gary remembered hitting the ground. He remembered rolling for cover as the Taliban assassins continued to fire. Gary rolled again, drew his sidearm and in the confusion, found himself behind the assailants. He emptied his magazine. If there were more of them than just the two that lay bleeding on the floor, Gary never knew.

The children, Ally and Andrew, clutched each other in the fireplace, their gut wrenching screams of terror resounding through the home. Gabe grasped his bleeding leg as he threw himself on top of Debbie, trying to keep her from the line of fire as Gary heard footsteps outside the front door. Gary grabbed the door handle as the man in the kitchen raced toward the living room.

"It has to be quick," Gary thought. "God, please let it work." Gary turned the handle and threw open the front door.

The gunshots were simultaneous. The man at the front of the house, shocked by the opening door, fired, peppering his accomplice's shoulder. The kitchen intruder pulled his trigger sending a wild blast into the front doorjamb as he staggered backwards, slamming into the kitchen counter.

At the sound of the second shot, Mike was up and through the picture window diving onto the front porch in a barrel roll. Mike didn't wait, didn't look...he sprang from his position, flinging himself at the attacker on the porch. Mike collided with the man's legs toppling him onto the stairs. The shotgun dropped from the man's hands and bounded to the dirt below. In an instant Mike was on top of the man, burying his fists into the man's face as the man fought to toss Mike aside. The man's nose exploded in a spray of blood, his eye socket collapsed from the force of repeated blows. Mike didn't stop. Mike wouldn't stop. The children were still screaming, Mike could hear them, and the sound drove him beyond his humanity…into unbridled vengeance.

Gary was on his feet, spanning the distance to the kitchen in the measure of a heartbeat. The attacker at the counter held the shotgun with one arm, the good arm. Gary could see the blood racing from the man's shoulder, dripping onto the tile floor. As Gary approached, the man raised the shotgun to Gary's chest. "If it's your will," Gary said, launching himself into the air toward the attacker.

The shotgun rang out and Gary felt nothing. The air rushed by his face, then, his body plowed into the man, sending the man sprawling against the counter and onto the floor. Gary looked up, to see Ryan, knife in hand, standing in the kitchen. Ryan had cut the man causing the shotgun to miss its target. Gary grabbed the shotgun, bringing the barrel in line with the man's head. But, it wouldn't be needed. The man writhed on the floor, clasping his throat as blood surged from the open wound. The man had only seconds to live. Gary raised the butt of the gun over the man's head and came crashing down with one solid blow. The man went limp, unconscious, the only mercy Gary could offer.

"Mike."

Gary spun around, seeing Debbie standing at the front door. Mike was still straddling the man, still punching. The blows were wet now, dull. Mikes hands and arms were covered in blood. The attacker's face condensed to a ball of bone and pulp. Gary rose, walking to Mike.

"Mike," Gary spoke calmly.

Mike continued to punch, even as his strength began to wane.

"Mike…" Gary touched Mikes shoulder, "… it's over, Mike."

Mike flinched at Gary's touch, the pause enough to distract Mike's obsession. Mike looked at his hands, bloodied, swollen and shattered then collapsed onto Gary, exhausted.

Lori walked past Ryan into the kitchen, looking at the man on the floor, soaking in the violence as the tears began to flow. Ally ran to her side and Lori snatched her into her arms, turning her away from the carnage.

"I want daddy." Ally sobbed.

37

9:05PM

Alice stepped out of the squad, leaving the lights on, examining the man on the other side of the front gate. This was a big guy. He was the kind of guy Marc Braden had told her about but Alice had to be judicious with her thinking. In Savannah, the majority of the population was African-American. She wasn't about to automatically assume that any big black man qualified as a threat. The rules on racial profiling were clear for Alice and this man didn't deserve any more or any less suspicion than any of the million other people she'd interacted with in her career. Still....

"My partner is acting awful funny, Officer," William said, pointing inside his vehicle. "He started puking and shaking. His eyes rolled back in his head." William's faked urgency was convincing enough.

"Stay with him. I'm going to call for an ambulance," Alice said, reaching for the microphone attached to her shirt.

"Fuck!" Ra thought as he heard Alice. Ra moaned loudly, hoping to keep Alice off the radio.

"He aint gonna live, Officer," William looked at Ra then back at Alice with pleading eyes. "You gotta come help him."

Alice stepped out from behind her door and walked toward William. If this guy, this sick guy, was in as bad a shape as he sounded, Alice could do little to help. She'd have a look, but the sooner she got him professional help, the better.

"I'm coming. But, we need an ambulance," Alice said, pressing the transmit button on her microphone.

As the first syllables came from Alice's mouth, Ra jumped out of the car. She had barely identified herself to the dispatcher when Ra opened fire. The first round hit Alice in the chest plate of her body armor, pushing her backwards into the hood of her squad. The second round struck her in the left leg, just above the kneecap. Alice crumpled.

"Dumb ass bitch!" Ra shouted as he cleared the gate and walked up on Alice, weapon leveled on her chest.

Alice did nothing. Ra had no idea she was wearing body armor and Alice wanted it kept that way. She closed her eyes to slits. "If that bastard can play sick..." Alice thought, "... then I can play dead."

William unlocked the front gate as Ra stood over Alice. He kicked her leg, sending tendrils of pain shooting through Alice's body. She bit down on her lip to stem the agony as the radio in her squad and on her chest came to life.

"All units, all units, 10-35 suspected in progress, U.S. Coast Guard Station on Cockspur Island, all units respond." The dispatcher's voice was urgent.

"The dumb bitch called it in, Ra!" William looked around nervously, expecting to see police appear from every angle. He could hear a car on the main highway but he couldn't see its headlights.

"Did you?" Ra kicked Alice again, harder.

Alice couldn't contain the pain, she winced.

"You sneaky little bitch!" Ra said, pointing his pistol at Alice's head.

Alice drew back her good leg and drove her boot into Ra's knee. Ra's leg bent back with a sickening snap as tendons and cartilage tore, forced in a direction never intended. Ra fell to the road in a fit of anguish, holding the shattered knee as William charged toward the squad.

"God Damnit!" William screamed as he produced a pistol from his jacket aiming at Alice as she reached for her sidearm. William never noticed the sound behind him. He never noticed the scream of the engine as it jumped into overdrive.

Marc Braden plowed the car into William, shattering legs, sending William catapulting through the air over the hood then over the roof. Ra spun on the ground, haphazardly firing rounds into Marc's car as Marc slammed the brakes.

"Die mother fucker!" Ra shouted as Braden threw open his door, leaping from the vehicle, Jeff Nguyen's pistol in hand.

Ra aimed, but never fired.

With an ear splitting report, Alice's pistol recoiled. A single, hollow point, 9mm round entered Ra's throat. A gurgle of blood surged from Ra's mouth as he reached out toward Alice then slumped to the ground.

Marc stood motionless. In front of him, Ra, the man he'd seen last night, lay dead. Behind Marc's car, some twenty feet away, the one who'd called him "nigger" was contorted on the ground in a broken mass.

"Alice…" Marc spoke, "are you okay?"

Alice didn't move. "Not really, Marc." Alice replied.

Marc rushed to Alice's squad grabbing the microphone, "This is Master Chief Marc Braden. I'm on Cockspur Island. There is an officer down. I need an ambulance here immediate...."

Braden broke off his transmission as he heard popping sounds, the sounds of gunfire. Marc ran to his car.

****

Hank chanced a glance over his shoulder. Whoever Rachel had fired at had jumped for cover inside the galley door.

"Go! Go!" Hank yelled. There was no more use for quiet, not now. Hank grabbed Rachel by the back of her shirt and flung her around him and through the watch room door. A random shot rang out from the galley door, buckshot carving into the wall across from Hank.

"Go to the hatch!" Hank pushed Rachel ahead, jumping into the room as another splatter of buckshot whipped through the air. They didn't have much time. Their position wasn't a good one. The bad guys could run around the outside of the building and shoot them through the room's window's if they were smart enough. The hallway was no longer an option, it was a death trap. It was the hatch, the crawlspace and then the woods. It had to be.

"Come on out and play!" a voice yelled from down the hallway.

Rachel crawled behind the communications console, finding the handle to the hatch. "You ready?"

"We have to stay quiet." Hank peeked over the console, watching as flashlight beams poked through the watch room windows. "Go, Rachel."

Rachel lowered herself through the hatch and onto the broken matt of seashells that were used to coat the earth under the Station. Slowly, Rachel backed away giving Hank enough room to climb down. Her legs and boots made scraping noises as she climbed over the shells. Cobwebs stuck to her face and hands as she crept ahead, praying not to encounter a snake.

Hank, on his knees in the shells, closed the hatch. The crawl space was, maybe, three feet high. Hank had been under the building a few times to retrieve errantly thrown footballs or chase out raccoons, but generally the area was off limits. Cockspur Island was full of snakes, nasty ones, and the crawl space was a perfect habitat.

"I'd rather take my chances with the snakes," Hank let the thought slip out.

"Me too," Rachel agreed.

Hank looked around. Moonlight filtered in through the hedges that hid the crawlspace for cosmetic purposes. Hank couldn't see any movement, man or animal, but he could hear the footsteps on the wood planking that surrounded the station's exterior.

"They'll think we're hiding behind the console," Hank whispered to Rachel. "We've got a few minutes before they figure out we're gone."

Rachel nodded understanding as Hank returned to hand signals. With an indication of his hand, Hank and Rachel started to worm their way across the belly of the station. The shells cut their hands and clothes. It was a hundred feet to the space's end, near the shop buildings, where they would be forced into the open and a perilous dash to the woods outside the station's back gate.

****

Dennis grabbed a large manual and tossed it over the Communications console. He wanted to solicit a response from whoever he had trapped. The book hit the floor with a thud and a ripple of pages. Another manual, another throw… same result.

Dennis grabbed one of his hired hands and pushed the man into the watch room. The man let out a whoop of surprise and terror. He didn't want to be shot but Dennis wasn't giving him any options. The room was still and the thug leapt behind the console, shotgun at the ready. Nothing….

"Empty," The man said, turning to Dennis.

"Well they damn sure didn't go out the windows!" Dennis yelled pointing at the other two thugs outside.

Dennis pushed his way past the man and examined the floor. "There's a hatch here. They're under the building!"

****

Hank looked out from under the building and his stomach turned. In the grass, off to his left, Jennifer Brooks lay motionless. Rachel looked, too, and was unable to contain a gasp.

"We have to check," Rachel insisted. She was right.

Hank skirted down the edge of the building, to the closest possible point to Jennifer, "Stay under cover!" Hank ordered Rachel.

Hank crawled out onto the grass, close enough to touch Jennifer's leg. He shook Jennifer, staying low, still partially concealed. Jennifer groaned. She was alive. Careless with exuberance, Hank crawled up next to Jennifer, examining her body. She'd been shot in the chest at point blank range. A blackened hole in her shirt marked the path of the bullet but there was no blood. Hank grabbed Jennifer's shirt, tearing it open.

"I'll be damned." Hank whispered as he stared at the body armor that covered Jennifer's chest, "You're pretty damn smart, lady."

Jennifer was alive, but she was barely lucid. Hank figured she may have broken ribs, maybe internal bleeding. Body armor would stop a bullet but not the wave of energy from the bullet's impact. Jennifer was lucky her attacker didn't pay better attention. She was lucky he didn't have a desire to see blood. The guy never realized she was still alive.

Rachel heard a creaking under the building and turned to see the flashlight beam shining down through the hatch. Rachel crawled out from under the building, hiding behind a hedge, as the beam probed the darkness.

"Come on!" Hank whispered his insistence to Rachel as he put Jennifer Brooks in a fireman's carry. They were in the open now and they had Jennifer to carry. They were going to be slow.

Hank handled Jennifer's weight easily enough. She was only a little over one twenty but, over time, he knew he'd wear down. They had to find a place in the woods to hide Jennifer, somewhere out of sight.

"Dennis…look!" the voice came from behind Hank.

Hank and Rachel darted to the back of the shop building as lights crisscrossed the ground where Jennifer had been.

"The woman's gone!" the voice yelled as hurried footfalls crossed the planking.

Hank eyed the woods, no more than fifty feet away, then considered Jennifer, "Rachel. I want you to run." Hank looked into Rachel's eyes.

"Without you?"

"I need you to run as fast as you can. I want you to distract them so I can hide Jennifer." Hank explained.

Rachel began to understand.

"I want you to step out there in the open and haul ass. Take two shots over your shoulder toward those bastards then run like hell."

"Run where?" Rachel asked, checking her boot laces.

"To the Fort, Rachel. You know that Fort, you know this island... take them through the woods, give me some time and I'll meet you at the fort."

"Find them!" Dennis's voice, close by, boomed into the night sky.

"Go!" Hank ducked behind an air conditioner unit, lowering Jennifer to the ground as he urged Rachel on.

Rachel paused, only for an instant. "Okay," Rachel said then bolted across the grass.

Hank never could believe how fast Rachel was. She moved like a gazelle, she was near the woods in a heartbeat. Rachel's gun went off twice. She actually had to stop running to allow her pursuers to see her and then she disappeared into the woods.

****

"Hank is still at the station," Laura shouted to the crew as the 942 approached the northern tip of the island.

"What's the plan then?" Shawn asked, over the crew's headpiece communications system.

Laura had channel 16 tuned in on both the 942's radios, the volume at max. She and the crew had been listening intently, trying to pick out the whispered conversations between Hank and Rachel as they attempted to make their escape from the Station. Rachel was headed into the woods then on to the fort. Hank was going to try to hide Jennifer Brooks then join Rachel. Laura's last orders from Master Chief had been to return to the station, to rescue anyone left there. That was her plan of action. Rachel was one of Laura's best friends, Laura wanted to help her but, Laura also knew how fast Rachel was, how well she knew the island. Laura would go after Hank and Jennifer first.

"We're headed for the station. Be ready!" Laura instructed her crew.

****

Paul Sulsky was listening, too, and his choice was different. He remembered the girl, Rachel. He remembered pointing her out to Evan back on Tuesday. She was a pretty young girl. She could have been his daughter. She was running away from what Paul had brought down on her and she didn't deserve it. None of these kids deserved any of this.

Paul motored on... past the station's piers. If that other boy, Hank, was there then he was in good shape. Dennis would be chasing after the girl. Paul was headed to the eastern tip of the island, near the fort. Paul knew a place where the water was deep enough to get close. He would run the Gina Marie aground there. He would jump off his boat and he would go help the girl.

Paul reached under the console and pulled out a brand new .44 magnum, the "Dirty Harry" kind. He'd never been able to afford one before, not until now, and he'd always wanted one.

"I'm coming little girl. Please, hold on."

****

Hank stayed in his spot, watching three men rush across the grounds and into the woods after Rachel. He could have stood up. He could have started a firefight with them. But, his chances weren't good. The men were well armed. Two carried shotguns. One carried an assault rifle that looked like an M14. It was better to hide Jennifer then chase after them slowly, silently.

"Come on, Jenn," Hank said, lifting Jennifer onto his back. He knew where he was headed. On the far side of the shops was the buoy yard where the Aids to Navigation Team kept their supplies. In the yard there would be coils of wire-rope, large plastic boxes used to hold batteries for shore-based ATON. Hank could bury Jennifer under a pile of this stuff and no one would ever be able to see her.

Hank skirted cautiously along the wall of the building. Off in the woods he could hear the sounds of the men crashing through the undergrowth. He heard the "Damnits" and "Shits" coming from the men as they ran, headlong, through the scores of briars.

"That's my girl," Hank said. Rachel was dragging these guys through hell. "She won't be easy to catch,

Jenn," Hank said aloud as he rounded the corner into the buoy yard and came face to face with the barrel of a gun.

"Thought you were clever? Didn't you, boy?"

Hank froze. The man held the shotgun level with Hank's chest. Hank lowered Jennifer from his shoulders, easing her to the ground.

"Show me your hands!"

Hank lifted his hands slowly. His pistol was tucked into his belt. If he tried to grab it… he was dead.

"Take it easy," Hank said. "Just tell me what you want?"

"Me?" the man laughed. "I just want to get paid. The boss on the other hand… he wants the money you stole from him."

"I don't have anyone's money," Hank replied.

"Of course not," The man replied sarcastically then changed his expression. "Why don't you just give it to me? Or we could split it," he suggested.

Hank felt a surge of intolerance and anger. "I said I don't have…." Hank recalled his training. Action was faster than reaction.

"Fuck you," Hank said

Hank jerked to the side, sweeping out with his forearm to knock the gun barrel off target. The gun went off, blowing a hole in loose fabric of Hanks sleeve. He grabbed the barrel as the man drove the gun into the air then ripped back hard. The front sights of the barrel tore through the palm of Hanks hand.

Hank didn't feel the pain. Adrenaline surged as he swung his other arm into the side of the man's neck, into the brachial plexus. At the force of the blow the man staggered backwards. The nerves bundled in his neck had been disrupted, the impulses fired irregularly. The man looked drunk, falling into the parking lot adjacent to the shop building. Hank rushed forward, grabbing the shotgun and tossing it across the parking lot.

"Son of a bitch, man," the voice startled Hank.

Shawn Jones was racing toward Hank followed by Laura and the remainder of the 942 crew.

"A perfect brachial stun! I've never seen that," Shawn said as he grabbed a set of handcuffs from his weapons belt and locked down Hank's attacker.

"You heard?" Hank indicated the radio, still at his side.

"We did," Laura responded. "You okay?"

There was no time for conversation. "Shawn, you need to see to Jennifer," Hank ordered.

"Get back to the boat, Laura," Hank gathered his wind. "Go to the fort. Ground the damn boat if you have to but get there and get there fast. Rachel needs us."

The sound of a distant gunshot bounced through the woods.

38

9:30PM

Rachel ran. She ran as fast as her legs would carry her. The tangle of briars passed by, ripping holes in her pants, scraping her legs. But, her legs wouldn't stop. She made half the distance to the fort in minutes, despite dodging trees and brush. The lights in the woods behind her were distant. She feared they would give up, turn back toward the station, toward Hank. Rachel wanted them to follow her to the fort, to a place she knew so well.

Rachel could hide in the fort, if she could get inside. The main entrance would be gated off, she knew as much. But, there was a gap in the top of the gate. Maybe, just maybe, she could squeeze through. If all else failed she would swim the mote surrounding the fort. She would crawl in through one of the firing ports in the side of the masonry walls. The ports weren't that high off the ground. Rachel could jump, get a hand-hold, crawl inside. She stumbled.

As her face hit the ground, plowing into a thick stand of burrs, Rachel gasped. Nothing was broken, she'd simply tripped and was still a good distance away from her pursuers.

"Keep going girl," Rachel whispered to herself as she darted off.

There were other buildings she'd passed in the half-mile she'd covered. There was a Fish and Wildlife office and an out building that belonged to the park's maintenance department. Neither was a good choice. She needed the fort, its walls and the time it would afford her while her pursuers found a way inside.

A shot rang out in the night. Rachel heard the sound of a bullet ripping through the air nearby, shredding the brush. As distant as they were; the men still had weapons, good ones, and bullets flew faster than Rachel ran. She sped up. Sweat poured down her brow and into her eyes.

"Just a little bit more," Rachel said as the lights of Fort Pulaski began to glimmer through the trees. Rachel broke from the woods and into the fort's parking lot as another random gunshot zipped through the trees.

Fort Pulaski stood majestic in the pale moonlight. The masonry walls, still pocked by the fire of Union cannon, dwelt as sentinels to history. Not even the strongest walls could hold, could protect. Forts, Rachel knew, were only as strong as the men who manned them or the determination of those who stormed their battlements. Rachel didn't have long to become the "bold defender." The parking lot, well lit, was large. She flew across the pavement faster than she ever thought she could move. In the wink of an eye she was across the lot and onto the mote's drawbridge, the sound of her footfalls reverberating off ancient walls. A look behind revealed lights approaching the edge of the woods.

"They really don't give a damn, do they?" Rachel thought. It was strange and terrifying to her…how driven these men were, how confident, how lethal. Her pursuers pushed ahead, like bulls in a china shop. They made so much noise. Rachel examined the gate.

"Crap!" Rachel said as she looked at the top of the fort's gate and the extension of wrought-iron bars that had been added. There was still room at the top, maybe just enough for her to get through but, the chances of getting inside without slicing open a leg or getting stuck on the bars was insanely small.

****

Dennis stepped into the parking lot, scanning with his weapon. His pants were shreds. Cockspurs had found their way inside his shoes and scratched relentlessly at his ankles and feet. He was out of breath. The Coastie girl they chased had lead them half a mile through the woods, barely breaking stride. Only once had one of his goons gotten a shot at her using the night vision scope on the rifle. She was fast, ridiculously fast. But, she would be caught and she would give him what he wanted. She was at the fort now. She had trapped herself.

"Nothing," the goon with the rifle reported as he finished scanning with the night vision. "I can't see her."

"She's inside," Dennis replied as he started toward the drawbridge.

"She could have run any damn where!" the other man insisted. "And there are two of them. Where's the other one?"

"It's her I want!" Dennis shouted, wheeling around, pointing his shotgun at the man's head. "She's being protected! She was sent ahead! She knows where the money is! The other one was protecting her!"

"You're fucking nuts!" the man replied.

Dennis lashed out at the man, swinging the butt of the shotgun into the man's midsection. "And you're being paid, convict! The only reason you aren't being bent over in some penitentiary is because I am protecting you!"

The man held his stomach, grimacing in pain. Dennis bent close to the man's face. "You'll do what I tell you, do you understand?"

The man nodded his agreement, he didn't have a choice.

Dennis jogged across the parking lot to the gate. It didn't matter that the girl had a gun. She was scared. She was running. She wanted to hide.

"There," the man with the rifle directed his flashlight to the top of the gate where a thin sliver of blue fabric hung from a pointed piece of metal. "She's in there."

Dennis pulled up his shotgun."You better know how to hide!" Dennis screamed as he fired two rounds, shattering the gates lock. "We're coming!"

****

Hank's lungs felt like they would explode. The woods were thick, full of snares. More than once he had stumbled, struggling to keep his feet like some half-drunk idiot but, he couldn't slow down. The lights of the fort were in view through the trees. He was only a few seconds from reaching the parking lot, then the drawbridge, then... what? There were three men ahead of Hank, three men that were infinitely better armed.

"Screw that," Hank thought as he plowed through the woods. "My insurance is paid up." Hank exited the woods at a sprint as Dennis shot out the lock and entered the fort.

****

Paul ran the Gina Marie, bow on, into the sand and mud bank that surrounded the east tip of the island.

From his pilothouse window he saw the orange-white flash of gunshots at Fort Pulaski's gates. He hoped it wasn't the girl.

The Gina Marie dug into the bank, pushing ever forward as she heeled over onto her port side, onto solid ground, sending Paul crashing into the pilothouse door. The engines choked and sputtered. Smoke belched from the engines as they strained to move propellers through solid mass. With a resounding "clank" the engines seized. Paul gained his footing.

"Damnit, Dennis! Don't!" Paul yelled as he grabbed his .44, raced out of the pilot house and jumped over the bow onto the soft earth below.

****

It was quiet. It was eerie quiet as Dennis and his henchmen walked onto the parade field inside Fort Pulaski. Even in the middle of August a chill tinged the air. The ghosts of a century past hung thick in the surrounding darkness of the fort's chambers. Invisible eyes stared from every parapet, every rust encrusted emplacement, as Dennis walked forward.

"We're in the open and she's armed," the man with the rifle went down to one knee, scanning the surrounding walls of the fort as he whispered.

Dennis turned to the man with rage-filled eyes. His insanity burned.

"She's scared," Dennis said, motioning for the men to spread out, to search the fort.

****

Hank crossed the parking lot and stopped at the edge of the drawbridge. He could see flashlight beams on the parade ground. If the men turned, they would see him. If he crossed the drawbridge, they would hear him. Hank's mind turned to Lori and Ally. What kind of a father would do this to his family? Wasn't it true that he owed more to them than Rachel, than anyone? Ahead, in this old, dusty relic from another time there were men that could, would, take his life. Rachel was in there too… his shipmate, his friend. He could save her from these men, if he tried. Did he have the nerve to try? Hank charged across the drawbridge as the water in the mote beneath his feet swirled.

****

Rachel slowly gained the surface of the murky water, gulping in air, filling her oxygen deprived lungs. The last thing she had seen were the men crossing the drawbridge. Her ruse had worked. They thought she had climbed over the gate and into the fort. She heard the gunshots under the water; she waited, struggling against her body's desire for air. She couldn't wait any longer and she came to the surface as quietly as she could, just in time to see Hank charge over the bridge and into the fort.

"Hank! Stop!" Rachel called out.

****

At the sound of running footsteps crossing the drawbridge, Dennis turned. Hank was silhouetted by lights as he entered the fort. The girl's cry came a second later. Hank ran forward, his pistol barking as he fired at Dennis and his men. The man to Dennis' right buckled to

429

the ground, hit in the chest. Dennis returned Hank's fire. The first shotgun blast bounced off the bricks at Hank's feet. He could feel the hot breath of the buckshot singeing the air around him as it careened into walls and ceilings.

Rachel bolted out of the water, praying that her pistol would still fire as she gained solid ground, rounding the opening to the fort's interior. The report of a rifle penetrated the night sending bit's of masonry cascading through the air. She dove for cover, pulling up her pistol as another shot rang out.

Hank's legs left the ground as he fell onto the edge of the parade field. A white-hot pellet from Dennis's gun had entered Hanks calf, ripping through tissue. Hank pulled his pistol up as he hit the ground, taking aim at Dennis.

"Stop!" Paul Sulsky screamed as he walked into the fort.

The pause was unexpected, the silence... deafening. Hank scurried for cover behind a bench as Rachel lay prone on the ground, unsure what target to acquire.

"This doesn't need to go any farther," Paul said, stepping between Hank and Rachel...and Dennis.

Dennis shifted his aim from Hank to Rachel and back again as Paul approached, "Get the hell out of our way you stupid redneck!" Dennis screamed at Paul.

"I can't do that," Paul stopped, turning his head to look at Hank and Rachel.

"That storm was pretty bad. It wiped me out," Paul began.

"The boats were both damaged. My livelihood was gone," Paul lowered his head as he heaved a long sigh. "I didn't think any of this would happen," Paul's eyes held an apology for Hank, for Rachel, for everyone who'd been hurt.

"Get to the point!" Dennis insisted.

Paul squared his shoulders, facing Dennis. "Did you like the upgrades to my store, Dennis? Don't you think the boats look good with all their new gear?" Paul moved closer to Dennis, sliding a hand behind his back.

Dennis barely heard Paul, his focus still confined to Hank and Rachel.

"I saw them out there the day after the storm," Paul indicated Hank and Rachel "When they left I went where they'd been."

Dennis' gaze slowly averted to Paul. Dennis could guess what was coming but didn't want to hear an evident truth. Dennis had made a mistake. He had made a series of mistakes. The Coasties on the ground before him, the one he'd shot earlier, none of it was necessary. None of them was the real target. Dennis leveled the shotgun on Paul with pride filled hatred.

Paul chuckled, realizing Dennis' emotion. "I took your damn money, you dirty son of a bitch! I've had it all along!"

"Damn you, Sulsky!" Dennis screamed as Paul pulled the .44.

The shotgun blast caught Sulsky in the chest as a round from his .44 smashed into the ground at Dennis's feet. Sulsky flew backward onto the hard stone of the forts walkway, blood coursing from the gaping hole in his chest.

"Holy Christ!" Hank yelled as he stared into Paul's lifeless eyes. "You murderous bastard!" Hank screamed.

"Kill them. Clean up the rest of the mess," Dennis said menacingly, directing his henchmen, not noticing the figures rushing onto the parade field.

The sound of gunfire rattled the night air. The rounds came fast, zipping through the air with manic reports. Hank and Rachel watched Dennis drop his gun. Blood sprayed from Dennis's chest as he stumbled backwards. To Dennis' side, the henchman's face exploded with a bullets impact. The man tipped backwards in a deadfall, hitting the cold ground.

Dennis' hands fumbled across the slick blood that ran down his chest. Fingers probed, fighting to plug seeping holes, fighting to stave off the darkness that clouded his vision. Dennis fell to his knees. His eyes fixed on Hank, eyes still filled with hate and arrogance. Then, those same eyes rolled over white as Dennis's body fell face-first into the damp grass.

"Are you two okay?" a calm, familiar voice came from behind Hank and Rachel.

Marc Braden tucked his pistol into his belt as he walked into the dim light of the parade field. Laura and Jennifer followed, still scanning the fort's interior.

"You're safe." Marc said, pulling Rachel from the ground, wrapping her in a bear hug.

"You gonna make it?" Jennifer smiled at Hank.

Hank nodded as he returned the smile, "You're awake?"

"Never felt better," Jennifer lied as she rubbed her chest.

Laura bent over Hank, examining his injured leg, as the wail of sirens flooded the night air.

"Where's Lori?" Hank asked, going limp with exhaustion.

Cockspur Island

Epilogue

An unbearably monotonous investigation followed the shootings. Coast Guard Officers from Headquarters, Area, District and civilian officials from the Department of Homeland Security had flooded into Savannah to sort out all the facts and render their educated conclusions. The incident was unprecedented and was treated as such. Hank, for some time, couldn't decide if he were the victim or the accused.

At first, Hank, Rachel, Master Chief and the rest had been sequestered to the confines of the Station. All of the families, though not stripped of their ability to move about, were essentially prisoners in Savannah. Interviews were intrusive and details were expected to be explicit. Waves of reporters crashed over Cockspur Island and the story of the occurrence was given every possible spin. In a quiet moment, away from the senior investigators, a junior officer informed Hank that he was being kept away from them to allow things to settle...that he was not being punished. Hank bought that. It seemed logical, but he missed his family all the same. There was talk of awards and medals, but Hank never got his hopes up. He didn't care. After facing the barrel of a gun, being alive was the greatest reward he could ever receive.

The days after the incident gave way to weeks and to months. It was May now, almost eight months later, and the warm air of spring was claiming its temporary province across the corn and soybean fields of central Indiana. Starlings bobbed and weaved across the top of Lake Mississinewa, barely skimming the surface as they plucked at stranded insects. It was a perfect day. There hadn't been one of these for some time. God willing, there would be many, many more.

The squeals from shore brought a smile to Hank's face. Ally splashed in the water, playing with Beauregard, the old Golden from Savannah. The two of them had become fast friends in the days after the incident. Jeff Nguyen refused to let the dog go to the pound so Lori volunteered to look after Beau while Jeff recovered at Savannah General. A couple of days turned to a week and more. Beau became family. Jeff had no complaints about Beau's adoption on the day he went home to Charleston. He'd handed Lori a huge T-Bone, insisting that Beau be allowed to eat the steak, cooked to whatever specification Beau desired.

Gabe and Laura had been transferred from Tybee shortly after the conclusion of the investigation. The Sector Commander and Master Chief thought it was in their best interest to leave things behind and start fresh. Ryan almost immediately smoked pot after that long-ago Friday night. After insisting that he be piss-tested, knowing what would happen, Ryan was discharged from the service. He didn't care. The last Hank had heard, Ryan was tending bar somewhere in Key West.

Marc Braden retired just before Hank transferred. The ceremony was tremendous but melancholy. Master Chief was never the same after that night. In the months before he retired he became very distant, letting Jennifer handle the majority of decisions. Master Chief saved Hank's life and he would never forget that. Hank wrote long emails to Master Chief, often. He didn't care if there was ever a response.

Mike, Debbie and Andrew went on their way to San Diego. Finally, for once, Mike decided to give his family a break by taking a recruiting job in the sun. The tears between Lori and Debbie had poured for days prior to their separation.

Rachel headed off to Detroit. Each of them had been given their pick of open units after what they'd gone through and Rachel picked Detroit. She was going to the sector office to drive a forklift around for a couple of years and, as Rachel insisted, "get serious" about running marathons and women's ice hockey. Hank hugged Rachel for what seemed like hours the day she left. He hadn't spoken to Rachel since.

"Come on in," Lori waved at Hank from the shore. "Lunch is almost ready."

Hank returned the wave then looked out over the water, to the bobber that hadn't moved since it landed.

"I hope they aren't expecting a fish fry," Hank's dad squeezed Hank's shoulder. "Let's go eat. I'm starved."

"Me too..." Hank patted his father's hand. The cancer had been treated and, for now, wasn't expected to return. Still, every second Hank had with his father had taken on a new meaning and was undeniably precious. Hank pulled in the canoe's anchor as his dad picked up an oar.

"What's it going to be like to be back on fresh water for a living?" Hank's dad asked as he paddled toward shore.

"It's another one of those buoy-boats, Dad," Hank picked up a paddle. "It's going to be a lot of fun."

"Will you carry a gun?"

Hank smiled, "No, Dad, not this time around."

For Hank and his family, the Coast Guard Cutter Sangamon in Peoria Illinois would be predictable and quiet. There wouldn't be any drug runners or stinky fishermen. There wouldn't be any shooting, no blood...no fear. All that Hank had coming from his new unit was consistency. It was his pick.

As the canoe touched the soft bank, Ally leaned over the side and hugged Hank's leg.

Beauregard wagged his tale.

ABOUT THE AUTHOR

Bradley Adams is twenty-five year veteran of the United States Coast Guard. Brad has served at numerous Coast Guard units in Georgia, Michigan, Illinois and California, spending eleven years as an Officer in Charge of Coast Guard Small Boat Stations. He is a graduate of Excelsior College, earning a Bachelors of Science degree with majors in History and Business Administration. Brad has been madly in love with and married to Michelle Adams for twenty-three years and is the proud father of three beautiful, intelligent and amazing daughters.

"Cockspur Island", is Brad's second work of fiction and the first to center on the Coast Guard and main character Hank Morgan. "Dark River", the second book of the Hank Morgan/Coast Guard series is set for release in 2013.

CPSIA information can be obtained at www.ICGtesting.com
Printed in the USA
LVOW131015271212

313432LV00001B/3/P

9 781477 464007